# Fem Dom

TONY CANE-HONEYSETT

## AUTHOR'S NOTE

In 2008, I started research on a documentary I was making about the psychology behind people who were into bondage. I was curious to learn why someone would derive sexual pleasure from being tied up and restricted. Why was pain and humiliation so necessary for them? Was it purely sexual? And how did they first get into what is still perceived as a taboo subject? I wanted to find out and what I discovered surprised me. During the course of this research and eventual filming, I interviewed many men and women who had adopted the BDSM lifestyle and were happily living it 24/7. Amongst my subjects were sex therapists, sadists, masochists and dominatrices and it was their experiences that became the central theme to my film, *Mondo Bondo* and, consequently, became the inspiration for *Fem Dom*. This book is a work of fiction but much of the story is based in a very real truth.

# CHAPTER 1

It was 10.00 a.m. and the hell months were over. The bitter, biting, bastard of winter had faded into a brief spring and now the very welcome beginnings of summer. The sleepy, upscale suburb of Eden Prairie was as pretty as it sounded. And so was one of its imported residents, 34 year-old Tara Drew.

Tara didn't have a job. Not a real *paying* job anyway. She didn't need to work as Clem's fat monthly paycheck more than provided for the two of them. But she wanted to do something to make herself feel useful instead of merely cleaning house and waiting for Clem to come home to a hot meal every night. To alleviate the boredom of her Groundhog Day existence, Tara played Good Samaritan, feeding those less fortunate than herself, because if there was one thing Tara could do well, it was bake. The lucky recipient of her culinary prowess was the Saint Augustine's homeless shelter in Bloomington and her twice-weekly deliveries there gave her a sense of purpose.

"Very nice," Tara said softly to no one in particular as she pulled a tray of piping hot banana and walnut muffins out of the oven. While they cooled, Tara finished wiping down the dark granite countertops in her perfectly color-coordinated designer kitchen. The brushed chrome Viking stove and matching cooktop beautifully complimented the vast Sub Zero refrigerator, which seemed to take up half a wall. Sure, she was house proud and why not? It was a house worthy of pride. What's more, keeping six thousand square feet of real estate tidy and clean kept her busy. This was Tara's world but she was going quietly crazy.

Downtown, the imposing glass façade of the Kemp building on Nicollet Avenue housed the opulent offices of the Bergenson & Adler Advertising Agency located on the forty-second, forty-third and forty-fourth floors.

Clem Drew swiveled around in his Herman Miller Aeron chair, kicked up both feet on the glass-topped desk and cupped his hands behind his head. Staring out of the floor-to-ceiling windows at the other faceless steel and glass monoliths, Clem was feeling very content about his life right now and he had good reason. The phone on his desk rang. Clem leaned back and grabbed it.

"This is Clem."

"You lucky bastard!"

"Mike?"

"Damn! How'd you pull that off?"

"What can I say?" Clem smiled, smugly.

"Let's go start our own agency. Bring that account with you."

"Very funny. Go into business with an old hack like you?"

"Fuck you. Hey, let's grab lunch this week."

"Love to."

Somewhere else in the Kemp building, a man wearing headphones listened.

Clem hung up and chuckled then resumed his view. The downtown skyline could've been any big city in North America. But it wasn't anywhere: it was Minneapolis, slap bang in the heartland. Yes, the land of ten thousand lakes and more Fortune 500 companies per capita than New York, Chicago and Los Angeles. Handsome Clem

Drew was senior VP and executive account director at Bergenson & Adler, the highest grossing advertising agency in the mid-west. He was forty-three years old with over twenty years experience in the ad biz and nearing the pinnacle of his profession.

Clem's sky-high office was modern and minimal. With its clean white lines, it could be said there was a touch of that German zeitgeist about it, though the only thing Clem had in common with Germany was his company-paid silver Mercedes S600. The week had been particularly rewarding for the hard working ad man. Thanks to his marketing savvy and strategic planning ability, Clem's team of creatives and account managers had landed a whopping account – the $200 million Rebakor business. The sports clothing and running shoe manufacturer was a global brand and this was a huge win for Clem's agency. And there it was in print on the cover of the trade magazine *Advertising Age* – *'Bergenson Runs Off With Rebakor Account.'*

They had indeed and Clem Drew was quoted throughout the article. It was a serious chunk of change for the company coffers but also terrific PR for the agency and for Clem. The kudos belonged to him. His agency had beaten out some tough competition from BBDO in San Francisco, Saatchi's in New York and Chiat Day in Los Angeles. Those agencies were heavy hitters but Clem's pitch for the Minneapolis agency had hit it out of the ballpark.

He was now clearly the heir-apparent to succeed the old man; ageing advertising supremo and CEO, Frank Bergenson. Frank was about to retire and he had yet to choose his successor. This win had put Clem in pole position ahead of the only man who could pip him at the post, Kurt Fitzgerald.

"Congratulations, Clem! You sonofamofo!" Earl Chambliss bellowed, as he walked into Clem's office. Earl was CFO and handled all the contracts. "They've signed all the paperwork. We are now officially the agency of record." Clem winked as Earl shook his hand.

"Thanks, Earl."

"Frank is pissing his pants he's so happy. What a way for him to go out, huh? Biggest fish he's ever landed. You're gonna enjoy that big office of his upstairs." Earl chuckled loudly as he wandered off down the corridor.

Clem Drew looked the personification of the successful business executive in his bespoke suits from Barney's, crisp white Brooks Brothers shirts and snappy silk ties. *Look sharp. Think sharp.* That was the Drew philosophy.

"Justine? Who's next?" Clem spoke into his desk intercom.

"Internal with media buyers. One o'clock," a young female voice replied through the speakerphone.

"Can you move them to noon? I have a two o'clock pre-pro downstairs."

"Sure. But that reporter from the Star Tribune is coming in at eleven to interview you, remember?"

"Reschedule that. Too busy."


Tara hurried back to her shiny black Lexus SUV still wearing her spandex yoga pants. Clem would be home in two hours and she hadn't put the lamb chops in the oven yet. She'd collected his three freshly dry-cleaned shirts, bought him some new socks from the Von Maur department store and had even remembered to pick up more of the frozen coconut lollipops she knew he loved from Kowalski's grocery store. All in a day's work for the man she loved.

As Tara drove from Bodyworks Fitness back to her home on Dunkirk Crescent, she planned the evening in her head. A nice dinner, accompanied by a 2009 bottle of Robert Mondavi merlot and then maybe a little 'hootchie-coo' as she liked to call it. It was yet another attempt to try and rekindle the flame that seemed to have gotten down to the candlewick for her and Clem. He'd been so obsessed over the past four months with winning the Rebakor business that their relationship and, particularly, their sex life had taken a back seat. Tara was putting on a brave face but inside she was not happy and her frustration was starting to show. The more she did to support her husband, it seemed the less he appreciated it. But she understood the pressure Clem had been under and, anyway, it was not in Tara's nature to mope. So, here she was once again doing her best to make him happy and perhaps he might start to pay her some much-needed attention. They just weren't communicating they way they used to. Clem was working late most nights and was too exhausted at the weekends to do anything with Tara.

The two had started their relationship in Los Angeles nine years earlier. Tara was just a few years out of UCLA and Clem was working his way up the corporate ladder at Ogilvy & Mather on Wilshire Boulevard. They'd met when Tara had interviewed at the agency to be an account planner. She didn't land the job but she landed Clem. They were a good match for each other and spent most of their free time outdoors, planning tennis and cycling along the beaches, from Malibu to Redondo.

Nowadays, southern California seemed a lifetime away. Tara had grown up in in the sleepy town of San Luis Obispo, just north of Santa Barbara and south of Big Sur. Those wonderful childhood summers in Morro Bay and Pismo Beach were now but a distant memory. She had good, traditional parents who both worked honest jobs but she remembered how her Dad never lifted a finger when it came to helping her mom around the house. But then he never really needed to. Tara's mom ran his life for him: cooking, cleaning, and waiting on him hand and foot. Funny thing was, her mom seemed to enjoy it and her dad certainly never complained. It often crossed Tara's mind that she might be turning into a carbon copy of her mother the way she doted on her father. No, Tara didn't want to be like that but in truth, she already was.

"Jesus, Clem. Are you allergic to art or something?" Silver-haired CEO Frank Bergenson huffed as he walked into Clem's stark office and looked around at the bare white walls. Clem swung around in his chair and smiled.

"Hi, Frank. You never come down to this floor."

"Now I know why. It's damn boring. Maybe I could lend you a Vermeer or a Brueghel to liven up this place. I don't like bland."

Clem smiled at his boss.

"Clear walls keep a clear mind."

"Don't bullshit a bullshitter, Clem."

The Bergenson & Adler CEO carefully lowered himself on the stylish but patently uncomfortable Le Corbusier black leather chaise.

"Crap, this thing's not butt friendly, is it? Guess this must be a piece of art after all because it certainly isn't a goddamn chair," Frank bitched, almost falling off. Clem stifled a laugh as Frank smoothed out his slightly crumpled dark brown suit jacket so it faced front again.

"I assume this rare visit is because you want to thank me for making you even more stinking rich than you are already," Clem winked as he stood up and walked over towards his boss.

"It is, it is. Thank you, Clem. You did the agency proud." Frank rolled off the Le Corbusier and stood up. "They just signed off on all the contracts, so now it's 'officially' official. We got the entire business. The whole kit and caboodle -- TV, print, all outdoor, radio, cinema, point of sale, even stupid fucking hats if they want them."

"Yeah, Earl just dropped by to tell me."

"Good. Because you're going to run the entire account...." Frank paused. Clem beamed the smile of a man who just be given two free tickets to the Superbowl on the fifty yard line.

"It's going to be a pleasure, Frank," Clem butted in exuberantly.

"...with Kurt Fitzgerald," Frank finished.

Clem's feeling of elation just got hijacked.

"What? Fitz? Why Fitz? He had absolutely nothing to do with winning the business. Fitz has his accounts, I have mine! That's how we work, Frank. You know that."

Frank put a hand on his shoulder. "Clem. You know how much I think of you. But this is a two hundred million dollar account. Even the brilliant Clem Drew can't handle all that."

"Try me," Clem said flatly as he took a step back and retreated back behind his desk.

"Clem. I want you to suck it up and work with Fitz. Put your ego to one side and consider the greater good – the agency."

Clem felt like he'd just been punched in the gut. He'd toiled for four months on the huge Rebakor presentation. This was his baby. Sure, it had been a team effort but Fitz's role had been zero. Clem's team had won them the business. But now it seemed like Frank didn't have faith in Clem's ability to handle the day to day running of the account. It was more than just ego on Clem's part. He didn't like Fitz and trusted him just about as far as he could throw him.

"Give me two months and I'll have the entire campaign buttoned down," Clem said with his usual gung-ho spirit. The Rebakor account would need graphic designers, web designers, copywriters and art directors working on it full-time to produce advertising campaigns from direct mail inserts and radio spots to television commercials and billboards nationwide. A group of IT guys would need to be hired to create a powerful interactive bulletproof website and to get webvertising campaigns rolling out. It certainly was a mammoth task.

"Clem, you're smart. Very smart. Jesus, I wouldn't have hired you if I didn't think that. But I also hired Kurt Fitzgerald and he's a different kinda smart." Clem wasn't buying Frank's argument. "When I retire next month, you two are just gonna have to learn to work together, so you might as well start now. If you want my job, Clem, you're going to have to be a leader *and* a team player. Learn how to manage Fitz and you two will get along fine."

"Fitz is too impetuous," Clem muttered as he walked back to his desk.

"And he thinks you're too conservative," Frank snapped back as he started to head for the door of Clem's office.

"Too conservative, my ass!" Clem frowned.

"Look. You have four other accounts to run, Clem. Have you forgotten that? You've been so focused on Rebakor for the past four months you've been ignoring them. Do you even know the status of those guys?"

"I'm working on the marketing plan for Best Buy and I've just briefed creative on Zell Travel. I have a meeting with the Delfry client on Thursday and Arkitrade are coming in for a meeting this afternoon," Clem said confidently, knowing he was totally up on everything. Frank smiled.

"Okay, okay. I know you can lead, Clem. Show me you can work with people who don't see eye to eye with you. Put on your Obama hat."

"I thought you were a Republican," Clem quipped.

"I am," Frank said. "And thanks again for all your hard work. The agency really needed that business. See you later." Frank walked out of Clem's office and down the corridor towards the elevator and back to the sanctity of his opulent corner office upstairs.

Clem banged his hand down on his desk in annoyance. It was no secret amongst the rank and file that he and Kurt Fitzgerald were rivals, now his boss was expecting the two of them to partner up. This didn't make any sense. Fitz was not a man to be trusted. Frank Bergenson had deliberately split his agency right down the middle and, in effect, created two ad agencies in one with their own separate accounts. It was a shrewd move on Frank's part. He knew the competitive nature of the two: Clem and Fitz were like two pit bulls, straining on their corporate leashes to continually out-do each other. And that meant bigger bonuses for the better team. The winner in all this was Frank, of course, as he saw his agency's billings grow and grow.

Clem was a west coast Pepperdine boy while Fitz was a Madison Avenue hard ass who'd worked his way up the corporate ladder more by Machiavellian shenanigans than any brilliant marketing know-how. That's how he'd ended up in the mid-west. He'd pissed off enough people in Manhattan to reach his sell-by date earlier than his ego had anticipated. Kurt Fitzgerald was smart but not *that* smart. He'd gotten headhunted to Bergenson & Adler two years earlier and coming from the big New York shop Doyle Dane Bernbach, he pulled in a great salary package. But he was here for more than the money – it was about the opportunity to run his own shop and get back at the boys on Madison Avenue that'd thwarted his ambitions there. What Fitz didn't know, or what his ego would never admit to, was that his last boss at DDB had paid a headhunter to find Fitz a job as far away as possible. Minneapolis was in the middle of *Bumfuck, Nowhere* from a New York perspective and Fitz had taken the bait.

Whether Frank knew that or not, or whether he cared in the slightest, was anybody's guess. But anytime he got a chance to bring in an employee from either coast, he saw it as an image boost for his mid-west located ad agency. Anyway, one thing was certain, Frank was a wily old fox who knew exactly what he was doing. His agency had quadrupled in size over the past decade and was showing no signs of slowing down even in the struggling economy. The Rebakor win was proof of that. But he was also smart enough to know it was time for him to get out of the business. It was a young man's game nowadays with the impact of the Internet and web advertising really kicking into gear.

Frank was seventy-four years old and too set in the traditional business model of advertising to embrace these new ways. He didn't know how to Google, Tweet, send an email or what a URL happened to be. Fact was, he should have retired years ago but the agency was his baby, his life's work, and he wanted to make sure his legacy was in safe hands. The question was, in whose hands?

As long as he could keep his two generals vying to become his successor, the agency would be fine. Trouble was, what would they do to each other once he was gone? Only one of them could sit on his coveted throne. And while Clem was seemingly the man who would be king in everyone's eyes, the only eyes that mattered were Frank Bergenson's.

The lamb was roasting, the potatoes were simmering and the peas were just coming to the boil. In fifteen minutes, her husband would walk through the door from the garage and dinner would be waiting. It was all about timing, as any half decent cook will tell you and Tara's timing was right on the button. She glanced up at the kitchen clock. Five minutes to seven.

Clem's silver Mercedes sped along Shady Oak Road and turned left into Cherry Lane. He was tired. It'd been a long day and he was still very irritated about the whole Fitz thing. It just didn't feel right. Something was going on and he didn't like it. Fitz hadn't put in the graft Clem had. Why should he now be on equal terms with him? Clem wondered. None of it made any sense.

Tara took the sizzling lamp chops out of the oven just as she heard the garage doors open. The island counter was set for two and culinary aromas floated tantalizingly around the kitchen to intoxicate anyone with even the faintest appetite. Clem walked in carrying his laptop in a shoulder bag and talking on his cell phone.

"Yes, Justine, I know but we need the final layouts ready to take to the client tomorrow. And no, I'm not doing a dog and pony show on Skype. No way. There's never enough damn bandwidth anyway."

Tara smiled to her husband as he walked through the kitchen towards the stairs. He acknowledged her with a raised eyebrow. She wasn't going to interrupt what sounded like an important call. Clem continued his phone conversation as he went up to their bedroom. It was obvious her husband was not in the best of moods but a glass of vino would soon fix that, or so Tara thought. She poured the Mondavi.

Moments later, Clem appeared from upstairs, minus jacket and with his tie loosened. Tara handed him a glass of the velvety smooth red nectar. She enjoyed working out and had a lean and toned body to prove it but boy, did she love a glass of wine in the evening.

"It's your favorite. Lamb chops with all the trimmings!" Tara announced with a proud smile as she placed the lamb chops with rosemary on two warm dinner plates. Clem took a gulp of wine and walked into the living room.

"Maybe later. Sorry, honey. I'm not remotely hungry."

Tara stared at the two perfectly prepared meals. She'd gone to a lot of trouble once again but this was not the first time this had happened over the past four months. Tara gritted her teeth. She wasn't going to make a big deal of it. After all, Clem had been under a lot of stress at work and if the guy wasn't hungry, he wasn't hungry. Tara walked into the living room and over to Clem who was now slumped on the couch with his feet up, shoes off and TV remote in hand flipping channels. He stared at the changing TV screen without any trace of emotion.

"Honey, you have to eat," Tara said, hoping he'd magically change his mind and suddenly develop an appetite.

"I'll heat it up later," Clem said, not bothering to look away from the television.

"How was work?" Tara asked, sitting down beside him and trying to hide her own frustrations. "You seem very annoyed about something."

"Same old bullshit." Clem hit the remote again, in no mood to engage in conversation. Getting Clem's attention when he was in one of these moods was an exercise in futility so Tara walked back into the kitchen. Clem continued to stare mindlessly at the plasma screen.

"I'll put both the plates back in the oven. We can eat later."

If Clem didn't want to talk, he didn't want to talk and she wasn't going to try and force a conversation out of him. He looked pretty wiped as it was. Tara opened the warming drawer of the oven and carefully slid the two plates onto the rack. She knew the chops would be tough as old boots and she was not a happy camper. Tara walked back into the living room and sat down beside her distracted husband.

"They work you too hard, honey. I thought all the pressure was off now that you've won the business."

"It's not the work, it's the fucking politics. Frank Bergenson's playing mind games with me and Kurt Fitzgerald."

"Oh, just enjoy your wine and chill," said Tara, as she topped up Clem's glass, hoping to lighten his mood.

"The old man is loving watching us both duke it out for his job.

After everything I've done for his agency, I *deserve* his damn job."

"Well, I appreciate you. I know how smart you are. You should be their next CEO. That Frank's an idiot."

Now that the Rebakor pitch was over, she'd been expecting Clem to be back to his jolly old self. Tara was a good wife and she had a deep love for her husband but it was getting increasingly hard emotionally for her to be supportive. Clem was putting so much energy and effort into getting the impending CEO position that he had nothing left for her. He was coming home a spent force. It was like he was turning into a different person.

While Clem was living his life in the fast lane, Tara's was plodding along. Every day was the same old same old for her, like Groundhog Day. She was tired of living her life vicariously through Clem. *And where was the affection?* Tara couldn't remember when they'd last had sex. It was time to get their marriage back where it had been before Clem had become so blindingly ambitious. *Hell, maybe Clem just needed a blowjob to get him to unwind.*

While Clem stared silently at two boxers beating the crap out of each other on ESPN, a seductive smile crossed Tara's face as her hands slid over his stomach and then down to the zipper of his pants. She slowly pulled at the zipper tab.

Clem flinched. "No, I'm shot."

He grabbed her hand and pushed it away. Tara pulled back from him feeling totally rejected. *What man turns down a blowjob?* Clem flipped the remote and the fighters were instantly replaced with a re-run of The Honeymooners and annoying canned laughter. It was in stark contrast to the mood in their living room at that very moment. Tara stared at Clem with an expression of anger and frustration. She got up, walked over to the television and yanked the power cable out of the wall socket. The screen turned black, so did Tara's mood. She stood defiantly in front of the TV with her arms crossed tightly. Clem took a very deep breath then puffed it out like a party balloon slowly deflating.

"It's all work, work, work with you, Clem. There's never any time for us anymore," Tara complained.

"Look, it's not you, Tara. That's the ad business. It's never been a nine to five gig, you know that."

"Come on, Clem. Do you work to live or live to work?"

Clem looked at Tara for the first time that night. "I've been in this damn business long enough to know when someone's fucking with me," snapped Clem. "If I don't make CEO then Fitz will. And the first thing that prick will do is fire me. Then what? Well, I'll tell you what. We'll have to up sticks and move. I got hired right before the recession hit and I'm on a big stick, you know that and there aren't a ton of jobs out there."

Tara felt a bolt of emotion shoot through her but she knew that arguing about her needs seemed useless and trivial when Clem was on a rant like this.

"I thought as you climbed the corporate ladder your working life would get easier," Tara said, getting a little choked up.

"That's funny," Clem said sarcastically. "I want CEO. And I deserve it. Jesus, I've earned it, dammit! It's my inheritance after reeling in Rebakor. Biggest account that agency has ever won."

Clem got up from the sofa and plugged the TV back into the wall. He sat back down and flipped it on again.

Tara spent the rest of the evening busying herself around the house rather then try to engage her husband who was obviously not even interested in talking let alone having an orgasm. Clem went to bed early that night after finishing off the bottle of merlot all by himself and popping a couple of pills. By the time Tara climbed into bed, Clem was asleep. She felt bad about their earlier confrontation that evening so she snuggled up against his warm, naked body and gently stroked his shoulder. She felt a lump on Clem's back. She studied it as best she could in the dark. It looked like a painful red welt.

*Strange that Clem hadn't mentioned it.*

# CHAPTER 2

Frank Bergenson took off his headphones and stood up from behind his desk. He walked over to the soft white mohair sofa in his corner office on the forty-fourth floor of the Kemp building where a deflated Kurt Fitzgerald was sitting. Fitz was a few years younger and heavier set than Clem. A rugged face with strong features, the biggest of which seemed to be his large mouth and big white teeth. When the moment took him, he'd flash his pearly molars into a smile that bore a closer resemblance to a manic grin. Though Kurt Fitzgerald was in no mood to smile today.

Frank eased himself into an armchair. "Y'know, you and Clem Drew are the two smartest guys I ever hired. A little healthy rivalry is a good thing."

If Fitz felt flattered he wasn't showing it. His fat ego had taken a huge hit with Clem winning the Rebakor account. Frank wanted to get his man pumped up again and working with his usual enthusiasm.

"The Rebakor business was totally up for grabs. Everyone knew they wanted to get out of L.A. They'd had it with the east coast agencies, too. Those guys gauged them for years."

"Oh, cool it, Fitz. You'll still get a nice employee bonus out of it at Christmas."

"So why y'wanna see me? We pitching anything else worth $200 million?" Fitz snapped impatiently.

"I know you're pissed I left you out of the whole Rebakor pitch, Fitz but I had my reasons." Fitz didn't respond. Frank glanced at the headlines on his copy of *Adweek*. "I want you to work with Clem on the Rebakor business."

Fitz gave Frank a quizzical look. "What?"

"You heard me."

"Have you told Clem that?"

"Yes."

"And he's cool with it?" Fitz asked with a suspicious glance.

"Who cares whether he's 'cool with it'? I'm still running the show here."

"It's not gonna work, Frank."

"Oh, it'll work. I'll make sure of it." Frank Bergenson stood up and opened the pages of *Adweek* as he walked over towards the large floor to ceiling windows.

Fitz stayed seated. He was intrigued by Frank's instructions. He started to grin. "Oh, I get it. The blue-eyed boy is up to something, isn't he?"

Frank tossed the magazine onto a coffee table. "Clem has a two hundred million dollar account in his pocket. That's dangerous. It can give a man ideas."

"You mean like walking out the door and taking that fat chunk of business with him?" Fitz suggested, quickly seeing where his boss was coming from. He chuckled at the thought that old man Frank Bergenson didn't trust his favorite son.

"Precisely," Frank grumbled.

"Then why'd you leave me out of the entire pitch process?"

"Because you and Clem would've been so busy beating each other up trying to get control that we would never have gotten the business. Now we have the account, you can move in. Sure, James Molinaire loves Clem. Make him love you, too."

"And how d'ya know I won't walk out with the Rebakor account in *my* back pocket?" Fitz said, only half joking.

"Clem wouldn't let you, just as you won't let Clem. You could say I'm splitting the risk." Frank spoke softly but firmly. He wasn't kidding. Fitz listened but wasn't sold on the concept.

"So you want me to keep an eye on Golden Balls and make sure he doesn't get too chummy with James Molinaire."

"That's not what I said, Kurt," Frank frowned. "We're ad guys, not fucking CIA operatives." Fitz chuckled but Frank's expression remained deadly serious.

"But I've never even *met* Molinaire."

"Get your team to come up with the new Rebakor ad campaign. Beat Clem to the punch. Get something brilliant in front of Molinaire before Clem's guys have even had a chance to write the creative brief. I'll set up a meeting with you and Molinaire and Clem doesn't have to know about any of this."

"Golden Balls will hit the fucking roof!" Fitz smirked but liked the idea of usurping his rival in such an unethical manner, especially as it had his boss's blessing. "But what about the ad campaign Clem presented to Rebakor at the pitch? I can't un-sell something that Molinaire's already bought into."

"Who said you have to?"

"Well, how the fuck did we win the business? Didn't Clem's team present various *brilliant* creative concepts at the pitch?"

"No. Clem sold us on the strength of our previous creative work and how brilliant we *could* be for them if they were smart enough to hire us. It worked."

"So we landed a $200 million account without even pitching a single idea?"

"You could argue the one idea he *did* have was not to show Rebakor any ideas at all. Clem Drew's one helluva salesman," Frank chuckled. Fitz was impressed Clem had managed to pull that off but wasn't going to admit to his boss. "They love him to bits, Fitz. That's what concerns me and that's why we're having this conversation."

"Okay, then I need the creative strategy to give to my guys. He must've sold them on some strategic planning going forward."

"Oh, I'm sure he did. But you'll have to get that from Clem," Frank smiled.

"And how do I do that?"

"You can always trying asking Clem for it. Maybe try a charm offensive for once, Fitz."

"Oh sure. He's gonna love that." Fitz was not impressed with Frank's suggestion.

"I'll handle Clem's ego but you've got to come up with the goods." Frank stood up to let Fitz know the meeting was over. "Get your very best guys on this, Fitz. And keep your mouth shut."

Fitz's shit-eating grin was still plastered across his face when he walked out of Frank Bergenson's office. Frank was a sneaky sonofabitch and but then that's what Fitz liked about him. The chrome nameplate on the granite façade of the Kemp building may have read Bergenson & Adler but this was Frank's show. No one at the agency ever knew exactly what happened to Frank's old business partner, Lewis Adler. He'd left the agency under somewhat sudden and mysterious circumstances thirty-seven years earlier and none of the employees had ever heard of him since. He was long gone and no ever talked about it other than whispers that Frank had actually had his business partner secretly bumped off and the body buried under the foundations of the Edina public library.

Kurt Fitzgerald was now a much happier man than when his day had started. In his mind, he'd been given the green light to go to war against Clem Drew. The flag was down, the whistle had been blown. Round one was about to begin and Fitz had old man Bergenson in his corner. Maybe Frank was being a little paranoid in his old age but now Fitz had suddenly jumped up the pecking order from also-ran to serious contender.

Clem Drew stepped out of the elevator on the forty-third floor and walked past the reception desk in the lobby. As usual, he nodded to

Dee Dee, the pretty, bubbly receptionist who had an obvious crush on him. Clem looked his usual sharp self though his mood was less jovial than usual. He glanced at the 1962 Bulova Accutron watch adorning his left wrist. It was eighty-thirty precisely. Perfect timing. No flashy gold Rolex for Clem. He was too cool for that. That was gauche and more Fitz's style. Clem was quiet money.

His trusty assistant, Justine greeted him as she did every morning with her perky smile and equally perky breasts. Slim and sexy as all get out with legs all the way up to her small, tight butt, Justine was the perfect personal assistant; pretty as a picture, sharp as a tack and as loyal as a puppy dog.

"Double-shot cap on its way, boss," Justine said with a cute, dimpled smile as she passed Clem in the corridor though she could tell her boss was not in the best of moods this morning. Clem's arrival was always Justine's cue to head down to the lobby of the Kemp building where a Starbucks was conveniently located. But this morning, Justine rolled her eyes towards Clem's door as she passed by him. He heeded the warning as he walked into his office.

"Good morning, Clement," smiled Kurt Fitzgerald as he spun around in Clem's Aeron chair. "Nice view."

"I'm so pleased," Clem answered sarcastically. On any given working day, Fitz never came near Clem's office. His locale was on the other side of the building and there was no reason why their paths would cross other than Frank's monthly account exec meetings and company parties. Clem was irritated Fitz was sitting in his chair behind his desk and showing no signs of shifting his derriere.

"You going to a wedding or a funeral today?" Clem asked the black suited intruder. Fitz didn't get the sarcastic humor of Clem's quip. Instead, he leaned back in Clem's chair and put his feet up on Clem's desk. "Gucci loafers? Are you serious? Get them off my desk and get outta my chair, Fitz."

Fitz smiled at his irked counterpart and stood up disrespectfully slowly. Clem reclaimed his faithful Herman Miller by taking off his suit jacket and hanging it over the back of it, as he did every morning.

"Technically speaking it isn't your chair. Company property," Fitz reminded his agency equal as he wandered over to the windows to get a clearer view of the dramatic downtown skyline.

Clem sat down and ignored him as he booted up his laptop.

"Your office is so bland. It lacks any pizzazz," Fitz opined, looking at the stark white walls, which Frank had noted earlier.

"Well, feel free to 'pizz' off back to your own office unless you've something you'd like to discuss. I've got work to do."

"Ever thought of putting some artwork on these lonely walls?"

"Jesus Christ, everyone wants to hang shit in my office. No, I don't want anything on the damn walls," Clem snapped. "What do you want, Fitz? I've got a tight schedule."

"I could lend you a Damien Hirst. He's highly collectible. Very contemporary British artist, y'know." Clem stared at his laptop screen as Fitz strolled around Clem's office.

"Slicing embalmed animals in half is not 'art.' The man's a *wanker.*" Clem flipped open his laptop and booted it up.

"Well, you know the art world. Talent isn't a prerequisite," Fitz jabbed back. Clem was getting impatient.

"Rather like the ad world. Okay, enough with the foreplay, Fitz. Get to your point then please leave. I've got a $200 million account to take care of in case you've had your head up your ass and haven't read Ad Age, Adweek and The New York Times and the Wall Street Journal. I assume you can read."

"I have a question." Fitz sat down on the black leather sofa. Clem was already typing on his laptop and not even looking at Fitz anymore. "That must've been one helluva creative strategy you sold to Molinaire."

"And your question is?" Clem kept typing.

"That was ballsy, not showing any agency creative."

"So, I have balls. Next?"

"And they are golden," mumbled Fitz. Clem stopped typing and looked up over his laptop.

"Yes, they are."

Kurt Fitzgerald was getting nowhere fast trying to finesse the mystical creative strategy out of Clem.

"So, what was the angle you took? I mean, their previous ad campaigns have been spectacular. I don't know what you could've pitched them that was so persuasive."

Clem stopped typing and glanced up at the outwardly smiling but inwardly frustrated Fitz sitting on his sofa.

"You want a lesson in pitching, now?"

"Hey, I've gotta hand it to you, dude. You really brought home the bacon for the agency." Fitz continued with the ego stroking, sensing Clem was about to open up.

"Okay, Fitz. I'll let you in on a little secret. There was no creative strategy. I promised them a lot of things while giving them nothing. And in return they gave me everything."

"Impressive. I'd be curious to see what you come up when you do actually write it then."

"*When* I've written it, Fitz I'll be sure to come running over to your office to personally hand you a copy."

Fitz headed for the door as Clem smirked and got on with his work. If he was going to be forced to work with a man he didn't trust or respect, he wasn't going to make life easy for him. And when he made CEO, Fitz would be the first firing on his watch.

"Why don't I write it?" Fitz suggested cheekily, poking his head back around Clem's door.

"Very funny. I didn't know you could spell."

"You're a busy guy. The agency doesn't want its star ad man all tuckered out."

"Y'know, Fitz. I'm sure the old man has his reasons for putting you on this account but I'm sure he didn't expect it to be particularly harmonious. But I will be compliant so there's no need to get your panties in a wad. After I've met with the planning department I'll write the creative strategy and yes, you'll be in that meeting too, Fitz. Justine has penciled it for next Friday."

Fitz smiled. "Actually, Clem the meeting's this afternoon if you wanna attend. Two o'clock in the main conference room."

"The meeting happens when I say it happens, Fitz," Clem glared. Fitz pulled out a document from his inside jacket pocket.

"Here are my bullet points. Might wanna read them before we meet." Fitz tossed the stapled white papers down on Clem's desk as Justine walked in carrying Clem's morning cappuccino.

"Thanks, babe," Fitz smiled, taking the frothy paper cup out of Justine's hand and walking off. Justine looked back in stunned silence at the departing Fitz.

"I'll go get you another one, Clem. Sorry about that." Clem's expression said it all. He didn't need a caffeine fix to get his heart rate up now. He knew the game Fitz was playing and he wasn't going to take the bait quite so easily.

"Don't worry about it, Justine."

"Everything cool? I mean --"

"Sure. Can you call David in down in planning and tell them we have to postpone today's Rebakor meeting?"

"What Rebakor meeting?" Justine asked innocently.

"Fitz scheduled a meeting for two o'clock this afternoon. Don't call David until one forty-five. I don't want Fitz finding out. He can show up and sit in the conference room on his lonesome wondering where everyone is. That should teach him to call a meeting without my damn permission."

Justine liked Clem's thinking. "Oooo, sneaky. You got it."

Fitz had really got Clem wound up. He knew Fitz was a shit stirrer of Biblical proportions and how he'd gotten his reputation in New York for being a very political animal. Yes, Clem knew he had a formidable adversary in Mr. Kurt Fitzgerald. For the past two years, they'd both jealously guarded their clients and team members. Having to accommodate Fitz under the old man's instructions was a recipe for disaster. Fitz's little gameplay moments earlier had got this new working relationship off to an auspicious start. After all, Fitz knew the drill. He just wanted to rattle Clem's cage in the hope of wobbling his perch a little. If he wobbled it hard enough, Clem might just fall flat on his face.

Clem snatched up Fitz's bullet points and ripped the document in half without giving it even a cursory glance. He ripped again. And then once again, for good measure.

Back on Dunkirk Crescent in Eden Prairie, Tara slid a tray of unbaked cookies into her piping hot oven and set the timer. She checked the dozen cakes rising in the lower oven and turned down the heat. The kitchen was filled with a deliciously sweet aroma as Tara sprinkled flour onto a second baking tray.

*Ding dong!*

Tara hurriedly shook off her hands and touched her hair into place, leaving a white dusting of flour on her forehead. She hurried down the hallway towards the front door, curious to know who her early morning visitor might be. Standing there on the doorstep was Lorraine Pink, one of Tara's few friends.

"Lorraine! Great to see you!"

"Thought I'd swing by as I was in the neighbor…damn, girl." Lorraine looked at the white powder on Tara's forehead. "You look like you've been snorting coke and sneezed."

"Huh?" Tara glanced in a mirror. "Oh, crap. I've been baking more stuff for the church." Tara said, genuinely pleased to see her friend but horrified at her unkempt appearance.

"Come in for coffee and please ignore the mess."

"Mess? Oh *puhleeze!*" Lorraine joked as she followed Tara into the spotless kitchen. "Girl, you don't know what mess is. Try having two teenage boys living with you. Then you'd know what a real mess looks like."

Now, Lorraine had something Tara really didn't have - attitude. It came with the territory of Lorraine just being Lorraine. You see, she was more than just a little bent out of shape when it came to the touchy subject of *men*. It seemed they were either always walking out on her, or cheating on her, or pissing her off in general. Not that Lorraine wanted anyone to feel sorry for her.

"Mmmmm….smells good. I need one those darn cookies."

Lorraine was a strikingly attractive woman and if Tara felt out of place being a west coast girl, she could only imagine how Lorraine felt being a black woman in a state as white as milk toast. Lorraine sat herself down on a barstool at the island counter and looked around the expansive kitchen with its professional grade chrome appliances all looking as if they'd just been unboxed.

"How are the boys?" Tara shouted, as the noisy coffee grinder smashed up some fresh Colombian beans.

"Spending the summer with their useless piece of shit father, thank the Lord."

Lorraine was fascinated with the immaculateness of the kitchen and Tara's obsessive cleaning ability. She ran her finger along the shiny, smooth surface of the pristine granite countertop.

"Well, he can't be that useless if he's looking after them," Tara replied in defense of a man she'd never met.

"Y'know sometimes, I think the only reason you never had kids is that you're such a freakin' neat-nik."

"Double or single?" Tara asked, readying a mug under the spout of the espresso machine.

"I'm good. I don't want you messing up the world's most perfect kitchen."

"It's no trouble, Lorraine."

Lorraine looked at a framed photo of Clem and Tara on the wall taken back when they were dating in California. They both looked so relaxed and happy. Lorraine glanced enviously back at Tara.

"So tell me, since when have you gotten religion taking food to the church?"

"Gives me some sense of purpose. St. Augustine's needs help to supplement their food kitchen."

"So now you're Lutheran?"

"Oh no. I just volunteer my baking services twice a week. I enjoy it. Baking's my creative outlet."

"You're a pleaser, Tara. That's what you are. Clem must adore you. You're cute and you cook and you've got no kids to wear you out and fuck up your quality time." Lorraine's voice had a distinct ring of envy to it. "How long have you two lovebirds been married now?"

Tara pushed the flashing blue button on her expensive La Pavoni Italian espresso machine.

"Six years this May," Tara said, raising an eyebrow at the thought. "Boy, time flies when you're having fun, doesn't it?"

"You're still crazy about him, aren't you?"

"Hell, yeah! He's still hot -- muffin?" Tara offered up a warm tray of macadamia nut muffins.

Lorraine took one and pulled it apart. The steamy inside gave off a deliciously sweet, nutty aroma. "You made these, too?"

Tara nodded. Lorraine took a bite and closed her eyes. Tara got back to work.

"Mmmmmm…damn. You make me wanna punch you, you're so domesticated."

"Aren't you teaching your yoga class this morning?" Tara asked, waiting for the La Pavoni to start spluttering steam to froth up the milk.

"Uh-huh, so I shouldn't be eating all these calories."

"Sorry," Tara smiled.

"So, how's that pretty boy husband of yours doing?" Lorraine asked as she grabbed another muffin and put it in her bag.

Tara huffed a quiet sigh. "Stressed out of his noggin, actually. Either he's gonna make CEO or get fired."

"Shit. No pressure there! I'm so glad I teach yoga. Stress free gig, baby. Maybe you should find something to do other than spend every day cleaning and shopping and baking shit. If his ass gets canned you can't *both* be jobless living in a house this big."

Tara cupped her mug and sipped the creamy foam. "I'll be honest, Lorraine, I'm bored to tears. I've got to do something useful with my time."

"Get a job and hire a maid! Jesus, with Clem's fat salary you could have permanent live-in help, this place is so big. Wal-Mart are always looking for greeters, y'know," Lorraine joked.

"I think I need more mental stimulation than that, thank you very much."

"Talking of stimulation…" Lorraine flashed a coy grin, which Tara duly noted.

"Oh, so that's why you wanted to come by. Who is it *now?*" Tara asked as Lorraine's grin broke into a broad, excited smile.

"Tara, I swear this man is an angel. Look, you know what I think of the male species. They're all egocentric assholes but this one is different I tell you. You have to meet him. His name's Curtis and he's just plain adorable. I met him at the club and we've been dating two weeks now and boy, does he have a body on him or what? O Lordy!" Lorraine fanned her face with her hand in mock sweat. Tara shook her head like she'd heard it all before, knowing how quickly Lorraine got through boyfriends.

"And what's that face for?" Lorraine asked.

"Let's just hope this one sticks," Tara mused. Lorraine jumped off the barstool.

"Well, we were sure getting sticky the other night!" Tara pulled a face as Lorraine broke into a belly laugh. "So, Mrs. Drew. What are you and Mr. Workaholic doing Friday night? Because we all need to go out to dinner and I'll introduce you to my new man."

Tara shrugged. "Friday? God. No idea. We never do anything anymore. I'll ask Clem if he can make it but I can't promise."

Lorraine checked her watch and grabbed her bag. "Gotta run. Listen, Clem and Curtis are really gonna hit it off. He's a big sports nut, too. Call him right now – Friday night at seven. Maybe we'll do McCormicks."

As she walked Lorraine to the door, Tara liked the idea of a double date night out on the town though she knew that was unlikely to happen. She and Clem hadn't had a single date in months, which pretty much guaranteed the odds of Lorraine's plan for Friday night actually happening were zero to none. Mind you, they were the same odds for Lorraine and Curtis's relationship lasting more than a few weeks. Problem was, Lorraine had a temper that could be triggered by pretty much anything. Lorraine would never admit that she was ever the problem though she taught yoga to help her relax, which at least showed that she knew she had some issues.

Tara had met Lorraine at yoga class. She loved the fact that Lorraine bitched out loud when things bugged her and didn't care who heard. It went against the grain of the quiet and polite Minnesotan persona. And it amused Tara that Lorraine didn't care whose feathers she ruffled. Not that she always agreed with her best friend's perspective on life and matters. Tara could never be that *Type A* personality. She just didn't have it in herself.

Not working nine-to-five, not being a soccer mom or attending church religiously every Sunday meant that Tara's networking abilities had been somewhat limited since she and Clem had moved to Minnesota four years ago. Her drop-offs to St. Augustine's were just that and she rarely met anyone there who was her generation let alone who she might want to hang out with socially. In all honestly, she was not particularly happy living in the mid-west with her family so far away back in San Luis Obispo but here she was and she really had no right to complain or feel sorry for herself and so she didn't.

Tara stood in the middle of her fancy kitchen and looked around at her sanctum. She was fortunate to have it so good. It was summertime and the living was easy. It was just her marriage that was looking shaky and to Tara, that meant more than anything else in the world.

Justine put in a call to David Lassiter, a senior planner at Bergenson & Adler who worked one flight down. It was one forty-five precisely, the exact time Clem had instructed her to call.

"David? Hi, it's Justine. Clem needs to cancel your two o'clock meeting."

"Cancel it?" David laughed. "It ended over an hour ago. Fitz re-scheduled it to noon. Thought it was weird Clem didn't make it."

Justine was not happy. She walked into Clem's office where her boss was typing on his laptop.

"Just spoke with David Lassiter."

"Great." Clem smiled, still engrossed in his work.

"Fitz switched the Rebakor meeting to noon. It's already over." Justine stood in the doorway, as it was a safe distance from whatever Clem was going to throw. He pushed himself away from his desk.

"Sonofabitch!"

"Want me to call David and tell him to ignore everything that was agreed? I can schedule a meeting with the two of you for later."

"And tell everyone Fitz pulled some stunt to screw with me? No thanks. I don't want the entire agency to know that the gloves are off between me and Fitz. Not good for employee morale."

"Might juice up the gossip level in the agency though," Justine smirked. Clem wasn't amused. "Okay, so what d'you want me to do then?"

Clem pouted, locked in thought. "Fuck it. I'll let Fitz win this one. Ask David to send up a copy of the minutes. I'll write the creative strategy before Fitz tries to. I'll call the prick's bluff."

"Got it."

"And call James Molinaire and set up an appointment for next week. I want to fly to Louisville and get some face time with him. I don't want Fitz charging down there with his fucking strategy in hand and big dumb toothy smile. That's the kind of stunt he'd pull."

Justine went back to her desk and got on the phone. Clem got back to his typing, still irritated. And it was only a matter of minutes before Clem's irritation level hit red alert.

*Ding!*

Clem checked his new email message. The subject line said it all: *Rebakor Creative Strategy/Kurt Fitzgerald.*

It didn't take more than a few seconds of reading before Clem was on his way upstairs.

Clem burst into Frank Bergenson's office, his face red with rage.

Frank was watching the stock market on a large plasma TV.

"Frank! This isn't going to work. That jerk's trying to run my account!" Clem stood over Frank's desk. Frank turned around slowly in his plush brown leather chair.

"Sit down, Clem." Clem was in no mood to sit anywhere.

"He's gone rogue -- calling meetings without my consent, writing creative strategy and leaving me out the loop. This is never gonna work!"

"Clem, Clem, Clem. Take a breath."

"I'm taking a fucking breath, Frank!" Clem yelled. Frank stood up and thumb punched the remote, turning off the TV. He wandered over to the wall of windows that looked down onto the Minnesota Twins spectacular new ballpark below.

"Calm down."

"He's pulling this shit to undermine me," Clem steamed. "He's just trying to push my buttons. That's how that asshole operates."

"Seems he's succeeding. Your buttons are all pushed."

"Damn right!"

"Tell me something. Who's the best ball player on the Twins team?"

"Who the fuck cares?"

"I'm asking you a question, Clem. Humor me. Who's the best player?" Frank turned and peered over his gold-rimmed spectacles at his fuming account director. Clem's jaw clenched.

"Joe Mauer," Clem seethed.

"That's right. Great pitcher. Wonderful hitter."

"Jesus, Frank. You gonna give me a speech about teamwork now? You might wanna have that conversation with Fitz instead of me! And I wouldn't use the Twins as an analogy. They suck."

"Yes, they do," Frank chuckled. "You know why? Because the rest of the team aren't as good as Mauer. You're my Joe Mauer but I need more players like you on my team to make it successful. Fitz just wants to be more like you. He's just trying too hard."

"Trying too hard?"

"They say you can always tame a wild horse but you can't revive a dead one. He just needs to be reined in a little."

Clem wasn't buying it. "You're having this conversation with the wrong guy! Call Fitz in here. Tell him I'm Joe Mauer and put him back in the dug out. Better still, trade him back to the minors where he belongs."

"Okay, Clem. I'll talk to Fitz."

"Make sure you do, *coach!*"

Clem stormed out of Frank's office with the same force he entered and with his ego still seriously bent out of shape.


One floor down on Clem's side of the building, Fitz strode past Justine into Clem's office carrying a folder.

"He's meeting with Mr. Bergenson," she called out as Fitz kept walking.

"That's fine. I'll leave this on his desk."

"Leave it with me," Justine called out but Fitz was already in Clem's office. She quickly got up from behind her desk and hurried in to see Fitz standing behind Clem's chair and staring down at his desk. His eyes darted across the various papers neatly laid out like a lizard hunting a scurrying insect.

"Looking for anything in particular?" Justine asked pointedly, standing in the doorway and blocking his exit. Fitz quickly averted his gaze and glanced up at her.

"That's okay, sweetie. It can wait." Fitz flashed her a smile as he walked slowly towards her. Justine stood her ground. She wanted to keep Fitz right where he was in Clem's office until her boss returned.

"Clem will be back any minute."

Justine didn't trust Fitz one bit and wanted to keep an eye on his every move. Fitz brushed his body against hers as he slowly squeezed his bulky frame passed her. He stopped and pinned her against the doorjamb with his chest pressed firmly against her breasts.

"Nice. Are those puppies real? They feel pretty natural."

Justine pulled herself away from him and the doorjamb. "I could report you to HR for that," she scowled.

"Oh, please. Get a life," Fitz scoffed as he strolled off down the corridor.

# CHAPTER 3

Clem's silver Mercedes sped out of downtown Minneapolis and along Interstate 62 towards Eden Prairie. He checked his watch. It was late and he hadn't had a chance to call Tara. It had been a strange day and he was feeling drained. He flicked the hands-free button on the steering wheel and made a call. A voicemail picked up. Clem left a brief message.

"I need to see you again. Thursday. Seven o'clock. Call me to confirm." He hung up and glanced at the car's clock. It was 10:34 p.m. He wanted to call his wife but didn't want to wake her if she was sleeping. He kept driving.

Back on Dunkirk Crescent, Tara got into bed and switched off the bedside lamp. She wasn't going to wait up for Clem. She'd done that too many times before, though she knew she wouldn't sleep either, worrying about where he might be. Tara leaned across the bed and turned the light back on. She grabbed a bottle of Tylenol PM from the bedside drawer.

By the time Tara had woken from her silent slumber the following morning, the other side of the bed was still empty, though the ruffled sheets revealed that Clem had finally come home last night. Tara sleepily ambled downstairs and wandered into the kitchen wearing only a long t-shirt. Clem was fully dressed and standing, eating his breakfast cereal. His eyes fixed firmly on the morning's emails popping up on his laptop in case one of them might have another inflammatory attachment that he would have to defuse.

From Tara's point of view, he was annoyingly bright-eyed and bushy-tailed for someone who seemed to be burning the candle at both ends. Tara headed straight for the La Pavoni, yawning on the way.

"I wish you'd call if you know you'll be coming home that late. I was worried sick," she mumbled.

Clem kept reading, not bothering to look up. "I know. I'm sorry. We're working on the first round of creative for Rebakor. Damn nightmare," Clem answered, still engrossed in his emails.

"Should've called," she repeated. Tara wasn't going to hide how ticked off she was as she put a mug under the espresso spout. She opened the fridge door and grabbed the milk, deliberately making as much noise as possible with her every action to show her annoyance. If it bothered Clem he didn't show it.

"Didn't get a chance," said Clem. "I was too distracted trying put out another fucking fire." Clem hit the eject button on his laptop and a CD popped out. He carefully tucked it in a plain CD case and placed it next to his laptop. "Hey, d'you pick up my shirts yesterday?"

Tara ignored the question and fired back with one of her own.

"Did you get my message about dinner at McCormick's with Lorraine and her new boyfriend for Friday night?"

"Yeah, no way that can happen."

"Figured."

"It's just too nuts with this first round of Rebakor creative coming up," Clem explained. It was nothing more than Tara expected. Nonetheless she was still disappointed.

"Clem, it's a Friday night. We have no social life anymore."

"Sorry, honey. But you've got all day to have a social life. I've got this thing called a job, remember?" Clem snarked. Now Tara was really getting pissed. This was familiar ground and she was getting fed up with it. Clem shut down his computer and dumped his empty cereal bowl in the sink.

"So how did you get that big red welt on your back?" Tara asked him, changing the subject and throwing a curve ball. Clem blinked. He looked at her for the first time that morning.

"Welt? What are you talking about?" Clem looked puzzled. Tara calmly put the milk back in the fridge and closed the stainless steel door.

"The one on your back. And there's another one on your shoulder," she said, more calmly this time, though very surprised Clem wasn't aware of his injuries.

"Didn't know I had any," Clem muttered as he bagged his laptop.

"Seriously? How can you not know? They look painful."

"Oh, yeah. I got dinged a few times last night playing squash courtesy of Jack Perkins," Clem suddenly remembered. Tara leaned against the counter and folded her arms.

"And since when did you start playing squash?"

"I played a bit in college. What's the big deal?" Clem blew off Tara's questions as he checked his reflection in the mirror and tightened the Windsor knot in his tie.

"Jack plays squash?" Tara asked, doubting the truthfulness of Clem's explanation.

"Badly. Gotta go." Clem grabbed his suit jacket and picked up his computer bag.

"So, you've got time to play squash. Huh. No time for dinner with your wife and friends but you've got time to play squash," Tara voiced sarcastically.

Now it was Clem's turn to be irritated. "Tara. I'm not really playing squash, I'm playing *politics*. Jack's an alibi, I mean, ally."

"Alibi?" Tara jumped.

"You know what I meant. I meant ally."

"Rather Freudian."

"What? Look, I don't have time for this, Tara."

"What's new? You don't have time for anything anymore. It's all work, work, work with you these days."

"Like I said, Jack's an *ally* and I need all the friends and support I can get now that Fitz has decided to go to war."

Clem headed for the garage. Tara was not alert enough for a full-scale argument so early in the day. Anyway, Clem was not playing ball this morning.

"I'll tell Lorraine we can't make it then," she shouted out dejectedly, conceding defeat.

Minutes later, Clem was on his usual rush hour route into downtown Minneapolis driving along Interstate 62. And, as always, the sheer volume of traffic slowed his commute to barely a crawl. This was Clem's time to think in relative peace. No company bullshit, no nagging wife, no meetings. Okay, so Tara wasn't really a nagger but she was really starting to bug him. He didn't need to be questioned every time he didn't call, got home late or had a small red blemish on his skin. Clem's focus was plainly on the financial security, the prestige and the kudos of Frank Bergenson's job and Kurt Fitzgerald was now Hell bent on derailing him. He needed a strategy. Winning such a huge account could have a negative effect on the agency's current roster of business. Clem knew clients got jealous if they felt they weren't getting the same care and attention they once enjoyed. Every client had now taken a step down the pecking order and there was probably a lot of backchat and politicking going on that he didn't know about.

Clem had to be careful not lose the respect and support of the company's other larger clients. There were three that billed over $50 million annually. Not close to Rebakor's size but still important clients to keep sweet. Clem wasn't sure how much influence they might be having or if any personal agendas were factoring into Frank's decision-making process.

Clem had to find out what these guys were thinking. *God, this company politics bullshit was so damn time-consuming.* It was an ego war. Clem's jaw started to clench.

The traffic started to pick up and the wheels of Clem's S600 began to turn quicker. Yes, a strategy was needed: Plan A with a solid Plan B backup. Maybe a Plan C too, come to think of it. *But what about Fitz? Which board members was he in bed with?* That sneaky bastard could be pulling any kind of stunts behind Clem's back. Maybe Fitz was merely a puppet being manipulated from above. Shit, maybe Fitz could meet with a mysterious accident and *die an ugly fucking death.*

Clem's mind started to race faster as his car gained momentum. He had to stop thinking like this. It was annoyingly distracting from his hectic work schedule. He needed to focus on the Rebakor account but his mind couldn't get off the subject of why Frank was pitting Fitz against him on such an important piece of business. Clem had to stand back and get a perspective on what this really meant. He realized that if he didn't deal with Fitz, he might not have a Rebakor account to concentrate on at all.

Putting himself in Frank's shoes, Clem figured there could only be one logical reason, though in Clem's mind it was totally illogical: it was too dangerous to leave a $200 million account in the hands of one man. But Frank had no reason in the world to think that Clem could ever betray him. *Why would he think that?* If it truly was the case then that really pissed him off. Clem was a loyal employee who'd worked his tail off for the agency. He'd never try to steal away any Bergenson account. Sure, plenty of fledgling agencies had started life doing just that. After all, that's a sound business move if you want to start your own shop but not Clem. There was no way he'd stab Frank in the back, and all the other employees at Bergenson, by running off with Molinaire's business. That's the kind of move Fitz would pull in a heartbeat but then that man had no shame. Fitz was very good at taking credit for the work done by colleagues. And he was very good at manipulating those below him and schmoozing those above him. Nosiree, it wouldn't be above Fitz.

What was galling to Clem was that if his theory about Frank was true then it showed a serious lack of trust from the old man. *So did that mean Frank Bergenson trusted Fitz more?* That was a ridiculous idea. Clem was the blue-eyed boy, the chosen one, the heir apparent. Kurt Fitzgerald was a conniving bullshitter. Surely Frank Bergenson must have garnered some inkling that Fitz was a prick after working with him these past two years.

Clem's mind was a jumble of thoughts, fears and ideas. He just had to keep his eye on the ball at all times from now on though the real issue was just how many balls did he need to keep juggling before something hit the floor hard?

On the sun-drenched patio at D'Amico's restaurant in Edina, Tara and Lorraine sat with menus open though neither was looking at any of the culinary offerings. They were deep in conversation. Lorraine looked particularly perturbed.

"So Clem said he can't make dinner tonight because he's too busy?"

"Apparently. But I'm not surprised. He's always busy. I'm sorry. I was really looking forward to hanging out with you and Curtis." Tara felt guilty, as if it was her fault.

Lorraine snapped shut her menu and slapped it down on the table. "And what's more important than taking his beautiful wife to dinner for once in a blue moon?"

"I agree, Lorraine. But he's got a business dinner somewhere with someone else," Tara answered flatly.

"What? Are you serious? Did he name the restaurant?" Lorraine was annoyed that Clem had screwed up her dinner plans with such an ambiguous excuse.

"No."

Tara closed her menu as a smiling young waiter approached.

"Are we ready ladies?" Lorraine and Tara spoke in unison as they handed their menus back to the waiter.

"Caesar salad."

"Coming right up," the waiter took their menus and departed.

Lorraine frowned at Tara. "No name of the person he's dining with or which restaurant he's going to?" Lorraine huffed. She was unimpressed with Clem's lack of divulgence but now Tara was also getting irritated.

"Oh, Lorraine, I don't know. Some new client. Who cares who it is? Look, I'm sorry we can't make it. How about the week after, maybe?"

"Tara, you need to get a clue, girlfriend." Lorraine pursed her lips and was starting to get herself wound up. Tara had seen that face before.

"He's busy. What can I say?"

"Well, it's pretty fucking obvious he's *busy*. Who's he getting *busy* with? Huh? That's what you ought to wonder about. When was the last time you and Clem got down to business?"

Tara looked confused. "You mean had sex?"

Lorraine rolled her eyes. "No, Tara. I mean played fucking checkers. Of course I mean sex!"

An elderly couple on the next table turned around and glared over at Tara and Lorraine. Tara felt embarrassed. She hushed Lorraine. "Shhhh….been a while I suppose. Couple of months ago, I think." Lorraine sat back in her seat in disbelief.

"You *think?* Are you serious? You know guys have a real hard time going a few days without getting any. He's nailing that personal assistant – Jessica - or whatever her name is," Lorraine boomed at a decibel level way too high again for Tara's comfort.

"Justine? No. She's very sweet," Tara whispered back.

"Oh, she's sweet all right. Clem doesn't need you if he's balling her!" The elderly couple gave their table a second glance. "I think you've been sniffing too much of those cleaning solutions, girl." Lorraine was on a roll now. "Stop cleaning your damn house and start getting Clem to clean up his act,"

"Oh, Lorraine you don't trust any man. You think they're all secretly up to something," Tara shot back.

"Okay, Little Miss Clueless. Call her right now. Call this little slutty Justine chick and ask her the name of the restaurant she booked for her boss tonight. Tell her that Clem left something at home that he needs for his important 'business meeting' tonight and that you'll take it to the restaurant."

"That's crazy."

"If he's really having a meeting at a restaurant, this Justine chick will have to tell you if she wants to keep her job. But if she doesn't tell you where's he's going it means she's up to no good with your husband."

"And what if she *does* tell me the name of the restaurant?"

"You're going have to go down to wherever she says Clem is having his little ol' dinner and see if everyone's telling the truth." Lorraine sat back in her seat, rather pleased with herself for coming up with such a foolproof plan to catch out Tara's cheating husband. Tara just shook her head.

"You just have an overactive imagination, Lorraine."

Lorraine jumped forward in her seat and leaned even closer into Tara. "Dammit, I'll call her then!" She fumbled around in her bag for her cell phone. "What's the number?"

Tara snatched at it. "No, you won't."

"I'll call information for it then."

"No, you won't!"

The two of them proceeded to grapple for dialing rights just as the waiter returned with their salads. Tara and Lorraine composed themselves as their Caesars were placed in front of them. Tara quickly snatched the phone from Lorraine's hands and called Clem's office.

Lorraine smiled. "Now we're getting somewhere."

"Hi, Justine. It's Tara. Hey, what's the name of the restaurant Clem's going to tonight?" Tara smiled at Lorraine as she waited for Justine's response. "Bella Luna, at seven? Okay, thanks so much, Justine." Tara handed the cell phone back to Lorraine with a told-you-so expression.

"Bella Luna at seven o'clock. Happy now?" Tara asked. Lorraine was not impressed.

"Double bluff. Trust me, they'll both be there tucked away in a romantic corner," Lorraine insisted.

"God, Lorraine. You're unbelievable!"

"Unless he lied to Justine and he's seeing someone else, just like my cheatin' dirt bag ex-husband did to me. Men are lying sons of bitches. They all think with their dicks."

And with that, Lorraine shut up at the very moment the elderly couple got up to leave, shooting Lorraine one last disapproving glare as they departed. Lorraine shot one back.

"What's your freakin' problem? Shouldn't listen in on private conversations."

For Tara, their conversation was now over, too. Lorraine had brought it all back to the same place their conversations always tended to end up: back to the men that had done Lorraine wrong. Tara munched on a ranch-dressed lettuce leaf.

"Yummy salad."


Clem sat on the edge of his desk listening to two media buyers give the details of the planned Rebakor media blitz that would launch the new logo and new Rebakor fusion-soled running shoes. The deadline for the presentation was approaching fast and Fitz was on Clem's back to see the projections.

Justine poked her head around the door.

"D'you want me to call in lunch for you boys?"

"Sure, we'll be a while," Clem replied. "Pizza good for you guys?" The two media buyers nodded.

"Remember you have a three o'clock with Katrina and Max and then a four o'clock with Jerry and Henry," Justine reminded her boss as she went to phone in the pizza order. Clem winced.

"Oh, shit. Yep, thanks Justine. Damn! I totally forgot about those guys."


Back on Dunkirk Crescent, Tara carefully packed up her latest baked offerings to take to St. Augustine's when something caught her eye. It was the CD that Clem had ejected from his laptop that morning. He'd obviously forgotten to take it with him in the kerfuffle over their somewhat heated exchange.

Tara picked it up. Scrawled in black magic marker was a name: *Britney*. Tara frowned. She took it over to her Mac in the living room. Tara had no idea what might be on the disk or who this Britney chick might be but Lorraine had planted a little seed in her head and now Tara's suspicions were growing.

She slid it inside her computer and waited. A screen appeared with an icon she hadn't seen before. Her computer didn't like whatever she'd just inserted.

*File Unrecognizable.*

The uncooperative file on the mysterious CD was protected. It seemed to be a text file of some sort but she still couldn't get it to open. Clem's computer was a PC so it was a compatibility issue she couldn't resolve. She needed to a PC to access whatever was on that disk. Tara grabbed her cell phone and dialed.

"Hi, Lorraine, it's me. Your laptop's a PC, isn't it?"

Thirty minutes later, Lorraine and Tara were staring at the screen of the PC laptop. Lorraine had a sarcastic expression on her face.

"I told you, didn't I? Men. All the damn same. Who the fuck's Britney?"

"No clue," Tara answered. A box on the screen asked for a password. Tara left it blank and hit the *enter* button in the hope the file might open but nothing happened. She was no techno geek by any stretch of the imagination.

"Hmmmm…" Tara sighed.

"Shit," muttered Lorraine. "Why the fuck does he need to password protect it? That's your evidence right there. Okay, let's figure this out. What's Clem's mother's name?"

"Louise."

Lorraine typed the letters into the password space then hit the *enter* button again. It didn't work.

"He ever have a dog?"

"Buster." Lorraine re-typed the password. Nothing.

"Crap!"

"Mother's maiden name?"

"Crowther."

Lorraine hit the keys. Nothing.

"Fuck!"

"Middle name?"

"James."

Nothing.

"Bullshit."

"We could be here all day trying to guess his password, Lorraine."

"Fuck. *I'll* go to the restaurant and *I'll* catch the bastard red-handed." Lorraine was starting to get on her soapbox again. Tara's eyes widened.

"No you won't, Lorraine."

"Tara, if Clem's cheating on you, wouldn't you rather know for sure than build a resentment that'll burn you up because he's never gonna tell you about her so you'll end up hating the very man you're so damn crazy about? Do you really wanna be as fucked up as me? Yeah, I admit it. I'm fucked up but that's what the male species has done to this girl!"

Tara looked downcast. Lorraine had made her point.

"Okay," Tara said quietly. "I'll go to the restaurant."

# CHAPTER 4

Tara didn't often drive into downtown, especially at night. If it wasn't for the GPS in her SUV she'd be totally lost. Her mind was racing as she sped north along Interstate 35. The skyscrapers of downtown loomed large on the horizon. She'd changed from her usual casual attire something more presentable; a chic black dress and heels. After all, what woman doesn't look cute dressed like that? She thought. And if she was about to catch her cheating husband with some tart, she was going to make sure said tart would see that Mrs. Drew wasn't some frumpy old stay-at-home wifey. But what would she do if Clem was getting all snugly with another woman when she got there? *That would be it. Over. How could she ever trust him again? There's no way she could stay in a marriage with a cheat and a liar. No way.*

What would she say to him? Or to this Britney slut? To the both of them sitting there like two little lovebirds? Would she create a scene? What if Clem got mad? No, he wouldn't. Clem was too cool for that. He'd try and weasel out of it with some damn lie that would sound so fucking convincing she'd have no way of knowing if he was telling the truth or not. *Shit. Lorraine was right.* The resentment was already building inside her.

"Take the next exit," said the dulcet-toned female voice of her car's navigation system.

"Okay, shut up," Tara mumbled through tight lips.

Friday night at Bella Luna was always packed with diners. This was definitely a 'reservations only' establishment. It was a large, stylish, upscale restaurant in the heart of the downtown business district. The décor featured deep orange walls with dark Japanese wood tables and chairs though the cuisine was decidedly Tuscan Italian. Its low lighting gave the place a distinctly warm and inviting ambience. There was the usual clientele of suited corporate types sitting at tables with a sprinkling of beautiful women.

A tall statuesque hostess greeted Tara at the front desk. "Do you have a reservation?" Her glossy red lips smiled perfectly like a model in a Revlon cosmetics magazine ad.

"No, no. I'm here to see, er…some people who are dining here tonight."

"Their name? I can tell you which table they're sitting at," the helpful hostess suggested.

Tara couldn't see past the bamboo partition, which separated her from the main room full of diners. She was nervous. This could be a very weird situation.

"Er….Drew. Clem Drew is the name," Tara replied, straining her neck for any sign of her husband. The hostess checked her list of reservations. A perfectly manicured fingernail stopped two thirds of the way down the page of her leather bound book.

"Here we are. Drew. Plus one." The hostess smiled at Tara. Tara's heart was pounding so hard she could hear it.

"This way." The tall hostess walked into the main room.

"No!" Tara blurted out, causing her guide to stop and turn around with a puzzled look. "It's a surprise. Just point out where they're sitting."

"Oh, okay. Table eighteen. Just through there to your right," the hostess indicated. Tara sucked in a lungful of air and walked slowly in the direction of the hostess's elegantly outstretched arm. Her eyes darted around the busy room like a nervous fawn surrounded by a pack of wolves. She walked as nonchalantly as she could muster past the various groups eating, drinking and conversing at their tables. There was a lively hubbub of chitchat as servers went about their duties. And there, right where the hostess had pointed, Tara spotted a pretty brunette: a young thirty-something sitting alone at a table for two.

With a cocktail in her left hand, the woman deftly texted on her iPhone with the other, obviously waiting for Clem. The brunette glanced up with an expressionless stare, noting Tara's approaching presence. It wasn't Justine but yes, that was her. *That was Clem's whore all right.* Maybe Clem was in the restroom or at the bar or maybe...

"Tara?"

The voice was unmistakably Clem's. Tara spun around to see her husband sitting with a very distinguished older gentleman.

"Oh! Hi!" Tara gushed with an embarrassed smile. "Glad I found you," she blustered as Clem and his dining companion got up from their chairs.

"What are you doing here? Is everything okay?" Clem looked genuinely concerned. Tara's Plan B speech kicked in on cue.

"Oh, no. Yes, I mean! Everything's fine. Everything's fine but I was worried you might have needed this." Tara pulled out Clem's mysterious CD from her shoulder bag. Clem smiled.

"Oh, honey. That's okay. No, I don't need that. I've already copied it onto my hard drive." Clem turned to his guest. "Hank, this is my wife, Tara."

"Good evening, Tara. Hank Britney, pleased to meet you," the older man smiled warmly, extending his hand to shake Tara's.

"Hank's one of our biggest clients."

"Used to be the biggest till the new guys came to town. Very thoughtful of you, Tara. Not many wives would go to so much effort just on a hunch."

Tara smiled weakly and shrugged. "No big deal. I just thought it might've been important."

"Care to join us?" Hank suggested.

Tara would loved to have joined them both especially as she was all dressed up for the evening and now in serious need of a stiff drink. She felt incredibly silly barging in on them like some jealous wife who thought her husband might be cheating on her. *Fancy that!* But Clem wouldn't want her to stick around. Tara figured if she sat down the conversation would be geared to include her and then the whole point of Clem meeting this Hank Britney character would be wasted. Tara looked at Clem for some clue that he might want her to join them.

"Looks like we're short of a chair," Clem said which was enough of a hint for Tara to leave.

"You two carry on. Love to join you both but I'm meeting Lorraine and her new flame at McCormicks," Tara lied. "Gotta get going. Nice to meet you, Britney. Sorry, Hank!"

"Likewise," Hank smiled.

Tara pecked Clem on the cheek and departed. She couldn't get out of the place quick enough. She felt so ridiculous. *How could she have been so wrong?* It was Lorraine's fault. That bitter, twisted woman had screwed up Tara's usually very levelheaded thinking. Her anger was now directed away from her innocent husband and focused on Lorraine as she hurriedly exited Bella Luna.

As Tara waited outside and waited for the valet kid to bring her vehicle, her blood rush subsided and she collected her thoughts. *Clem was just having a business dinner. He wasn't having an affair after all.* She was happy. Okay, that was all rather embarrassing and unnecessary back inside the restaurant but her worst fears were not realized. Tara was hugely relieved. That was the first and last time she would ever let Lorraine warp her thinking. Clem was a good, hard working husband and she needed to remain supportive through this difficult time for him. She would not be so easily manipulated again. Tara was mad at herself for listening to Lorraine in the first place. That woman was damaged goods when it came to the male gender. Her instincts were always wrong and she was wrong again this time. She wanted to call her right then and there and tell her she'd figured it out all cock-eyed but Tara knew she was in too much of an emotional state and might regret what she'd say.

Back in the sanctuary of her travertine tiled bathroom, a calmer Tara soaked in her Jacuzzi tub with its air jets gently pumping out bubbles, merlot in hand. She hummed along to the soothing tones of a Nora Jones CD playing softly and tried to mellow out before Clem got home. She'd been soaking for nearly an hour and was ready to get out but was just too relaxed and warm to move.

"Hey, you." Clem threw his tie in the closet and walked over to the tub causing Tara to snap out of her meditative state.

"Oh, hi, honey. I'm sorry, that was so dumb of me tonight." Tara said quietly, still feeling guilty for thinking Clem might be cheating on her. Not that Clem any inkling of Tara's motivation for showing up at Bella Luna. Or did he?

"Sorry? What for? Hank Britney was impressed. He thought you were my secretary at first. Even Justine's not that efficient."

"I was worried I'd made you look like some forgetful idiot," Tara lied. She was more worried Clem had found her out. He pulled off his shoes and sat on the side of the bathtub.

"Britney had already seen my Power Point presentation for the direction I want to take the agency next year. He loved it. That guy carries a lot of clout so it's good to have him in my corner. Any of that merlot left?"

"On the kitchen counter." Clem headed downstairs. "Clem?" Tara called out.

"What?"

"I love you, honey."

"Ditto."

Tara slid her shoulders back under the foamy water, relieved that Clem wasn't mad at her and that he hadn't figured out her ulterior motive. Seemed he was in a good mood for a change, too. A rare occurrence indeed. Maybe things on Dunkirk Crescent weren't so bad after all. A warm and fuzzy feeling drifted through Tara. Okay, maybe she was a little drunk but so what? She felt good.

By the time Clem came back up to the bedroom, Tara was already in bed asleep. Maybe Clem might have had carnal thoughts on his mind but that wasn't going to happen now. He got undressed quietly and got into bed. Leaning over, he gently kissed Tara on her brow so he wouldn't wake her, and then rolled over to turn off the bedside lamp and go to sleep. Tara turned over slowly and sleepily to snuggle up a little closer to Clem. As they spooned together silently in the dark, she slid her arm around his stomach. She felt a slightly raised bump on his skin.

"No more squash," she whispered.

Next morning, Tara was feeling particularly perky as she stood over by the toaster waiting for her hot cinnamon bagel to pop up. Clem walked into the kitchen, immaculately dressed as always and in Tara's eyes looking even more handsome than usual. Clem was carrying a dark blue suit.

"Morning, honey." Clem dumped the suit on the counter. "Can you drop this at the dry cleaners today, sweetie?"

"Sure. I'll take it in this morning."

The toaster dinged and the two bagel halves popped up, filling the kitchen with a delicious cinnamon aroma. Clem leaned across Tara, grabbing one of the halves and pecking her on the cheek.

"Thanks. See you later." Clem headed for the garage.

"What about dinner tonight?" Tara called out.

"I'll call you later!" Clem shouted back. Well, at least that was better than 'don't wait up.'

Tara's Lexus pulled into a parking space outside Cho's Dry Cleaners. She felt good that Clem's mood seemed so much lighter than it had been over the previous three nights. Obviously, the dinner with Hank Britney had given him a sense of security which had also alleviated Tara's sense of insecurity. How quickly feelings can change over the shortest time, Tara thought.

Tara grabbed Clem's suit and walked into see Mrs. Cho, an elderly Chinese woman who had apparently lost the ability to smile many years ago. She appeared through a rack full of cellophane wrapped garments with a pen behind her ear. Tara dumped the suit down on the counter and gave Mrs. Cho a particularly big smile, which had absolutely no effect on the Asian laundry owner's po-faced demeanor.

"Good morning, Mrs. Cho. I need this by tomorrow, please."

"Okay. Drew, right?"

"Yes, Tara Drew. Oh, wait..." Tara quickly checked the jacket and pants pockets. "My husband always forgets to empty his pockets," Tara smiled, finding nothing. "Well, he proved me wrong for once."

She handed over the suit to Mrs. Cho who checked the jacket's lapel pocket that Tara had missed. Mrs. Cho handed a business card to Tara.

"Check all pockets."

Tara looked at the white business card while Mrs. Cho took Clem's suit to the back of the shop. It was a rather nondescript card with just a name, number and description printed in black Garamond type: *Mistress Krystal – Professional Services - 952-941-5051.*

Tara stared at it then flipped it over. Handwritten on the back in Clem's distinctive handwriting was written 'Tuesday, 5pm'.

As Tara drove home she felt numb inside. *Professional services?* No, it couldn't be what she was thinking it might be. This wasn't right. Surely this couldn't be a real business card. *But then again.*

Maybe Lorraine wasn't so far off the mark after all. Just when she thought everything with her and Clem seemed hunky dory again she finds what was looking like a smoking gun. Maybe she was over-reacting. *No, that card was pretty clear.* She had to confront Clem about this. She wanted some answers. God, what a shock to her system this was, especially after the events of the previous evening. Tara slammed on the brakes and pulled over to the side of the road. She rummaged through her bag for her cell phone and placed a call to her best friend.

"Lorraine?"

"Hey, honey. How'd it go last night?"

"We have to talk. Are you at the club?"

"Yeah, come on down."

Tara waited in the café of Bodyworks Fitness as a spandex clad Lorraine walked towards her carrying two large protein smoothies. She was anxious to learn how Tara's evening had gone.

"You caught the sonofabitch red-handed, didn't you?" she asked a pensive Tara. By the expression on Tara's face, Lorraine figured she knew what Tara was about to say. "I knew it."

She sat close to Tara to comfort her. "Here, try this -- Blueberry with whey protein. It's good for you. Full of anti-oxidants." Lorraine handed Tara one of the enormous purple drinks.

"I'm very confused.'

"Dammit, who wouldn't be?" Lorraine commiserated.

"I felt like a complete idiot last night. I walked in on Clem like a crazed jealous wife and he's there with some sweet, older gentleman having a business meeting."

Lorraine was taken aback. "Really? Then why are you so pissed off?"

"Because I found *this*."

Tara handed Lorraine Mistress Krystal's business card. Lorraine studied it.

"Ooo, kinky. Where d'you get it?"

"It was in Clem's jacket pocket."

"Clem's into kinky shit?" Lorraine asked rhetorically, keeping her voice low as club members mingled about them.

"What does that card say to you?" Tara asked looking straight-faced at Lorraine. "And that's Clem's handwriting on the back."

"Oh, fuck. Like I said, it says to me that Clem's into kinky shit." Lorraine handed the card back to Tara.

"This is one of those dominatrix people, isn't it?" Tara asked her more sexually experienced friend.

"Well, I'm guessing she ain't a babysitting service but I could be wrong again."

"Who else could this person be? I mean – this card..." Tara continued.

"Honey, if that card is genuine, then someone's due for a whupping on Tuesday at five o'clock. That's what that cards says." Tara suddenly lost all interest in her protein shake. "Hey, I got plenty of ex's who deserve an ass whupping," Lorraine quipped.

"Why would Clem want to go to someone like that? That's disgusting." Tara seemed shell-shocked.

"Fucked if I know. But there are a lot of creepy guys out there."

"You're saying Clem's a creepy guy?"

"Honey, most men are sex freaks. So many of them are damn perverts who just get off on this kinda sick shit. Masochists, sadists, gangbangers....y'know, men in general."

Tara felt repulsed. "Clem's not a sex freak."

Lorraine was back on her soapbox talking about her favorite topic and she wasn't listening to Tara anymore.

"Yeah, that kinda porn is *all* over the internet. Fetish stuff. All kinds of crap like you wouldn't believe. Some guys like to wear diapers. They get off dressing up like a baby and sucking on a bottle for Chrissakes! I don't get it."

Tara was horrified by the visual imagery Lorraine had just put in her head. "So after this Mistress Krystal whacks her clients do they have sex?"

"Beats me!" laughed Lorraine, enjoying her own zinger though Tara didn't see the funny side.

"I don't know who I'm married to anymore," Tara mumbled.

Lorraine tried to console Tara with a friendly arm around her shoulder. "Sorry, baby. It's not funny, I know.

"I mean, there I am trying to be a good wife, being supportive, running his errands, cooking him his favorite meals...and he's seeing some woman for sex. Why doesn't he want to have sex with me? What am I? Nothing more than just his cook and housekeeper?" Tara blathered.

"You don't know that for sure." Lorraine squeezed Tara tight.

"I've seen the marks on his body."

"What?"

"Big red welts."

"Shit. That's not good." Lorraine's sour expression triggered Tara's waterworks. "But that doesn't mean this Mistress Krystal chick did it," said Lorraine, unintentionally coming to Clem's defense in an attempt to comfort Tara.

"Don't stick up for him!"

Lorraine sat back and picked up her drink. "Well, did you ask Clem *how* he got these marks on his body?"

"Playing squash."

"So he got the marks playing squash. There you go."

"Clem doesn't play squash. He doesn't even have a bat," Tara shot back.

"Racquet." Lorraine corrected her.

"Bat, racquet, who cares? If he's been lying to me and cheating on me then I'm going to catch him. I deserve better than this," Tara snapped angrily.

"Well, if it was me, I'd taser his balls. Yeah, that's what I would do but then I'm no Dr. Phil." Lorraine slurped on her straw. "Mind you, he'd probably get off on it."

"Lorraine, you have no idea who I'm dealing with here. This could've been going on for years without my knowledge. Clem is in the bullshit business. He's mastered it. That's why he's been so successful. He'd spin me a mile of bullshit that's so good I'd end up believing him because he's always so damn convincing,"

Tara tossed her protein shake in the trash. "It's disgusting."

"You wanna try the banana strawberry?" Lorraine asked stupidly as Tara stood up and headed towards the exit.

Lorraine had never seen Tara angry before. She was always the personification of calmness. Now her eyes were glaring and there was a fire in her voice that Lorraine could relate to. In fact, she felt like she'd finally found a kindred spirit. She scurried after her friend.

"Okay, Tara. This is what you do. Photocopy the card. Put it back in his jacket pocket. Don't mention it. Then file for divorce."

*Divorce?* That really wasn't what Tara needed to hear at that moment. The reality of her situation suddenly caught up with Tara. She'd stopped crying but her eyes welled up again.

"But I don't want my marriage to end!" Tara blurted.

They walked quickly outside into the parking lot towards Tara's Lexus. Tara was now damping her tears with a scrunched up tissue.

"Honey, in my experience, you can't kick the kink out of a guy. It's like a disease, an addiction. You're going to have to deal with the fact you married a kinkster."

Lorraine's frankness had all the subtlety of a dentist with a jackhammer. It certainly wasn't what Tara wanted to hear but it had the effect of turning off her waterworks and giving her a moment of sheer clarity.

"Well, I'll deal with it then. I'm going to cure him," Tara said, defiantly.

"Of course, there's always marriage counseling too but if I was you, I'd be calling a divorce lawyer instead of a therapist," Lorraine continued her tactless train of thought though she could tell Tara wasn't interested in that route of treatment for her and Clem.

"I know what to do," Tara said firmly.

# CHAPTER 5

Clem was holding court in his office with Creative Director Chuck Svensen and various writers and art directors from downstairs.

"Okay, guys. We need a concept that'll play across the board in all media – TV, radio, billboards, hot air balloons, you name it."

"Hot air balloons?" queried the freckled art director.

"That was a joke, Suzie."

"I thought Fitz and his team were meant to be in this meeting, Clem," pointed out Jerry, the senior writer in the group. Clem handed out six creative briefs.

"Don't worry about Fitz. Here's the creative brief. Everything you need to know – demographics, previous taglines, you already know the strategic positioning of the brand and where we need to take it, and last of all…budget."

"Wow! We could get Spielberg to direct with this kinda money," said Rachel, another of the art directors, staring at the dollar amount on Clem's brief.

"Chuck, I need to see something from these guys here that we can approve internally by the end of next week."

"Okay," grunted Chuck, jotting notes on his iPad.

"What's this client like?" asked Herman, a chubby writer on the team.

"Conservative," Chuck Svensen informed the room.

"So no wacky alien monkeys, angry nuns or tattooed babes in bikinis," Clem added, to a collective groan.

"You account executives have no clue about decent creative," Jerry complained. "My alien monkeys campaign could have won me a Clio."

Clem was used to dealing with all the egos of the creative department. "Don't make my job any harder trying to sell the client stuff we all know he isn't going to buy. That'll just piss him off."

"Heard this speech before," Herman mumbled to Rachel.

"Come on, guys. You know my job is to sell clients campaigns that actually increase sales and not just give you golden gongs. How about that for a concept?"

"Yeah but Clem," Herman butted in. "My buddy at Saatchi's in London won the Palme d'Or at the Cannes Advertising Awards two years back. He got a week in the south of France on the friggin' French Riviera! Parties, Euro chicks -- all expenses paid!"

"Holy shit! Are you serious?" said Eric, the youngest copywriter in the department.

"That's what we're talking about!" Jerry cracked.

Everyone in the room knew that accolades led to awards and that awards led to pay raises and bonuses plus a grand old time to boot. In the creative department, there was a healthy competitive environment as each two-person team of art director and copywriter wanted to out-do the others but Clem needed all these guys to pull together now. It was up to Chuck Svensen to rally his creative troops and come up with several stellar campaign ideas but he was being unusually quiet.

"I'm leaving it up to your collective creative brilliance to show me some campaigns that'll work in all media across the board from TV to point-of-sale. Just make the product the hero and if it has your blessing Chuck, I'll present it to Rebakor. Let's have an internal meeting early next week and maybe I can present to Molinaire down in Louisville the following Friday." Clem smiled at the eager creative teams perusing his paperwork. "Okay, any more questions?"

"Yeah," Chuck tapped his finger on the table. "Not sure this creative brief jives with the strategy Fitz presented the other day."

"Just work to *this* creative brief," said a stone-faced Clem.

"You guys are working together on this, right? I mean, I don't want my department cranking out concepts to a brief that doesn't fit the strategy."

Suddenly all eyes were drilled on Clem.

"Work to the strategy in this brief, Chuck. Right – so are we done?" Clem asked bluntly to the group. The room stayed silent. Everyone knew what was needed. "Thanks, guys. Meeting over."

Tara propped up Mistress Krystal's business card on her computer screen. If it was a gag card of some sort it certainly looked very authentic. *And why would there be a time of day scribbled on the back of the card in Clem's handwriting?* Tara grabbed the card and looked at the number. She just had to get her nerve up. What would she say if she called this mysterious woman? Tara couldn't stop herself from turning back to look again at that photo of her and Clem in Santa Monica. It made her sad and angry.

*Call, dammit!*

Grabbing her cell phone, Tara dialed the number on the card. A female voice answered almost immediately.

"Hello…"

"Hi. Is this Mistress Krystal?"

"…leave a message."

Hearing the flat tone of the voicemail message caught her off guard. Tara hung up abruptly. *Did she really think someone in this line of work would pick up a call?* No, that wouldn't be very discreet at all. This woman was a pro. She'd have to be very circumspect with whom she spoke to on a phone line that might be tapped. After all, this service couldn't possibly be legal.

Tara spent the rest of the day surfing the web Googling one word after another all with the same theme – Mistress, Dominatrix,

Fetish, Sado-masochism, BDSM - the list of terms seemed endless. She understood the basic concept of this sort of thing did but she wanted to know if actual sexual intercourse was involved. It was bad enough that she'd discovered Clem's secret desire to be beaten and dominated by a strange woman but what was eating her up was whether his motivation was for the pain or for the sex. Or both. Either way, he had broken the trust between them and Tara was feeling betrayed.

The web spilled its secrets to Tara. There were thousands of websites and blogs dedicated to bondage, domination, submission and masochism. Some of the pictures were hard for her to look at, as they were so graphic. Some of the videos she watched were painful to even listen to. But she wanted to know about this fetish of pain and humiliation and why so many people seemed to find it pleasurable. Tara had to understand why the man she thought she knew so well would go seeking what seemed such a strange sexual perversion. She continued to read a blog written by a Dominatrix who called herself Madame Magdalene....

*You know I'm talking to you. Mister macho. All strong and powerful. You have an insatiable desire to become a slave to a beautiful, arousing woman such as myself. Like all my male slaves, you desire to be punished, humiliated and exposed in intimate sessions for your deviant needs to really be fulfilled. You might appear to be in control of everything in your life, but to me, you are worthless. You do exactly as I tell you, no matter how belittling, how embarrassing, or how emasculated you might feel while performing such acts of sexual depravity. You are mine, to use, torment and tease and you will obey my every instruction.*

Tara soaked up the information on the screen. What was this freaky, warped world she had discovered? While it might seem alien to her, it obviously wasn't to Clem.

The more she read, the angrier she became. She felt an inner rage. Tara realized she could no longer trust this strange man she shared her life with. Had he been living a lie all this time? How long had this been going on? Was their marriage just a sham? Was this the reason their once exciting sex life was now non-existent? So many questions ran through Tara's mind but the thought that Clem found her sexually inadequate was killing her. Clem was her dream man. He was everything to her, in and out of bed. *Why would he jeopardize their marriage over this twisted, kinky shit?*

Looking up from her computer screen she glanced again at the picture of her and Clem laughing together on the pier at Santa Monica back when they were dating. Where was *that* man? That fun-loving, sweet-talking guy with the big smile and California tan? What had he become? What had happened to that relationship when everything was so wonderful and normal? Even back then when they had little money they still seemed to have everything. Now they were financially in great shape but it seemed they really had nothing after all.

Tara continued to read, searching for the psychological reasons why anyone would seek out this type of behavioral weirdness. Much to her surprise, she began to learn that it was people in positions of power and authority who were more likely to enjoy being submissive. It seemed they wanted to relinquish responsibility albeit for just brief moment in their lives. Instead of telling others what to do, they wanted someone to tell them what to do. *So, it was the submissives who were really in control, not the person dominating them.*

Relating this to Clem all seemed to make some kind of sense. He fit the profile perfectly. After all, Clem had a lot of power at work and a great fear of losing that power. But would that explain his need to explore this kinky way of behaving? Obviously, he was ashamed of it otherwise surely he would have expressed some of this to Tara. *Why did he feel he couldn't share this intimate side of his nature with his own wife? Was he scared she would leave him? Was it about the sex? Was sex even involved?* Getting tied up and beaten is a far cry from the simple pleasures of good old-fashioned fucking. Tara started to feel sexually inadequate. She thought about what they did in the bedroom. He liked oral sex, giving and receiving. They mixed it up pretty often so it never got repetitive. She would straddle him sometimes while other occasions they'd do it doggie style. *That was pretty edgy, wasn't it?* Obviously, not kinky enough for her more needy husband. So, was it her fault that she didn't satisfy Clem in the bedroom? Endless questions were spinning through her mind.

One word kept coming up again and again: *Control.* It was all about *control.* This need was *controlling* Clem, Clem was *controlling* her, and she had no *control* over any of this. Fact is, she'd let Clem's career *control* her life. She'd never wanted to move from sunny California to freezing Minnesota but she did for him. Now Tara felt like she really didn't have control of her own life anymore. That would change from this day forth. Right then and there, Tara decided it would be *her* turn to take control of matters now.

Tara knew the knee jerk reaction for any woman in her situation would be to simply confront Clem and let him explain his actions. But in her mind, she could see Clem reprising Jack Nicholson in *A Few Good Men* yelling at her *'You can't handle the truth!'* which she feared might also be true. Confronting Clem was always an option but she had other ideas how to discover an even greater truth that would serve her better because this was now about Tara taking control of her marriage and her life, with or without Clem.

A shot of adrenalin coursed through her veins. It was like a thousand watt light bulb had just exploded in her frontal lobe. Grabbing her cell phone again, Tara suddenly felt empowered. If she didn't like the situation it was up to her to change it.

Frank Bergenson and Kurt Fitzgerald waited floor for the elevator. "I like the campaign. It's solid," Frank nodded approvingly.

"Solid? It totally rocks!" Fitz shot back, surprised by his boss's faint praise.

"Well, to tell you the truth, I don't get it. But who gives a shit whether I get it or not? I'm not meant to get it. I'm not the target market. If kids can relate to it, that's all that matters."

The two men stepped in to the elevator and descended to the

underground parking garage. "I can't remember the last time I jogged anywhere come to think of it. Has Clem seen this?" Frank asked.

"Very funny."

"Good. Then I want you to fly down to Louisville. Take Charlie Knutson with you. No one else needs to know."

"What about Clem? He's bound to find out."

"Get the ball rolling. Go sell the campaign to Rebakor and jump start the approval process. I'll handle Clem. Tell Molinaire and his marketing department that Clem's out sick or something."

Back on Dunkirk Crescent, Tara's hand was getting clammy holding the card for so long. She paused and thought some more, searching for Dutch courage. She called the number again and once more the voicemail picked up.

"Hello. Leave a message," said the anonymous female voice at the other end.

"Hi, I'd like to make an appointment. My name is…" Tara paused. A copy of last week's *People magazine* was on the table beside her with a photograph of Brad Pitt and Angelina Jolie holding a baby on the cover.

"…Angelina. My phone number is……." Tara paused again, suddenly feeling very uncomfortable revealing anything about herself, especially her own cell phone number.

"I'll call back." She panicked and hung up quickly. "Shit!" Tara said out load to no one but herself realizing that this wasn't going to be as straightforward as she'd first thought.

She was opening a door to a whole new world. *But what was she so scared of? Fear of the unknown?* Now she was annoyed with herself. This was stupid. She needed to be stronger than this. *She was trying to save her marriage, dammit!*

Tara rang again. "Hi, I just called. My number is 952-615-4040." Tara hung up.

Now what? She wondered. Just sit there and wait for a phone call that might never come? That was no good. That wasn't being in *control.* She thought for a minute, then grabbed the *Yellow Pages* from a cupboard. She started flipping through it. Maybe this would require some professional help. She stopped at *Private Detectives* and scanned the list of names. There was only a handful. A small box ad for ex-cop Jack Kelsey caught her eye.

# CHAPTER 6

Kurt Fitzgerald and Charlie Knutson, a junior account executive at Bergenson & Adler, walked out of the Delta terminal at Louisville International Airport and straight into a waiting limo.

The car sped away towards downtown and the headquarters of Rebakor. Fitz had a large leather portfolio with him. Power Point presentations were all fine and dandy when it came to strategy and planning meetings but when it came to judging creative work, most clients preferred to see and feel hard copies in their hands.

Fitz knew this was his golden opportunity to shine. He had to maximize this moment to steal some of the glory Clem had been basking in. Buddying up to Molinaire was not necessarily going to be a walk in the park. The Rebakor marketing chief had to really like the campaign Fitz and Charlie were about to show him. But Fitz also needed to drive a wedge between Molinaire and Clem and then step in between them.

An angry Clem was an unstable Clem and an unstable Clem was exactly what Fitz wanted. Hell, he'd even blow Molinaire if he had to in order to win him over. Any opportunity to screw Golden Balls was too good to miss. He was going to grab that opportunity by the balls and squeeze for all it was worth. The prize? Running the show at Bergenson & Adler and Clem Drew would be history.

The fear of Clem taking the Rebakor business away with him and starting his own agency was obviously more than a concern to Frank Bergenson: it was becoming all-consuming. He'd seen it before and never clearer than when he looked in the mirror. After all, that's what he and his young advertising partner Lewis Adler did. They started Bergenson & Adler with an account they'd stolen from the extinct Fullwell & Partners ad agency where they both worked. Maybe that was why Frank was showing signs of paranoia. What goes around comes around.

Frank was leaving a legacy that depended on his agency remaining intact and flourishing. He'd gotten his reputation for being a wily old fox by making the big decisions based more on his gut than logic. And even though Frank had absolutely no evidence that Clem had even contemplated pulling a number, that little voice inside him was talking and he was listening. Sure, Clem was bound to learn of Fitz's Louisville trip soon enough but that was the idea. It would take Clem down a few pegs and scupper any convictions that he had Molinaire in his pocket. But the trick was to not piss off their new and biggest client in the process.

Frank Bergenson teed off at the third hole and landed his shot in the brush though he didn't seem too bothered. After all, the purpose of this game was not golf. It was more a game of chess. Frank was far more complex than he appeared. His easygoing, grandfatherly charm worked wonders with clients. They felt safe with him at the helm of the agency. But now that he was stepping down, the clients on his agency's roster were expecting Frank to orchestrate a smooth transition as power shifted to his successor.

All those years building the agency up into the marketing powerhouse it had become could so easily be destroyed if he continued to rock the boat by playing Clem against Fitz. The two princes could tear Frank's playhouse down with their infighting if he wasn't careful. But Frank knew exactly what he was doing. These were merely the chess moves playing in Frank's head and he was enjoying every minute of it. Sure, Clem and Fitz were two smart cookies but not in *his* league. He could outwit the two of them together. This was Frank's last little game of manipulation before putting himself out to pasture. He'd spent his entire career becoming a puppet master and he still knew how to pull all the strings.

Clem took a few practice swings with his Ping driver as Frank tugged his wooden tee out of the ground.

"I don't like cell phones," Frank grumbled. "They ban them at this club. They introduced a 'no cell phone' rule for all golfers. Doesn't affect me, I don't have one."

"I didn't plan on making any calls, Frank," chuckled Clem.

"You'd better turn yours off, or I'll have to report you for being an asshole." Clem duly obliged with a wry smile.

"Very pleasant afternoon to be playing hooky," Clem said, looking relaxed and not having one iota of a clue as to why his boss had suggested they play a round. In four years, Frank and never once invited Clem to join him on the links.

"All work and no play makes Jack a dull boy," Frank grinned.

Clem placed his ball on the tee and took a few more practice swings. "Can't remember the last time I played." He took an almighty swing and smacked his ball perfectly straight down the middle of the fairway. "Hmmm...not bad."

"Doesn't seem to have affected your game any," said Frank as he admired Clem's fine shot and shoved his Calloway driver back into his bag. Frank got in the driver's seat of their banana colored golf cart. "You should get out and play more with our clients."

Clem pulled a face. "Not enough hours in the day. Always seems like goofing off, to be honest. Then we bill the client for playing golf with them? Doesn't seem fair."

"Fair? We're a business, not a charity."

"Come on, Frank. Golfing is for fun, not business. You start playing with clients and then all the enjoyment goes out of the game. Anyway, I don't like deliberately losing to massage their egos."

"Jesus, Clem. You're missing the point. The client gets to know you, then he trusts you, and when he trusts you, you become friends, then you keep his business for life."

"That's one way of looking at it."

"What's the other way?" Frank asked, steering their little cart down the fairway.

"Client gets to know you, you get to know him, then you start to understand him, then you end up thinking like him and then you're useless to him. He's hired us to *not* think like him."

"Pah! Maybe I'm old school." Frank huffed as he headed over to his ball hidden somewhere in the tall grass by a large oak tree. As they drove to where his shot had landed, Frank pulled a spare golf ball out of his pants pocket and dropped it cleanly on the fairway. Clem watched Frank blatantly cheat.

"Hey, there's my ball! Not such a bad shot after all," Frank exclaimed as he stopped the cart and got out to grab his five iron.

"Are you cheating, Frank?" Clem frowned at his boss.

"Hell, yeah. I'm seventy fucking four. If I didn't cheat I'd lose. I don't like losing, you know that, Clem."

Clem rolled his eyes. "Why did you ask me to play out here today?"

"Because you need to lighten up. It's not always about winning all the time."

"Why are you cheating then?" Clem laughed.

Frank leaned into his shot and sliced it badly. "I'm probably going to cheat on every hole and you're still going to beat me," Frank shouted as he watched his ball fly across the fairway and land in a sand trap. "But I don't care. I cheat because it's fun. Sometimes playing by the rules is just too fucking hard."

Clem was enjoying his time with Frank and being out on the golf course on such a beautiful day. But he knew this wasn't about golf. Frank was a lousy golfer anyway. This was Frank's way of apologizing and reassuring him that the job, which Clem coveted, was indeed going to be his. Maybe Hank Britney had done his part and got

Frank's ear. *Yes, that was it.* This was just part of Clem's initiation. They got back in the banana golf cart and set off down the fairway towards Clem's ball. "Yep, sure is a great day," grinned Clem, feeling good about life.

Meanwhile, down in Kentucky, Kurt Fitzgerald and Charlie Knutson sat in the glass walled conference room at the Rebakor corporate headquarters. Young Charlie was Fitz's protégé and was excited to be playing in the big league with an international client meeting about to take place. But he seemed perplexed by the wait.

"Where are these guys? They knew we were coming, right?"

"Relax," Fitz reassured him.

"I feel like a guppy in a fish bowl sitting here."

Just at that moment, six casually dressed hip, young Rebakor executives walked in chatting amongst themselves. They took their seats around the large circular conference table without engaging Fitz or Charlie Knutson.

"Hi guys, Kurt Fitzgerald," Fitz smiled across the table. There were a few cursory "hellos" and "hi's" in Fitz and Charlie's direction but there was a chill in the air. One seat remained empty.

As Fitz was about to get the conversation rolling, the tall, svelte figure of James Molinaire entered the room. Kurt Fitzgerald stood up and flashed his customary pearly white smile.

"So, you are Mr. Fitzgerald."

"Yes, sir." Fitz shook Molinaire's hand and sat back down.

"Mr. Bergenson set this meeting up. He said he wanted us to be introduced."

"Thank you for taking the time to see us at short notice, James. I'm very excited to be here and to meet you and the Rebakor team. This is Charlie Knutson, who is also now assigned to your business."

Charlie smiled and nodded.

"Now before we get into the creative presentation I'm about to show you for the next campaign roll-out....."

"Hold on one minute." James Molinaire raised his right hand to halt proceedings. Fitz froze in mid-sentence. "Now excuse me, Mr. Fitzgerald. I'm confused. I agreed to meet with you this afternoon as I understand you are now going to be working on our business. But I really wasn't under the impression you were going to be presenting creative executions today."

"I thought Mr. Bergenson...."

"This is important. Clem should be here. Why isn't he here? I believe I have a meeting set up next week with him." Molinaire turned to one of his young executives. "Put in a call to Clem Drew." The executive immediately left the conference room.

This wasn't going to plan right off the bat. Fitz had to think fast.

"Clem thought this might be a good opportunity for you and I to touch base as we've not yet been formally been introduced," Fitz fidgeted, seeing that James Molinaire was looking rather miffed.

"Yes, I get that. But he should be at this meeting. Why did he set up something for next week if you're here presenting creative to me today?"

Molinaire shot Fitz a decidedly steely look. He didn't like to be bamboozled like this. This was rapidly developing into an awkward situation. Fitz had to get proceedings back on track so he took the opportunity to twist the knife in Clem's back before Molinaire had a chance to remove it.

"I believe Clem has other client commitments...so there was the possibility that he was going to have to cancel your meeting next week. Rather than risk that happening, we felt it was important to push forward ahead of schedule." Fitz was so impressed with his own bullshit he actually started to believe it himself.

"No one cancels me. I do the canceling."

The executive returned. "Voicemail," he said, looking at his boss. Molinaire's lips pursed. Fitz shrugged apologetically.

"Probably playing golf with Mr. Bergenson," Charlie Knutson quipped under his breath, loud enough to be overheard by everyone. Charlie made a good wing man. Molinaire bought it. The wedge had been successfully driven. Fitz had played it well.

"An auspicious start to our working relationship, I must say. All right. Mr. Fitzgerald, show me what you've got inside that portfolio of yours."

"Delighted to. And call me Fitz. Everyone does," Fitz smiled.

Over the next two hours, Fitz and Charlie Knutson put on a dog and pony show for the Rebakor marketing department. Charlie held up the artwork for the print campaign that would run in magazines and newspapers as Fitz read out the headlines and body copy. They showed the outdoor campaign that would run on billboards, bus shelters and bus sides. Then they read three scripts for television and Internet commercials and radio spots that linked up with the TV message.

After a slick and impressive presentation of all the creative, James Molinaire seemed impressed. He shook Fitz's hand as they walked out of the conference room. The meeting may have gotten off to a rocky start but Molinaire seemed in a much better mood now.

"Hmmm....*God Speed*. I like it. Compelling line. Compelling. Good work. Of course, the focus groups are what really count. If they responded as positively as you say they did, that's really what matters. Those numbers were impressive."

Molinaire walked Fitz and Charlie Knutson towards the entrance of the Rebakor building. The six executives had scattered back to their cubicles and Fitz was now in bullshit overdrive.

"Focus groups were 93% positive. The other 7% is pretty much wiggle room anyway. One group even stood up and applauded after we presented to them," Fitz beamed.

Charlie Knutson flashed a confident smile for added credence to reassure the Rebakor marketing chief.

"Absolutely loved it," Charlie gushed.

Fitz and Charlie knew damn well there had been no time for any focus groups. Setting up qualitative and quantative research like that took weeks to organize and process. His team had thrown together the campaign at the last minute with no time to spare. Fitz was walking a tightrope now. And Molinaire was now behind a campaign that Clem Drew knew nothing about and with only bullshit numbers to support it. This could cause some serious repercussions back at the agency.

Molinaire checked his watch. "So what if I hadn't bought into the campaign?" he asked the two Bergenson men. "You would've wasted your time and my money on focus groups."

Fitz's expression turned serious. That was a very good question.

"The agency felt very strongly about this campaign. We're all behind it one hundred percent so we took the precaution of testing it before presenting it. If the numbers hadn't supported it, we wouldn't have shown it to you."

"And what if I had shot it down in there? You would've wasted my ad dollars on unnecessary testing."

"Not at all. Valuable insight into your demographic and how your brand is perceived by your users and non-users is never a waste of money."

Molinaire nodded approvingly. It seemed he had warmed to Fitz's directness.

"I'll be straight with you, I'm disappointed Clem wasn't here today, whatever his reasons. I know you and Clem are probably close friends but I like consistency."

"Absolutely," Fitz nodded.

"I don't want you guys flipping point person on this. I don't like voicemail. I don't leave messages. I like to know the person handling my account is always available whenever I might need to speak with them. Understand?"

"Here." Fitz handed Molinaire his business card. "Call me, text me, email me, 24/7 I'm always available."

"I don't email and I don't text."

"Got it." Fitz grinned.

The three of them walked outside where the Rebakor limo was waiting to take Fitz and Charlie Knutson back to the airport.

"Good meeting. Good job."

"It's gonna be epic! I'll get back to you with our director and photographer recommendations."

Molinaire glanced again at his watch. "Sounds good. Tell Clem to call me."

"Will do." Fitz shook James Molinaire's hand, with absolutely no intention of passing on his message. Fitz had done his homework on the Rebakor boss. He now knew something about James Molinaire that Clem didn't; Molinaire was a deeply religious man. The campaign appealed to Molinaire's sensibilities. The tagline *'God Speed'* that ran on all the ads, billboards, TV and radio had hit a perfect bulls eye on Molinaire's religious bent.

It wasn't a particularly brilliant or original tagline but James Molinaire bought it and that was really all that mattered. In reality, it was a corny old line and one of the most over-used in the business and certainly lacked the creative originality for which Bergenson & Adler was renowned. If there was a golden rule in advertising creative departments at every agency it was to be original. Innovative thinking won awards, awards got an agency recognition and recognition got business walking in off the street. Unoriginal concepts were a dime a dozen and usually the result of interfering clients who wanted to be part of the creative process. Of course, the easier option was letting the client dictate the creative. That way an agency could keep meddling clients happy and simply take the money and run. And there were big agencies that did that. Bergenson & Adler had built its reputation for innovative creative – up until now.

Clem and Frank wound up their game by 5.15 p.m. and the two of them headed back to the clubhouse. Frank had cheated on almost every hole but Clem had still finished way ahead and only just over par for the course. It had been a long five hours in the sun and Clem had been waiting all afternoon for Frank to bring up the subject of the impending changing of the guard but it hadn't been broached yet. Instead, Frank had kept the conversation flippant asking all those small talk questions: *"How's the wife doing? - Where you two going on vacation?"* Mindless chit-chat stuff. But no word on the only topic of conversation Clem cared about.

"Join me on the nineteenth," Frank suggested, as they parked their little banana boat and unloaded their golf bags. Maybe this was the moment Clem had been waiting for.

They headed into the bar and sat at a quiet table that looked out onto the practice range. A waitress took their drink orders and Frank lit up a fat Cuban Cohiba cigar.

"You can smoke those things in here?" Clem questioned.

"Let them try to stop me," Frank frowned. "Hell, I've been a member here since 1972. Do you have any idea how much money I've paid them over the years in club dues and bar tabs? Damn, this is the only place left where I *can* smoke these babies."

The waitress returned with a Glendronach for Frank and a Sam Adams for Clem.

"Enjoy yourself today?" Frank asked, sipping his whiskey.

"Sure did. This is a pretty swanky place."

"Yep," Frank answered. The conversation was going nowhere. "Lets take a look at the menu. How about the Lobster Thermidor?"

Clem knew Tara probably had dinner waiting for him but didn't want to go rushing home if Frank was finally going to spill the beans.

"Sure, why not?" Clem smiled. Frank called the waitress back over as Clem pulled out his cell phone and powered it up.

"You can't use that thing in here. I told you that earlier," Frank scolded.

"Just checking messages, that's all." Clem scrolled down a list of missed calls. "Hmmm…"

"What?" Frank asked, peering over at Clem's phone.

"That's a Kentucky number."

"They leave a message?" Frank asked casually.

"No."

"Well, it couldn't have been that important."

It was now close to six. Clem was annoyed he'd missed the call.

It made him look bad as it was now after office hours and too late to call back. His patience with his boss was wearing thin.

"Okay, Frank. Are you going to cut to the chase or not? We've run out of things to talk about and you're still not saying anything about who's going to be filling your shoes."

Frank gave Clem a weary look. "Clem, you're a worrier. Cut it out. Stop thinking about Molinaire for half a second and stop being so concerned about Fitz. Hell, you've been uptight all afternoon about your damn cell phone being turned off. Lighten up."

"*Concerned,* Frank. I'm *concerned.*"

"Same thing," Frank argued.

Over dinner, Frank and Clem talked about The Minnesota Vikings, Joe Mauer and the Twins, how to make the perfect Martini and the best Caribbean island to vacation on - everything except the six hundred pound gorilla in the room. By the time Frank had added their dining expense to his club tab it was past eight o'clock.

They walked out to their respective vehicles in the parking lot pulling their golf bags behind them. Clem was curious why Frank was playing it so close to his chest at this late stage of the game.

"Look, Frank. I know you might not want to discuss this but for a seamless transition of power...."

"Have fun today?"

"I did. Thanks."

"Two weeks, Clem. Then it's all yours. See you at the office tomorrow." Frank walked off towards the trunk of his black Lincoln town car where a chauffeur was waiting for him.

Clem smiled. That's what he'd been waiting four years to hear.

## CHAPTER 7

Kurt Fitzgerald was beaming as he left Frank Bergenson's office. He walked past Rose, Frank's matronly secretary giving her a wink and firing a finger shot at her.

"Bye, Kurt," Rose smiled.

"See ya, hot pants," Kurt smirked, though the thought of seeing Rose in hot pants was certainly not on his agenda. That, however, could not be said of Justine who stepped out of the elevator and was now walking towards Rose's desk. Fitz had made more than one pass at her during her two years at Bergensons. She could've filed a sexual harassment report against him on more than one occasion but Justine had decided to always let it go in the interest of company harmony. If Clem knew Fitz had made sexual advances on her he'd have made a big deal of it and Justine didn't want that. It would probably result in her being branded a trouble-maker and terminated, so Justine's policy had been to just try and avoid the man altogether, whenever possible.

Seeing Fitz leave Frank Bergenson's office in such a good mood was enough for Justine to put two and two together very quickly and get a resounding four. She'd had this nagging feeling that Fitz and Frank Bergenson had been a little too tight these past weeks. Fitz's wink at Rose had been duly noted plus the obvious fact that whatever the reason was for Fitz and Bergenson's meeting, Fitz was visibly pleased with the outcome. He walked towards the approaching Justine.

"Hey, baby. Looking as hot as ever."

Justine shot him a sarcastic smile and kept walking. This time it was Rose's turn to note Fitz's behavior. Rose was mother hen to all the young chicks at Bergenson & Adler and was protective of her brood. Justine and Rose exchanged affectionate smiles as Fitz exited back down to the floor below via the elevator.

"Hello, Justine. We don't often get to see you up here. What's the special occasion?" asked Rose, genuinely pleased to see one of her favorite girls.

"That man creeps me out, Rose." Justine glanced back to make sure Fitz had gone.

"He's not so bad."

Justine pulled an expression that strongly suggested she felt otherwise. "He's always hitting on every woman in the agency."

"Well, maybe not every woman here gets quite so upset about it as you do, Justine. We don't all have your cute looks and slim figure."

"You're sweet, Rose but he's a freako. Anyway, I'm not here about that. It's Clem's birthday next week and I'm planning a little party for him in the office on Wednesday. So I was wondering if you and Mr. Bergenson might want to come."

"Oh, that's sweet of you. I'll ask him. Let me check his calendar and I'll get back to you. What time?"

"Four o'clock," Justine grinned like an excited Girl Scout as Rose scribbled down the info.

"Okay. Well, I can't guarantee Mr. Bergenson will make it but I'll be there for sure. Clem is such a terrific guy. Though the last time I saw him up here he was steamed about something."

Justine puffed her cheeks. "He's been so busy on the Rebakor business….so, why is Freako always in such a good mood these days? I don't get it."

"He's been up here to see Mr. Bergenson a few times recently. I think Mr. Bergenson is just trying to reassure him," Rose said quietly in case there were lurkers listening.

"Reassure him?" Justine sneered again. "About what?"

"Well," Rose whispered. "I think his ego took a big hit with all the praise and acclaim Clem has been getting, you know."

"Oh, poor baby! Gimme a break!" The phone rang and Rose signaled to Justine that she had to take the call. "See you Wednesday then?"

"You got it, honey," Rose gave Justine a motherly smile as she picked up the phone. "Mr. Bergenson's office."

Justine walked away. "Okay, thanks. But keep it under wraps. I want it to be a surprise."

"Mum's the word," Rose mouthed, covering the mouthpiece.

The traffic downtown started to get busy after four o'clock and Tuesday was no exception. The early shifters were getting off work and either heading out for happy hour at their favorite watering holes or heading back home to the burbs.

A green Chevy Malibu waited on a metered parking spot outside the Kemp building as various cars and SUVs pulled out of the huge skyscraper's underground garage. Private investigator Jack Kelsey was an ex-cop who'd been around several blocks many times. He was a heavy-set guy, tough and savvy. The deep lines etched in his face seemed to suggest that he'd seen it all before and then some during his time as an officer of the law. This line of work was easier on the heart and the lower back, and a whole lot less stressful.

Kelsey sat patiently in his Chevy Malibu studying each vehicle that drove by him. But the only car he was looking out for was Clem's silver Mercedes. His alert gray eyes kept constant watch. In the front passenger seat were the simple tools of his trade: digital camera with telephoto lens, video camera, Colt snub nose handgun and, most importantly, a notepad and pencil. Pens were unreliable – they ran out of ink. Names, numbers and times, that's what he'd been asked for. A photograph of a certain Mr. Clem Drew was propped up on his dash to make sure he could I.D. the guy. He waited patiently.

A silver Mercedes sped out of the underground parking garage and quickly turned right onto Nicollet Avenue. The one-way traffic flow meant the green waiting Chevy was already pointing in the same direction. Kelsey clocked Clem's face. He quickly turned the key in the ignition and pulled out into the steady flow of vehicles but stayed a few cars behind his target. The silver Mercedes weaved in and out of the traffic moving at a slightly faster clip than everyone else. Kelsey kept track but stayed his distance.

The Mercedes turned a quick left onto Hennepin Avenue and then a right on Eighth Street, escaping the busier thoroughfares. The green Chevy followed as Clem headed south out of downtown towards the older neighborhoods that blended downtown with suburbia. After a short while, Clem's car seemed to be staying at a more constant speed which made Kelsey's pursuit easier.

Clem's car slowed down as it turned onto Calloway Avenue, a quiet street of small shops and residencies. After a few hundred yards, the silver Mercedes pulled over and stopped outside an old brownstone apartment building. Kelsey kept driving. With one hand on the wheel, he reached for his video camera. He filmed Clem step out of his car and stuff a handful of quarters into a parking meter then recorded Clem walking the few yards to the apartment entrance.

Kelsey stopped his car and started to slowly back up. He was out of Clem's line of sight but Kelsey's zoom lens had its target clearly in focus. While he filmed, he narrated what he observed.

"Subject's arrival time at location…5.48 p.m. Subject has exited vehicle and is proceeding to entrance of apartment building located on Calloway Avenue."

Clem disappeared inside the brownstone. All Kelsey could do now was wait. It was anybody's guess which apartment buzzer Clem had pressed once inside. Kelsey scribbled down the address and noted the time just for good measure. Then he reversed his Chevy into a parking space which gave him a clearer view to the entrance to 1611. Kelsey switched off his car's engine. Now he just had to remain vigilant and that meant no shuteye. That was the trouble with these kinds of jobs. He was hungry. Flipping open the glove compartment, he leaned over and grabbed a bag of toffees. That should keep his blood sugar high enough to keep him awake until Clem emerged, whenever that might be.

It was just after eight when Clem got home that night. He'd called Tara to give her a heads up that he was running late this time. She was over preparing anything elaborate for dinner since Clem had started acting so strangely disinterested in her cooking as well as her body. Tara hadn't had a face-to-face conversation with her husband since Mrs. Cho had found the card in his jacket and she wasn't quite sure how she was going to react when she saw him. She'd written several speeches in her head, most of them extremely angry and she wasn't sure which one was going to blurt out of her when Clem walked in.

Tara sat quietly in the living room reading, or pretending to read, when she heard Clem enter the kitchen from the garage. She was still in her shorts, t-shirt and Nike running shoes. She knew that the two of them wouldn't be going out anywhere that evening as they never did that anymore, so there was no point dressing up in anticipation. And considering the mood she was in, a public place would not be a good idea right now.

Tara heard Clem put his laptop case on the island counter but she stayed out of sight in the living room. She waited for Clem to at least call her name but he didn't say a word. All she heard was the sound of his footsteps as he walked across the hardwood floor in their kitchen towards the carpeted staircase. Tara could hear his muffled footsteps ascend the stairs up to their bedroom so she put down her book and walked quietly to the foot of the stairs.

She waited, and then heard the shower running. *Should she confront Clem before he showered, during or after? And why was he showering before the dinner she hadn't made him?*

Tara's beating heart and racing mind were getting the better of her. She felt she was on the verge of losing control of her emotions. Control was the key. Tara knew that. But she had so much pent up angst inside she had to vent it somehow or she'd explode. Tara couldn't just stand there waiting for Clem to stroll back downstairs all in his own good time. She was ready to fight but her opponent wasn't coming out of his corner. That gave *him* control and she didn't want that. Tara opened the front door and ran outside. She was like a volcano ready to explode so she decided she might as well keep running. And that's exactly what she did, all the way around the leafy trails of Caribou Lake.

Clem stood in the shower soaping his body from head to foot as if cleansing himself of a contagious skin disease. Physically, Clem was in great shape and took pride in his appearance but his apparent 'squash' bruises from the other night were giving him quite a banged up look. The steaming hot water blasting out of the large circular showerhead drowned him in a cascading waterfall, like a baptismal purification washing away his sins. Clem closed his eyes and turned his face upward so the water drenched his face. He stood there for fifteen long minutes lost in a mental no man's land. It felt good, so good.

After toweling himself dry and putting on his bathrobe, he felt more spent than usual on this particular night. He went downstairs to the kitchen and poured himself a large brandy then went looking around the house for his wife. Finding no one home, Clem sat down on the sofa and started flipping through the TV channels on the remote as he usually did to unwind. Nothing grabbed his attention. He turned it off and went back upstairs to the bathroom.

Rifling through the cabinet drawers, Clem found a red plastic canister of Oxycontin. It was an old prescription from when he'd torn his meniscus on the basketball court a few years back. The pills were an easy way to zone out and while he didn't need them for his knee injury anymore, they sure helped him relax quickly and mixed with some booze it was the perfect cocktail for a very good night's sleep. Clem gulped down a single pill with the remains of his brandy and got into bed. If that didn't send him into a deep sleep nothing would. He didn't know where Tara was and was really too tired and woozy to worry about her right now.

Outside, the June night sky was a beautiful deep blue hue. The last glows of sunlight illuminated the soft edges of the motionless puffy and darkening clouds. By the time Tara got back to the house it was past nine and the last vestiges of daylight were clinging to life. The run had burned all the adrenalin out of her system and calmed her somewhat. It had given her time to think more clearly about what she needed to say to Clem but there would be no confrontation tonight with Clem now sleeping as soundly as a hibernating grizzly.

Tara awoke the next morning in the guest bedroom. She'd had a bad night tossing, turning and thinking. But downstairs in the kitchen, Clem was already up and getting breakfast. She could hear the La Pavoni spitting out an espresso. Tara pulled on her pink robe and headed downstairs. She was still barely awake as she ambled into the kitchen.

Her husband looked his usual immaculate self in his dark gray suit sporting a lemon silk tie over a crisp white shirt. He was feeling good about life again after a very good night's sleep and Frank's reassuring words.

"You sleep in the guest bedroom last night?" Clem sipped the hot foam off his cappuccino.

"Uh huh," Tara mumbled as she contemplated the opening gambit of her verbal assault. Still drowsy from her turbulent night, she already felt at a disadvantage for any early morning mental jousting. If they were going to get into it she was already behind on points with Clem so annoyingly perky, alert and caffeinated.

"Why?"

"I couldn't sleep."

"Man, I slept like a baby. I took an Oxycontin and crashed. Hey, d'you pick up my suit yesterday?" Clem asked, rather flippantly.

"No." Tara snapped back as she headed straight for the bagels.

She wasn't going to admit that she had. Clem took another sip of his cappuccino as he quickly flipped through the business section of the Star Tribune.

"Oh, okay. No biggie."

His off-the-cuff response got Tara's heartbeat going but she refused to make eye contact with him. *No biggie?* Little did he know. She stared into the toaster, watching her bagel heat up. Clem poured his cappuccino into a to-go mug then pecked Tara on the cheek.

"See ya tonight. Be home about seven." And with that he was gone.

*Ding!*

Tara's bagel popped up in the toaster. She was annoyed her husband was in such a damn good mood when she was still furious with him. Their confrontation would have to wait until he got home.

Clem sat in the morning traffic on Interstate 62. It gave him an opportunity to reflect on his dinner with Frank two night's earlier. It was nagging at him that Frank's only reference to naming him as his successor was just a glib remark at the end of the day. It was almost as if Frank finally said something only to pacify Clem. After all, what could have been Frank's motivation to waste an entire afternoon and evening talking about absolutely nothing? Unless there had been an ulterior motive on Frank's part.

Wily Frank Bergenson didn't do anything without a reason or an objective. *Why did Frank want Clem out of the office that day? What was going on back at the agency that he should know about?* Clem was starting to suspect that something was rotten in Denmark.

# CHAPTER 8

Jack Kelsey and Tara sat in the green Chevy Malibu in the strip mall on Flying Cloud Drive outside a Subway sandwich shop. The interior of Kelsey's sedan stunk of stale cigarette butts. Staring at the screen of a laptop, Tara watched the video Kelsey had shot of Clem. Her brow furrowed as she watched her husband arriving at the old brick apartment building. But Kelsey could care less how Tara felt. He'd done his job. He just wanted his money and he preferred cash. The camera work was a bit on the shaky side but so what? His resume highlights were murders and heists not winning an Emmy for any production values. The video zoomed in on a close up of Clem's face. There was no mistaking it was Tara's husband and she knew exactly what he was up to.

"1611 Calloway Avenue. Older neighborhood over on the south side. I clocked him departing the premises at six fifty-eight. He was inside for...let me see..." Kelsey checked his notebook. "One hour and ten minutes. I followed him back on the freeway to your home address. I've got pictures too, if you want."

"No thanks," Tara mumbled.

"Tough finding stuff out about your spouse when you thought you knew them. Everyone has secrets, I tell ya that. But not everyone gets found out." Tara was getting more upset and emotional listening to Jack Kelsey's blunt little soliloquy. She cut him off.

"How much do I owe you?"

Kelsey handed her a folded piece of paper. "Six fifty. Here's my invoice. Prefer cash if ya got it."

Tara opened her bag and took out her checkbook. "It'll have to be a check." Tara angrily scribbled it out.

"That's fine." Kelsey tapped out a Marlboro and reached inside the glove compartment for his lighter.

"Can't you just wait thirty seconds before you light that thing?" Tara snapped, shooting him a look.

"Sure."

Kelsey put his smokes back in his pocket. Tara ripped the signed check out of her checkbook and handed it to him.

"Thanks."

Tara stood in the parking lot of the strip mall as the green Malibu drove away. Kelsey had given her a mini DV videotape which Tara didn't really know what to do with but as she'd paid for it she might as well keep it. It wasn't exactly incriminating. Video of Clem getting out of his car and entering a building was not something any divorce attorney would call a smoking gun. But it could be used against him to help build her case.

Evidence in hand, Tara walked over to Mrs. Cho's laundry. Tara slipped the tape in her bag and entered to the aroma of freshly steamed clothing: a significant improvement over stale Marlboros.

Mrs. Cho was busying herself arranging the plastic wrapped garments on the electric rails that seemed to run in every direction.

"I've come to pick up. Drew. Blue suit," Tara announced, still pissed from her meeting with the dour Kelsey.

"You got ticket?" Mrs. Cho barked back, sounding more like a drill Sergeant than someone in a customer service business. Tara was in no mood for any attitude from anyone this morning.

"One ticket! One blue suit!" Tara barked, slamming the ticket down in front of Mrs. Cho. The two women locked eyes like two stray cats in a stare down.

"Twelve dollar," Mrs. Cho said flatly, looking at the ticket and ringing it up on the cash register. Tara opened her purse and counted out twelve single bills. She slammed each one down in front of po-faced Cho. "One! Two! Three! Four! Five! Six! Seven! Eight! Nine! Ten! Eleven! Twelve dollars!"

Mrs. Cho pressed a button and the electrical rail behind her started moving the vast array of freshly steamed clothing. Clem's dry-cleaned dark blue suit arrived like a train pulling into a station. Mrs. Cho yanked it off the rail and handed it over. Tara grabbed it and headed for the door as Mrs. Cho muttered under her breath.

"Have a nice day."


Across town, up on the forty-third floor at Bergenson & Adler, Clem quickly scanned through the pages of *Advertising Age* and *Adweek* to see if there was any mention of the agency, Rebakor or himself.

"Here ya go, boss," smiled Justine, handing Clem his morning cappuccino and his second caffeine fix of the morning.

"Thanks, Justine."

In her tight white cotton shirt and gray mini-skirt, Justine was looking like a naughty Catholic schoolgirl and Clem couldn't help but notice there was an added sexiness to her.

"What's going on upstairs?" Justine asked, as she hitched up her skirt and sat herself down on the edge of Clem's desk, exposing more of her bare thigh. As Clem rocked back in his chair, her tight, pale skin was directly in his eye line but he tried to avert his gaze.

"Upstairs? Is there something I need to know about?"

"Fitz and Frank seem awfully buddy-buddy these days." Justine raised an eyebrow. "I just don't trust Fitz. He's such a slime ball."

"What's new? We all know that," Clem replied as he tried to focus on work and not Justine's thighs.

"I went up to see Rose about something and he was coming out of Mr. Bergenson's office with that big sleazy grin on his face like he'd just won the lottery or something."

This was not what Clem needed to hear but he didn't want to let down his guard in front of his loyal assistant.

"I can't worry about it, Justine. What's my schedule looking like today?" Justine slid of the desk and her skirt rode up revealing a hint of her white thong. Clem couldn't help but notice this time.

"Oops, that wasn't meant to happen," Justine apologized, slightly embarrassed. Clem smirked but said nothing as Justine pulled down her skirt.

"Okay...Jerry, Suzie and Chuck Svensen want to show you some campaign ideas for Rebakor and they want Fitz to be in the meeting too so everyone's on the same page and they don't have to have a separate meeting with him. Is that cool?" she asked.

"Is *what* cool? The meeting? Or Fitz being in the meeting?" Clem replied.

"Either. Or both, I suppose. Not sure. What shall I tell them?" Justine stood by the window with the morning sun backlighting her hair and tight white shirt. She was looking like a page out of *Playboy* but Clem wasn't about to let that distract him.

"I'm cool with the meeting on creative but I don't see any damn reason why that prick Fitz needs to be there."

At that second, Frank Bergenson walked in to Clem's office.

"Fitz will be in the meeting because I want him in that meeting. I'll be in the meeting, too. You don't have a problem with that, do you Clem?"

Frank Bergenson's abrupt entrance and announcement had sufficient emphasis to suggest that he wasn't expecting any dissent. Justine took the surprise offensive as her cue to depart very quickly and return to her desk.

"Good morning, Mr. Bergenson," she smiled as she hurried off. Frank ignored her.

"Actually, Frank, yes I do have a problem with that," Clem said defiantly.

Frank Bergenson closed the door to Clem's office and walked past the Le Corbusier 'art chair' and sat himself down on the more comfortable sofa. Clem stood up from behind his desk.

"And why is that?"

"That man is so disruptive it's detrimental to the account. I can't manage effectively if he's undermining everything I do!"

"Sit down, Clem. I was hoping we weren't going to have this conversation."

"I'm quite capable of having a conversation standing up."

"Calm down and sit down."

"What conversation do you want to have that necessitates me sitting down?" Clem's attention was now very focused on his boss. Frank leaned forward, the lines in his forehead creased deeply.

"Either you work alongside Fitz or I'm taking you off the account altogether."

"What?" Clem was incredulous. He was being threatened by the same man who only just the other night had told him he was going to become king. *Where was this directive coming from all of a sudden?*

"You heard me."

"You'd let that prick run the account on his own? You can't be serious."

"I never said that, Clem. No one person can run that piece of business alone. I said I'd take you off the account."

Clem paced across the room then turned back to face his seated boss. "What's gotten into you, Frank? One minute I'm the guy taking over the show and now you're threatening to take me off the account that I won for the agency?"

"It was a team effort, Clem and you know that," Frank said, maintaining his composure and appearing quite unfazed by Clem's outburst.

"Sure it was a team effort, Frank. But who put the team together and who led the team? Yours fucking truly and *you* know *that*. Fitz wasn't even a bit player. Gimme a Goddamn break."

"Clem, shut up and sit down. It's hurting my neck looking up at you. Stop acting like a junior executive having a hissy fit."

"No, I'm not going to sit down, Frank. I'm not sitting down

until you give me a satisfactory answer."

Frank Bergenson stood up and rubbed the back of his cricked neck. He sighed wearily.

"Clem, I've been thinking long and hard about this and I'm saying this for your own good. No other reason. Listen to yourself. Look at yourself -- You're pushing too hard. You're over-doing it. Frankly, I'm concerned you're gonna burn out."

"Burn out?"

"Yes. And then what? Huh? -- If that happens, you're not only no good to this agency, your detrimental to its operations. I can't let that happen."

Clem let Frank's words sink in. Maybe Frank really did have his best interests at heart. And Clem's outburst had just proved his point. Clem sat down on the sofa and now it was Frank who stood over the young lion.

"Why the heck do you think I dragged you outta here to play golf?"

"I haven't figured that out yet. I'll get back to you on that one." Clem's mental chill pill was kicking in but he was still quietly seething inside.

"I want you to slow down and smell the roses. Lighten up. Don't focus all your energy on work."

"Frank, I'm fine. I'm at my best under pressure. I revel in this stuff. I'll take a break when we've got Rebakor up and running but this is a crucial time for the agency and I don't want to fall at the last hurdle." Clem was still very irritated that even the thought of being taken off the account was on Frank's mind.

"You know as well as I do that until they start writing those checks for the media buys we won't be getting agency commission. And they won't be writing any checks at all until this year's ad campaign is in the can. Now I don't care what you say or want or think right now Clem, I want Kurt Fitzgerald and you to work as one cohesive unit because two fucking heads are better than one, excuse my fucking French."

Frank finished his speech and strolled over to the window to let his words sink in. Clem slumped back in his seat.

"Okay, I get it. Fine. Jesus Christ. Fitz will be in on the meeting if that's what this is all about."

Clem conceded to his boss's wishes rather than rock the boat but Frank was sounding more like an incoming CEO instead of one about to put himself out to pasture.

"All our other clients are cutting back their budgets for the rest of this year heading into Christmas. That's never happened before. This shitty economy is killing us and yes, I know you need to advertise out of a recession but everyone is running scared."

Clem heaved a sigh as he listened to Frank's diatribe. "And...?"

"And when Molinaire signs off on our first campaign and the creative budget is finally approved, you need a vacation and I'm not talking about a long weekend in the Hamptons. You need a good couple of weeks down in Cabo or somewhere so you can unwind and come back refreshed. And spend some time with your wife, dammit."

Frank had a point but Clem was starting to think that maybe the old man was just getting twitchy about wanting everything hunky dory before he left the building for good. And it certainly would be *for good*. If Clem wanted to wear the crown he sure better tow the line until Coronation Day.

"Okay, Frank. You're the boss. I'll work with Fitz," Clem said emphatically, finally putting an end to Frank's tiresome monolog.

"Good. That's settled then."


Tara sat in her parked car and dialed Mistress Krystal's number. Her call went straight to voicemail once again.

*Beep!*

"Hi, this is Angelina. I called earlier..." she was interrupted by a calm, low-pitched female voice on the other end of the line.

"I don't do women. Don't call again." The line went dead.

"Hello...? Shit!" Tara re-dialed. This time the woman picked up Tara's call right away.

"I said I don't..." This time Tara did the interrupting.

"I want you to teach me," Tara blurted out quickly before the woman could hang up on her again. There was a momentary silence. The female voice spoke again.

"Teach you what?"

"Teach me what you do," Tara replied, nervously.

Silence.

"And what exactly *do* I do?"

"You...er....hurt people?"

Silence.

"I please people. And I don't give lessons." The line went dead again. Tara dialed back immediately. This time the voice messaging system answered. Tara waited for the beep then left a message.

"I'll pay your going rate. I want to learn. I want to know how to do what you do. I'm serious," Tara said, sounding focused and levelheaded. She waited on the line hoping the woman at the other end would pick up. She didn't. Tara hung up.

She was now feeling really frustrated. Did she honestly think this Mistress Krystal character would teach her how to smack people around? What was she thinking? This woman wasn't normal: she was a twisted human being. How could anyone who does this kind of thing to make money have any kind of rational thought process, let alone take on a student? She wondered. And what kind of student was she asking to be? To master the art of inflicting pain for pleasure? *How fucked up was that?* This wasn't like calling to schedule an art class, this was a whole other world. And a very dark world at that.

Tara started to argue with herself but the cold, hard truth was that this woman was giving her husband sexual pleasure of some sort, which was something Tara certainly hadn't done in a very long while. *What magic spell was this Mistress Krystal casting that Tara couldn't?* Tara sat in her SUV and pondered life for a split second before her cell phone's ring snapped her out of it. She snatched at her phone.

"Hello?"

"Okay. Three hundred dollars a hour. Meet me at the Starbucks on Grandview and Pine at three o'clock. Wear red shoes."

Before Tara had a chance to respond the caller hung up. She looked over at the clock on the wall – it was close to one. She knew she was getting in deep but Tara was now on a mission: find a pair of red shoes in the next two hours.


In the executive restroom on the forty-fourth floor of the Kemp Building, Kurt Fitzgerald washed his hands in one of the porcelain sinks then dried them off. He carefully checked his perfect white teeth in the mirror for any remnants of the huge burrito he'd just stuffed down during lunch with Charlie Knutson. Life was good and everything was going swimmingly. He ran a comb through his dark hair, slicking it back behind his ears. He was now looking perfectly coiffed.

"Molinaire is so up his own asshole," Charlie Knutson chuckled as he zipped up his pants and walked over to the sinks.

"That was great timing, Charlie," Fitz snickered, while admiring his own reflection. "Molinaire's expression when you said Clem was playing golf! Just fucking perfect."

The two men high-fived each other just as the door swung open. Clem walked in and glanced over at them without saying a word. He headed straight over to the urinals. Fitz was ready to leave but turned a faucet back on while Clem unzipped his pants and took a piss. Fitz was the last person Clem wanted to see right now.

"Working the old man pretty well, aren't you, Fitz?" Clem said, with his back to the two men. Fitz winked at Charlie.

"Now, what exactly does that mean?" Fitz looked at Clem's peeing reflection in the mirror.

"Like you don't know." Clem flushed and zipped up. He walked over to wash his hands.

"Just cleaning up after you, that's all." Fitz shot Clem a sarcastic grin as he yanked out a paper towel. Clem fired a look at Charlie Knutson.

"How's it going, Charlie?"

"I'm good, thanks," Charlie grinned.

"Are you aware your boss is delusional?"

Charlie Knutson flashed a nervous smile over at Fitz who was not so amused. Knutson knew he was out of his league. He wasn't going to start verbal sparring with Clem Drew because he couldn't win that battle. But with these two heavy-hitters calling each other out, he was in no hurry to leave the restroom either, though he made sure he was a safe distance from both of them. This could turn ugly.

Fitz ambled away from the sinks and stood by the door as Clem grabbed a paper towel and dried his hands.

"Ever thought the old man might be working both of us?" said Fitz. Clem wasn't buying it.

"Y'know, Fitz. You're standing in the right place right now because you're so full of shit."

Charlie Knutson blurted out a snigger that neither Clem nor Fitz appreciated. Charlie got the hint.

"I'd better get going. Catch you later, Fitz." Charlie made his exit, leaving Fitz and Clem facing off.

"You just don't get it, do you Clement?' Fitz smiled. Clem scrunched up the paper towel into a ball.

"What don't I get, Fitz?"

*"You can't always get what you want."* Fitz sang softly to the Rolling Stone's tune as he moved slowly towards Clem. Clem threw the screwed up paper towel at Fitz's head, narrowly missing him and bullseyeing the trash can.

"Don't get cute with me, Golden Balls," Fitz warned as he got in Clem's face. Fitz was bigger and stronger than Clem though probably not as fast. The two stared each other down.

"Aren't you late?" Clem said, goading his visibly irked rival.

"Late for what?"

"For Frank's two o'clock ass-kissing. You don't want to let him down." Fitz curled the fingers of his big right hand into a fist. "Go ahead," Clem goaded. "Take your best shot. Of course, it'll mean instant dismissal but it'll probably be worth it, don't'cha think?"

There was a momentary silence that lasted a few seconds but it seemed a helluva lot longer to both men as they got their emotions in check. They both knew the repercussions of anything resembling fisticuffs.

"Whatever it takes to get the job done," grimaced Fitz. He tuned towards the door and swaggered out of the restroom down along the hallway. Clem followed right behind him and headed in the opposite direction. He was fuming. The only thing he knew for sure right now was that he was being out-maneuvered and he didn't like it. He didn't like it one bit.

# CHAPTER 9

Tara entered the Starbucks on Grandview wearing a pair of red Converse sneakers. She looked inconspicuous enough in her tight blue jeans and gray hoody but felt the whole world was staring at her as she arrived for her clandestine rendezvous. Tara stood in line to place an order though she was already jittery and any caffeine coursing through her veins might cause her to hyperventilate. Her eyes darted around the café at the seated customers. She wasn't sure how she was going to react to seeing the woman who had been beating up her husband for his sexual gratification – not that she had any idea what this person looked like.

Just how sexually intimate this Mistress Krystal had been with Clem, Tara wanted to find out. This was the only way to learn the truth. Her plan, if she could pull it off, was masterful. If carried out to the letter, she would come face to face with Clem at the scene of the crime. *But what then?* Tara couldn't think that far ahead just yet.

"Can I help you?" a voice behind the counter asked Tara.

"I'll get an iced Chai, please," Tara blurted. She handed the young barista some change and waited at the pick-up counter for her drink to be made. Again, her eyes flicked around, clocking the faces of everyone in the place – an assortment of coffee drinkers, book readers and laptop users. Over in a corner sat an attractive blonde wearing a short skirt with knee high leather boots. *That had to be Mistress Krystal.* She stood directly in the blonde's eye line to make sure her red sneakers could clearly be seen. The blonde was too engrossed in her magazine to even glance up.

Tara collected her iced Chai and took it over to a window seat, in full view of anyone who walked in. It was three minutes after three and not one of the dozen or so patrons looked remotely like anyone who might be called Mistress Krystal. Not that she was expecting someone in fishnets and bullwhip to walk through the door. In fact, she didn't know what to expect.

As Tara leaned across to pick up the crumpled copy of *USA Today* on the wooden chair next to her, a husky female voice caught her off guard.

"Let's go, Angelina."

Tara jumped. "Oh!"

Dropping the newspaper, Tara turned around to see a stocky, middle-aged woman wearing sunglasses and a pretty summer dress walking away from her and out of Starbucks onto the street. Tara left her drink behind and followed quickly.

Out on the sidewalk, the woman kept walking briskly, not even bothering to look back. Tara quickened her step and caught up to her, glancing at the woman who obviously wanted to remain incognito.

"Let's walk and talk," the woman said, moving at a steady clip along the busy sidewalk.

"Okay," said Tara, not sure where they were both going.

"How'd you get my number?" asked the woman in sunglasses. Tara certainly didn't want to reveal the truth but was stumped for an answer.

"Oh, it was...y'know...friend of a friend. Where are we going by the way?" The two women stopped at the curb waiting for the light to change. "Look, are we being followed or something?" Tara asked anxiously.

"I don't know. Are we?"

"How would I know?"

"I don't advertise in The Yellow Pages. You can't Google me and find me. How'd you get my number?"

"Why is it so important?"

Tara was feeling under pressure to fess up. The lights changed and the '*walk*' sign illuminated. They crossed the street.

"Why is it so important?" The woman repeated. "Let me think about that for a nano-second. Oh yeah, I remember now – because you could be a cop, a private investigator, undercover reporter or maybe, just maybe, the jealous wife of one of my clients. That's why it's important."

Tara was indignant at the accusation of being a jealous wife even though she had just been nailed straight out of the gate.

"That's not true. I'm not even married," Tara lied.

"And that's not a wedding ring on your finger, I suppose?" the woman remarked, not even looking at Tara. Tara glanced down at her wedding band. She was annoyed with herself.

"Oh, shit." Tara mumbled under her breath. "Yes. Okay, I'm married. That's not a crime is it?"

The woman slowed down to a stroll as she pretended to window shop past various shop fronts and boutiques on the block. "Okay, so we've established you're married. You part of the scene?"

"Scene? What scene?"

"Jesus." The woman turned to face Tara. "You're a newbie."

"Newbie? Huh. Well, I guess I am."

"But you're into B and D?"

"Well, you know -- I've read stuff about it on the web," Tara said, sounding distinctly naive.

"So you want to learn my trade yet you know nothing about it. You're already proving to be a very poor student."

"Well, er -- look, Mistress Krystal…"

"I'm not Mistress Krystal," the woman announced.

"What? Then who are you?"

"I'm a cop working undercover and you're busted."

"What?! No!" Tara yelled. She spun around to see if a SWAT team or a gang of FBI agents were about to move in and surround her. The woman smiled and started walking again. Tara didn't follow this time. She just watched nervously as the woman walked away.

"Stop!" Tara yelled. "Stop screwing around with me whoever you are!" Tara was frozen to the spot and looked terrified.

The woman turned around and walked slowly back towards her, smiling. She obviously hadn't expected Tara to get freaked out quite so easily.

"See, hun? I have to be extremely careful. I have to be totally discreet. My clients are high-end. They want complete privacy and they have to trust me in more ways than one. If I'm going to let you into my world, I have to be able to trust you, too."

"So you *are* Mistress Krystal?" Tara said, feeling relieved.

"Only when I'm role playing."

"I'm a very trustworthy person," said Tara, looking straight into the woman's black sunglasses and hoping to make up for lying about her marital status. "I don't tell lies."

"Well, Angelina, you've already proved you're not smart enough to be working undercover but where d'ya get that name? See Miss Jolie and Brad on the cover of People magazine? Not very original."

"Angelina is my real name," said Tara, lying again but trying to sound as believable as possible. Mistress Krystal took off her sunglasses and looked Tara in the eyes.

"Listen, hun. My professional name is Mistress Krystal. I'm forty-seven years old. I was born in Chicago. Raised a Catholic. Studied business management at Vanderbilt University in Nashville, Tennessee. I've never married. I don't have any kids and that suits me fine. I'm a sole proprietor, a one-woman business. I do very well. My only marketing and advertising is that card you have of mine. That's me and that's all you need to know. You'll learn nothing about my clients. Discretion is in my DNA. That's why all clients are high end. They know they can trust me. Get it?"

"Got it," said Tara, obediently.

"Play straight with me and I'll play straight with you. Cut out the bullshit. I can see through it a mile away. In my business, if I want to *stay* in business, it's a job requirement."

"Uh huh." Tara listened wide-eyed.

"Now, if you insist on being called Angelina then fine, I'll call you Angelina but tell me how you found me or this meeting is over because I have a client showing up at five o'clock and I still have a very sneaking suspicion that you're a jealous wife."

Tara was disarmed by Mistress Krystal's candidness and intuition. She felt like she'd just been verbally assaulted and certainly a little chastised. *Boy, this woman was a piece of work.* She was not someone Tara had any intention of being friends with – quite the reverse, in fact -- but there was something about her directness and honesty that Tara liked. It compelled her to tell the truth -- well, almost. She still couldn't get her head around the fact that this woman could well be regularly fucking her husband.

"I found your card," Tara said, being truthful for a moment. Mistress Krystal was still skeptical.

"Really? I'm very selective who I give my cards out to. Sure it was lost when you found it?"

While Mistress Krystal's speech had hit home, Tara was still not ready to totally spill the beans on herself. "I found it in the back of a taxi, actually. I swear," said Tara, hoping for all the world that this woman would believe her now.

Mistress Krystal quickened her pace. Tara knew lying was futile with this woman. Either she was a lousy liar or this woman really did have some kind of psychic ability to know when people were not being truthful. Tara caught up with her. It was almost as if she was now in too deep with a woman she'd only just met and who was responsible for tearing up her marriage. Tara figured if she was going to lie she might as well go all in.

"Look. Okay, I'm just a bored housewife trying to spice up my marriage. My husband hasn't so much as kissed me in the last two months let alone wanting to have sex. I've got to spark it up somehow. I found your card in the back seat of a yellow cab. It was down the side of the seat. Honest. I've had it for months and just kept it. I've been trying to get the courage up to call you for weeks."

Mistress Krystal cracked a small smile. Tara didn't know if the woman was buying her story or not. They walked in silence for a moment then Mistress Krystal spoke.

"Like I said. Three hundred an hour. Cash."

Passing a few mom and pop stores, Mistress Krystal walked with Tara down a residential street. They were now several blocks away from the Starbucks where they'd met. Along one side of the road were a row of ranch houses and ramblers while across the street were the backs of several apartment buildings. Mistress Krystal led Tara behind a group of large buildings and under an old iron stairwell attached to a 1930's apartment building. Tara had lost her bearings. She rarely came to this part of town and wasn't sure she'd ever find this place again on her own. Tara figured this must be the backside of the place in the video Jack Kelsey had shown her.

"Where are we?"

"This is the rear entrance to my place. I always come and go this way." They climbed the iron stairwell to the next level. At the top, she turned a key in the lock of a heavy dark green door.

"But what street is this?" Tara pressed.

"That's Jackson behind us. Always park there." As they entered, she glanced back over her shoulder at Tara. "You never know who's watching the front entrance," she added, rather cryptically.

"Like who?" Tara asked, following closely down a hallway and feeling a little anxious that the cops might be staking out the place.

"It doesn't hurt to be circumspect."

She led Tara to another locked door, red in color this time. Mistress Krystal unlocked the double and pushed it open. The two of them entered a gloomy apartment.

"This is it." She removed her sunglasses. Tara wanted to get a better look of this mysterious woman but it was too dark. Bamboo blinds and brown walls made the room appear more like a dungeon cell than a large living room. The woman flicked on a light switch, which barely made a difference. A single bulb hanging from the center of the ceiling lit the room dimly. A solitary kitchen chair was the only recognizable piece of furniture.

Tara felt a chill run down her spine. So this was the scene of Clem's sordid sexual dalliances: this nasty, ugly room in dire need of an HGTV makeover. The place was just plain skanky and Tara felt dirty being there. Mistress Krystal turned to face Tara and smiled like a realtor showing off a beautiful room. Tara looked into the eyes of this woman she secretly despised for the first time. Her eyes were slightly almond shaped and a beautiful light green color, almost hypnotic. Tara quickly averted her gaze.

"Welcome to Mistress Krystal's playroom. For adults only, of course. I keep it dark and stark. Clients like it like this. Helps create the right mood." She walked across the dreary room. Tara stood speechless as she eyed the racks of whips, crops, paddles and shackles that hung on the far wall. There was a set of standing stocks, and a strange looking seat contraption.

"So you make it look this bad deliberately?" Tara asked, for want of something to say and careful to avoid eye contact again.

"It's not to my tastes but it's not about me, it's about them."

"I guess so."

"Got three hundred bucks on you?"

"Er – yeah." Tara fumbled through her bag for her purse. She handed over three crisp one hundred dollar bills.

"Okay. Let's get started. Here's your first lesson -- know your equipment." Mistress Krystal walked over to the far wall where a variety of 'toys' were hung across several metal racks. "Here's my arsenal. My tools of the trade. Usual stuff. Cuffs, collars, leashes and chokers. These are my floggers -- deerskin, bull leather, rubber, horsehair and rabbit. This one's fox fur." She waved her arm towards a neatly hung row of whips.

"Wow."

"Now, I've no idea what your husband's kink is…."

*Oh, I bet you do!* Tara thought.

"Neither do I," Tara replied truthfully.

"But…over here are my paddles -- leather, fur, rubber and wood. Over there are various types of cane -- English boarding school type, bamboo, rattan and acrylic. Then over here in the whip department…."

Tara interrupted, pointing back to the floggers.

"I thought that was the whip department over there."

"Oh, those -- they're just for warm-ups and pussy clients. These guys are the big boys. I have single-tail four footer, four-foot bull whip and six-foot snake whip."

Tara wondered if Clem might be one of her 'pussy clients.' She pictured Clem in the soulless space and shuddered. Mistress Krystal was on a roll now, like a salesperson running through her inventory to a prospective buyer.

"As for hoods, take your pick – I've got leather, latex and a gas mask. We got these funky looking leather head cages, straight jackets, arm binders, wrist to thigh restraints, suspension harness, body bag and a sleep sack."

"Sleep sack?" Tara winced.

"Wrap 'em, bag 'em and hang 'em. That's a bit more involved. Only got one guy into that. He likes severe restriction."

"Do I need to be taking notes or something? I mean, there's a lot more to this than I realized."

Tara was bewildered by the vast array of devices and implements but Mistress Krystal wasn't finished yet. It seemed she was enjoying playing teacher and showing Tara the ropes, along with everything else.

"Electrical items -- Eros-Tek 312, violent wand, that's a tens unit, those are restriction implements, gags, and a few more kinky luscious toys I keep in a closet under the stairs. Okay. Questions?"

"What's that Eros thingy for?"

"For when you want to shoot a few hundred volts of electricity through nipples or genitals."

"Ouch! What's that?" Tara pointed to a crudely built wooden contraption.

"Spanking bench for the naughty ones."

"Oh, right."

She pointed towards a small kitchen behind a bamboo screen. "Kitchen is over there and so is the bathroom. I need to get changed. Go feel that stuff -- hold them, swing them about. You can get a sore arm cracking a bullwhip over and over."

She left Tara standing in the middle of her medieval torture chamber. Tara picked up a flogger. Her hand gripped the leather handle. She squeezed it tight and was surprised how comfortable it felt. *So this was it.* This was where Clem came to get his rocks off. And this was the woman who was marking his flesh with these painful looking instruments.

She felt angry now. *What in God's name was Clem thinking visiting a woman like her in a place like this?* And what was *she* doing in a place like this? Why had she come here? She wasn't into this crap. This was a place for perverts and pain freaks. But surely Clem wasn't one of those types, *or was he? How could he be?* And what on earth had she gotten herself into?

As her mind started questioning everything in her life at that one moment, her anger began to subside. Now she was feeling anxious alone in the room. This woman could be some kind of crazy nut job. She could beat Tara to a pulp and no one would ever know. Nobody knew she was here. She hadn't told Lorraine and obviously not Clem. She hadn't even planned on being here herself. *Hell, this woman could even kill her right there and then and dispose of her body before she was ever missed.* She should have at least told Lorraine.

Tara put down the flogger and picked up a riding crop. She waved it in her hand and walked around the room swinging it wildly through the air in case she might have to defend herself from the woman getting changed in the next room. Tara was way out of her comfort zone. She needed to leave.

"It's later than I realized. I'd better be heading out," Tara called out. "I'm sure your client will probably be here soon."

There was no reply. Tara put the riding crop back in its correct place on the wall. *What if the next client to ring the buzzer was Clem?* She had to leave right now. "I'll come back another time for the rest of my first lesson," Tara called out again as she headed towards the hallway.

A dark figure appeared out of the other room and blocked Tara's exit. Mistress Krystal stood under the door arch looking nothing like the woman Tara had met at Starbucks. This was a sexually charged *Glamazon* dressed in black leather and stockings. Her blonde hair was now blown out high and wild. Her make-up had taken a dramatic twist with her green eyes accentuated with dark mascara and deep blue eye shadow. Her lips now reddened and glossy. She wore black silk gloves that ran all the way to her elbows and in her hand she held a strange electrical device that sparked a blue crackle of light: a violet wand. She looked like she'd stepped out of the pages of a kinky X-Men comic book.

"You're not leaving yet. We haven't even started."

"Holy shit!" Tara blurted out in both shock and awe as she took several steps backwards. Mistress Krystal's stilettoed heels stepped forward into the playroom and circled Tara.

Tara's eyes followed her every move as she stood motionless like a petrified possum.

"*Now* I'm Mistress Krystal."

"I gotta leave," Tara said, almost apologetically. Mistress Krystal acted as if she hadn't heard a word Tara had just said.

"Class is still in session."

"You look quite different," Tara said quietly, making the understatement of the century.

"This is a violet wand. It shocks in varying degrees of intensity. You can adjust the wattage."

Mistress Krystal turned a small voltage controller on the handle of the futuristic looking fairy light then touched it against Tara's bare arm, sparking a blue neon flash that shot an electrical charge into Tara's bare skin.

"Oww! Jesus!" Tara rubbed her burning arm.

"Oh, don't be a baby, Angelina. That was on the lowest setting. Okay, now where were we?"

Tara took a deep, relieved breath. It appeared Mistress Krystal had no intention of murdering her today after all.

Mistress Krystal walked over to the racks of assorted weaponry on the far wall. Her heels sounded loud with each step across the wood floorboards. "These are what I'll be using today -- Paddle. Cuffs. Collars. Whips. Crop. Cane. Flogger. Slapper. Strap."

"What's that little whippy thing over there?" Tara pointed to a small leather tasseled handle as she continued to rub her sore arm.

"That's a cock whip." Tara pulled a face.

"Oh, okay. Quite a selection."

"My clients have eclectic tastes."

It really made Tara wonder what Clem's preference might be. Of course, there was no way she could ask without totally blowing her cover. She just couldn't imagine him sitting in that lonely chair in the middle of the dingy room.

*Bzzzzzzzzzz!*

The door buzzer sounded. Tara went into a cold sweat.

"And that'll be my five o'clock," Mistress Krystal announced casually.

"What? How do I get out of here without him seeing me?" Tara asked in a panic.

"You're not going anywhere, Angelina. Just go sit behind that screen and don't make a sound. You'll be able to watch everything that goes on from there and he'll have no clue. Look, listen and learn. It's showtime."

Any thoughts of Tara leaving evaporated. Indeed, she wasn't going anywhere. Tara did as she was told. *But what if it was Clem? How freaky would that be?* How would she react if her husband walked in right there and then? Mistress Krystal walked down the hallway to answer the door. Tara snuck behind the screen and knelt down in dreaded anticipation.

As she waited, hidden in the darkened room, she could hear the sounds of someone in the hallway but no words were spoken. Tara was freaked out about the entire situation she had gotten herself into. She felt like an unwilling voyeur. If Clem walked in and stripped off she would have to jump out and bring everything to a very dramatic halt. It would, without question, be the most embarrassing moment of her life and surely for Clem as well but at least it would be the truth. On the other hand, if this person *wasn't* Clem, she was about to witness some poor schmuck getting the living daylights beaten out of him and that wasn't a very pleasant alternative either. She was definitely in a lose-lose situation. Tara suddenly realized she really hadn't properly thought everything through. But she'd paid her three hundred bucks and now the show was about to begin.

What if there was blood? *God, no! Please don't let there be blood.*

Several minutes passed. Crouched behind the screen she heard noises but still no talking. Then Mistress Krystal entered the room holding a leash, which was attached to a leather-studded collar around the neck of a scrawny elderly man. He was naked except for a baggy pair of white underpants. He shuffled into the room like a boney old dog being led outside to take a dump. In her high heels, Mistress Krystal stood at least half a foot above him.

"On your knees!" Mistress Krystal barked. The man obeyed and got down on all fours. Mistress Krystal straddled him and slapped his skinny buttocks.

"Move!" she ordered. The frail looking man did his best to carry her around the room on his thin white back. Her sizeable bulk was quite a load and Tara wasn't sure the poor man could handle the weight. He grunted as he moved slowly around in a small circle while Mistress Krystal continued to spank his ass. Each slap would cause the elderly man to grunt louder. This went on for a good ten minutes until he was close to collapse. Tara stared wide-eyed wondering what would happen if the old geezer actually suffered a heart attack. *How would they explain that to the ER staff?*

When Mistress Krystal finally stood up, Tara felt relieved for him. *How could this be pleasurable for anyone let alone a paying customer?* The man stayed on his hands and knees panting hard. His mistress seemed to show little concern for his lack of oxygen intake and certainly wasn't about to do anything to ease his situation.

*Smaaack!*

Mistress Krystal kicked the winded man hard in the ribs.

"Oooooffff!" He gasped as he fell over on his side, groaning in pain. His inflictor straddled him unsympathetically.

"Get up!" Mistress Krystal demanded.

As he lay on his side, he seemed in too much pain to move but he obeyed, getting back on his hands and knees.

"Thank you, Mistress," he said quietly. As soon as he seemed composed again, Mistress Krystal slammed her shoe into his soft white underbelly.

*Smaaackkk!*

The man let out a moan and collapsed again. Mistress Krystal waited and watched. "Aren't you forgetting something?" she asked him but he was too winded to answer her. It seemed he could barely breathe now.

"Thank you, Mistress," he gasped, getting back up on his knees.

"That's better."

As he panted quick, short breaths, Mistress Krystal pushed him over with the sole of her stiletto shoved hard against his hip left leaving the room to give him some recovery time. The old man curled up in a fetal position and didn't move. Tara remained fixated on him. It was like she'd just witnessed a bizarre crime take place. She wanted to dash out from behind the screen and help the poor old bastard but she was too shocked to move. Though this was an assault on a willing victim. In any other environment the cops would've been on their way. To think that this man was paying good money for this scandalous treatment seemed unfathomable to Tara as she stayed cowered behind the screen almost too petrified to breathe.

All sorts of noises were coming from the kitchen. *What was this mad woman cooking up next?* Minutes passed. The man barely moved. Slowly, he managed to pull himself up on his knees, breathing deeply. He rubbed his belly where he'd been kicked and looked a very sad, lonely figure of a human being. What a pathetic creature he was. It was then that she noticed the bulge of an erection in his underpants.

*Brrrrnnnng! Brrrrnnnng!*

Tara's cell phone rang loudly. She jumped. The elderly man looked over at the screen. Tara panicked. She flipped the mute switch on the side of her phone to silence it just as Mistress Krystal walked back into the room.

"Oh, so I see you're pleased to see me," she said, staring at her victim's hardened package. She grabbed his wrist and led him over to the medieval looking wooden standing stocks over in the corner. He was like putty in her hands, obediently allowing her to do anything she wanted with his weak body. She stuffed a ball gag in his mouth and buckled it tight behind his skull.

With his head and hands both locked in the heavy stocks, Mistress Krystal perused the array of weaponry on the wall racks. She selected a long bullwhip as her weapon of choice and cracked it in the air.

Tara shuddered at the idea that she was about to witness a whipping. Surely not, it'll kill him, thought Tara as she stared at his bare boney back. Mistress Krystal gently caressed the flaccid leather tassels across his body, letting the soft tip of the bullwhip gently touch against his skin. She slowly waved the beautifully crafted *inflictor of pain* under his nose so he could smell the essence of leather she was gripping so tightly in her hand. Mistress Krystal smiled, knowing what was coming next. She drew back her arm and threw it forward.

*Craaaack!*

The long black lash slashed across the man's pale back. A long, bloody welt instantly appeared across his spine on his old flesh. The man let out a muffled yell.

*Craaaack!* Another bloody streak.

*Craaaack!* And another.

*Craaaack!* And another.

Behind the screen, Tara winced with every stroke of the lash. Ten strikes later, the man's back was patterned in blood red streaks. Mistress Krystal dropped the bullwhip to the floor with a loud thud and walked towards Tara. With a beckoning finger she summoned Tara out from behind her cover and pointed towards the small kitchen. Tara silently slunk out of the dimly lit room to the safety of her new locale where Mistress Krystal filled a kettle full of water, put it on the stovetop and lit the gas.

"I'll let him stew there a while. He enjoys that."

"What are you doing now? Pouring boiling water on him?" Tara said, horrified at the thought.

"No, I thought you might fancy a cup of tea." Mistress Krystal replied casually.

"Jesus Christ, that was just brutal," Tara whispered in case the elderly man might hear her and was still reeling from what she'd just witnessed. "Who is that guy? Is he okay?"

"He's fine. He's one of my regulars. Been seeing me for years now and I haven't killed him yet. Comes here once every four or five weeks."

Tara was still incredulous. "But that's gotta really hurt."

"That's the point. That's what turns him on." Mistress Krystal took two pink mugs out of the cupboard. Tara sat down on a stool exhausted merely watching.

"This is what I do. You told me you wanted to learn. You still want to do what I do?"

"I guess." Tara's shell-shocked expression said otherwise.

"Boy, I don't know if you're cut out for this. Don't think you've got the stomach. Sugar?" Mistress Krystal grabbed the sugar bowl and opened a drawer in search of a teaspoon. Tara didn't reply. "You get used to it very quickly. It's kinda fun after a while."

"No thanks," Tara said, waving away the sugar bowl.

"I'll unlock him from the stocks in a moment and let him go.

I've got another client coming in after him." Mistress Krystal picked up the steaming kettle before it had a chance to whistle.

"But doesn't he want to have sex with you?" Tara asked.

"It's not always about sex, hun. Sure, some of them like to jerk off every now and then and I could have sex with them if I wanted. That's my call, not theirs. I do this gig to get paid, not to get fucked. I better go unlock him and get the old fart outta here."

Mistress Krystal walked back into the playroom to release her prisoner. Tara looked at her cell phone to check the caller I.D. It was her mother. She was the last person on earth she'd want to talk to right now. Walking back into the kitchen, Mistress Krystal rummaged through the cupboards.

"God, I'm famished. I need a cookie or something." She looked at Tara, "So, that was your first lesson. Was it worth it to you?"

"Is he okay?"

"He's still alive, if that's what you mean."

"You could've killed him!" Tara replied, genuinely concerned.

Mistress Krystal smiled. "That's why I have rule number two – do not kill your customer. Very bad for repeat business. Rule number three -- do only what the client requests. Don't go off script."

"He agreed to all that?" Tara asked, somewhat disbelieving.

"Every detail. It's always the same, every time he comes here."

"Who is he? I mean, do you know his real name?"

"Names aren't important unless they say so. I usually give them names unless they want me to call them something in particular. With him, it's pretty straightforward stuff. He doesn't really like to talk much."

"He looks like a homeless man."

"Don't let looks deceive you. He's a circuit court judge."

"A judge? You've got to be kidding me!" Tara rolled her eyes, incredulous. "God. What's rule number one?"

"Cash. Up front."

*Slaaam!*

The front door smashed shut as Mistress Krystal handed Tara a mug of tea. "Thanks. I hope he's okay," Tara said.

"Are you a reporter working undercover, Angelina?"

"What? No! Like I said -- my marriage has gotten stale. I want to spice it up a little," said Tara, coming from a place of truth this time.

"Well, hun, my bullshit meter isn't totally buying your story." Tara was lost for words. The cogs in her brain spun rapidly in the hope that her mouth might spit out some plausible response but Mistress Krystal beat her to it.

"Be here Friday at noon and we'll start getting serious."

# CHAPTER 10

Clem walked briskly past Justine's desk towards his office. "Clem?" she called out, looking up from her computer.

"Yep?" Clem turned back and looked down to see an envelope on the desk with his name on it. "What's that? Don't tell me you're handing in your resignation?"

Justine smirked. "Very funny. Rose wanted me to give you this. You've won."

"Won what?"

"Two tickets for two weeks in Mexicali. Ya ya! Lucky man."

Justine handed Clem the envelope. He ripped it open and pulled out two Delta airlines first-class tickets and a brochure for Capella Pedregal, a luxurious beach resort in Cabo San Lucas.

"Guess that's Mr. Bergenson's way of rewarding his big shot employee," Justine grinned. "Is my name on the other ticket by any chance?"

Clem studied the tickets more closely. He wasn't happy.

"Next week? These tickets are for the 15th. Frank can't be serious. We're in the middle of getting the creative ready for Rebakor. What's he thinking? No, I can't go anywhere!" Clem tossed the tickets back onto Justine's desk and walked into his office. Justine pulled a face. "They're all yours. Take your boyfriend."

A floor below in the creative department, Creative Director Chuck Svensen looked at the numerous Rebakor concepts thumb-tacked to the wall of the conference room. It was a colorful mix of print and billboard campaign ideas. Three creative teams sat facing the wall looking at all the work on display anxiously waiting for their work to be judged. They knew only three campaigns would make the cut.

"Good stuff, guys. Some nice ideas here." Chuck looked around the room. "Is Leo coming to this meeting?"

"Yeah, he's on his way," said a voice in the room. Chuck looked back at the work and counted.

"Okay, we've got...what? Twelve, thirteen campaigns up here. Clem wants to take three but I'm only giving one of these our agency recommendation. This. I love *this* concept." Chuck pointed to a print campaign parodying *Gulliver's Travels* with a giant pair of running shoes in the middle of Lilliput's town square.

Leo walked in looking pissed. Chuck glanced at his watch. "Glad you could join us, Leo. Take a seat." Leo stood.

"I've just been speaking with Gerard and Patrick. They told me Molinaire loved *their* campaign and that Rebakor are going with it."

A collective groan went around the room. Chuck smiled. "Don't be an asshole, Leo."

"I'm not kidding."

"What do those two goons know? They're just jealous they're not working on the account."

"They did some Rebakor creative for Fitz. Charlie Knutson told them they got the green light to proceed and start getting production bids."

"You being serious?" Chuck's smile vanished.

"As a fucking heart attack."

"When did all this go down?"

"Last week, apparently. Charlie said he flew down to Louisville last Tuesday with Fitz. Met James Molinaire and the entire marketing department."

"What the fuck!? We worked all fucking weekend busting our fucking balls to get this finished," shouted one of art directors.

"I had tickets for Maroon 5 on Saturday night at Target Center! I coulda fucking gone!" grouched a very pissed off copywriter.

Chuck Svensen was livid. As the agency's Creative Director, he was supposed to authorize every piece of creative that left the agency. If it didn't have his blessing then it didn't leave the building.

"Okay, guys. Meeting over. Let me find out what the fuck's going on here." Chuck Svensen stormed out.

Within minutes, he was marching past Justine and straight into Clem's office. Justine stood up and followed as she could tell by the expression on Chuck's face that this was not going to be good. Clem was typing an email.

"Are you screwing with us down in creative, Clem?" Clem stopped typing and looked up at the furious Creative Director.

"Clue me in. What's going on?"

"Fitz went down to Louisville and sold Rebakor an ad campaign. Who the fuck approved the creative?"

"Whoa, slow down, Chuck. What are you talking about?"

"My guys have been busting their asses working all week and over the weekend and now we find out it's all been for nothing."

"What do you mean Fitz went to Louisville? When?"

"Fitz and Charlie Knutson presented a campaign to Molinaire in Louisville on Tuesday."

"Bullshit! Who told you that? That's total bullshit." Clem's mind started to race. Where was he that Tuesday? *Fuck! Golfing with Frank Bergenson.* The penny dropped. Now Clem was livid.

"Talk to Leo. He heard it from Gerard and Pat. Makes me look pretty fucking stupid!" yelled Chuck.

"Chuck, believe me, if that's true, you're not the only person who's looking stupid right now."

"Damn right. I got six very mad creative teams downstairs who want to know who's running the show here!"

Clem pulled out his cell phone and started to make a call. "I'm calling Molinaire. Right now."

A female voice answered the call. *"Rebakor Corporation."*

"James Molinaire."

A second female voice answered.

*"Marketing."*

"Can I speak with Mr. Molinaire, please. This is Clem Drew at Bergensons."

A third female voice answered.

*"James Molinaire's office."*

"Hi, is James there? Clem Drew, Bergensons."

*"Hold for a moment, please."*

The voice at the other end put Clem on a long hold. He covered his cell phone and shot a look at Chuck Svensen.

"If this is true....."

The voice at the other end came back on the line. *"I'm sorry, Mr. Drew. Mr. Molinaire is unavailable at this time. Can I take a message?"*

"Yes. Please get him to return my call. Thank you." Clem was even angrier than before he placed the call -- now he was getting blown off by the client.

"I'll fix this, Chuck. I'm very sorry."

Clem left an irate Chuck Svensen in his office and charged down the corridor towards the elevator. All the dots were suddenly connected. The timing of the tickets to Cabo started to make perfect sense now, too. Frank wanted Clem out the way for Fitz's campaign to get up and running. He was being manipulated and undermined and he *wasn't going to take this shit.*

Up on the next floor, Clem headed down the corridors towards Frank Bergenson's office. There were no signs of life. Even Rose had left for the day. Clem headed back to the elevator. If Frank couldn't answer his questions then he'd have to go to Fitz.

Clem paced towards the account executives' offices on the floor below, glancing into each of them as he hurried by. It was now gone five o'clock and so, it seemed, were most of the senior account execs.

Even Charlie Knutson's office was empty. Clem got to Fitz's office. The door was locked and there was no sign of his secretary. The cleanup crew was already doing the rounds.

"Fuck!" Clem shouted loudly enough for the bemused Somalian cleaning crew to hear.

Without question, this had been the most bizarre day of Tara's life. A day of revelations that would certainly stay with her forever. First, the meeting with Jack Kelsey, then the violent world of Mistress Krystal.

She walked out from under the iron stairwell behind Mistress Krystal's apartment and took the back street back to Starbucks where she'd parked her vehicle. Tara made sure not to go anywhere near the front entrance of the apartment building in case 'someone' saw her. Her main concern was that Clem had been next on Mistress Krystal's client roster to show up that evening. She wasn't ready to come face to face with him just yet. She needed more lessons in discipline and domination first. Tara turned her cell phone back on and checked her voicemail as she walked quickly passed the hotchpotch of houses. She saw Clem had called. He'd left a voicemail.

*"Hi, honey. Shitty day. I'm gonna work out at the club this evening and blow off some steam. Wondered if you wanted me to pick something up for us tonight for dinner on the way home? Call me."*

Tara wondered if he was really going to the club or not. Maybe she'd just so happen to drop by and find out for sure. She was in no hurry to call him back. Why should she? He rarely called her these days and this sounded like one of those alibi calls. She wasn't certain she believed him.

Crossing the street at Grandview she walked to the Starbucks lot where she'd parked but there was no sign of her Lexus. Tara looked around the lot and saw several signs all with the same message:

'*One hour parking. Violators will be towed.*'

"Shit!"

This was the last thing she needed. What a way to finish off this crazy day, she cursed. It was the last thing she needed. Tara entered

Starbucks feeling mentally exhausted. It had been a long day already and now it was about to get even longer. She walked up to the barista who'd served her earlier in the day.

"Was there a tow truck out here?"

"Yeah. Every day. They're brutal, man. Not cool," the spotty kid sympathized.

"Fuck. Get me a grande double shot cappuccino," said Tara, as she dialed the towing company's number.

Over at Bodyworks Fitness in Eden Prairie, the workout warriors were showing up after their work days. Clem grunted as he lifted a barbell off his chest and pushed a hundred and sixty pounds of heavy metal up in the air. Ten lifts later he crashed the bar down on the support posts and laid on the bench staring up at the ceiling. Beads of sweat ran off his forehead and into his hair making his neck glisten. He didn't want to move. A muscular, tattooed guy half his age stood over him.

"Hey, man - - can I work in with you?" Clem got up slowly, his t-shirt so soaked in sweat it stuck to him.

"I'm done. It's all yours."

Clem toweled down the sweaty bench and ambled wearily over to a rack of dumbbells by the mirror. He started swinging hammer curls with a couple of twenty-five pounders. Clem's body was in good physical shape and just the thought of Fitz's smug smiling face helped him work out even harder than usual. He was still reeling from the stress of his day. He rarely lost his cool but it seemed he was living some crazy kind of emotional rollercoaster ride. *How could everything that was so good turn so one-eighty in the blink of an eye?*

Clem winced as he swung the dumbbells into a wide fly curl, straining the sinews in his deltoids. He felt a burning twinge shoot through his left shoulder, almost causing him to drop the weight on the rubber mat.

"Owww," Clem grunted, as he let both weights fall to his side. He struggled to put the dumbbells back on the rack. He rubbed his painful shoulder and ambled slowly out of the weight area back towards the men's locker rooms.

Clem stripped off, wrapped a white towel around his waist and entered the empty sauna. He sat up on the top wooden bench in the soothing heat, staring down at his toes. He ran the day's events back through his mind, reliving the conversation with the angry Chuck Svensen. As his mind began to drift, a familiar face entered the hot room.

"Hey, Clem? Long time no see!" Clem looked up to see Finlay Johnstone, a man younger than Clem and one of the fitness fanatics at the club. There wasn't an ounce of fat on his lean, muscular body.

"Finlay, you fat bastard!" Clem had known Finlay long enough to trash talk him.

"How you been, dude?"

"Been better. Think I fucked my shoulder."

"Rotator cuff probably. Ice it tonight. You still hacking it in the bullshit business?" Finlay sat down on a bench opposite Clem.

"Hanging in there, yeah. You still wasting your life exercising everyday?"

"Damn right. Got another Iron Man triathlon coming up in two weeks. Down to six per cent body fat. I'm lean and I'm mean!" Finlay beamed with youthful vigor. He had a sparkle in his eyes.

"You're nuts." Clem shook his head in amusement as beads of sweat dripped off the tip of his nose.

"*Me* nuts? Au contraire, mon amis. You're the one who's nutso sitting at a desk nine to five. I'm having fun, baby!"

"You found a real job yet?"

"No time for that!" Finlay laughed. "Too busy keeping my body toned and my mind alert."

Clem found Finlay's enthusiasm for working out impressive but he wasn't going to say that to someone who seemed brimming with more than enough self-confidence and motivation for five people.

"What's your big secret to surviving, Fin?" Clem asked, in all seriousness.

"I could ask you the same question, my friend." Finlay laid back against the cedar wood slats and sucked in a deep lung busting breath of burning air. "Nutrition. Lots of whey protein. Cut the carbs. Fat falls off you. And glutens! They're assholes. Rule them out of your diet."

Clem was fascinated with Finlay's seemingly carefree attitude and lust for life. "Seriously, how do you earn a living?"

"Odd jobs here and there. Y'know. Fix stuff. Enough to get by and feed my fitness addiction."

"You're a piece of work." Clem smiled.

"Keep life simple, dude. Humans waste so much time acquiring crap they really don't need. People are greedy motherfuckers."

Finlay closed his eyes and beamed a broad smile, appearing to not have a single care in the world. Clem felt envious. While he had everything he'd ever wanted in a material sense with his big house, flashy car and great job, here was a man who had nothing but who seemed far happier than he could ever remember being in his entire life. In fact, Finlay Johnstone was just about the happiest sonofabitch Clem had ever met.

"Well, good luck in that triathlon, Fin," said Clem, getting up to leave.

"Luck? You make your own luck in life, Clem." Finlay smiled as sweat poured off his body and he closed his eyes again.

"Catch you later, fatso."

Clem stepped out of the heat and into the coolness of the locker room. Finlay shouted to him through the window of the sauna.

"Get back to the grindstone, old man!"

By the time Tara arrived home, Clem had finished his take-out and was sitting with an ice pack on his injured shoulder. Tara walked in looking exhausted. It was as if their roles had been reversed for once.

"Hi, honey. There's a chopped salad I picked up for you in the fridge!" Clem called out hearing Tara walk in from the garage. She was starving and that was exactly what she needed, along with a glass of something alcoholic but she said nothing. She felt strange, as if she was returning from something very bad. Tara was furious with Clem yet guilty at having acted so deviously that afternoon. Now she was wondering who on earth she was married to if Clem had been leading this secret life. She had no idea how long it had been going on but she was going to find that out. Even if it meant leading a secret life from now on in order to catch her cheating husband. But until she could find him guilty, she would reluctantly have to act as if he was innocent.

Tara opened the fridge and found the take-out.

"Did you get my message? I didn't hear back from you so I went ahead and got it anyway," called out Clem, sounding like he'd just been magically domesticated. Tara still didn't answer. She grabbed a fork and walked into the living room where Clem was nursing his shoulder. It was gone eight but Clem didn't ask where she'd been and Tara wasn't about to tell him. And she was way too tired to make something up that sounded believable. If she'd told him about her SUV getting towed he'd be wondering why she'd been in that part of town so it was best she didn't mention it. But it had been a long day and she was feeling wiped.

"What happened to your arm?" she asked, really not caring if Clem was in pain or not. After all, it seemed Clem enjoyed being smacked about so why should she be concerned? She sat down on the ottoman and dug into her salad.

"Pulled something at the gym lifting a dumbbell," Clem grumbled. Tara couldn't be sure if he was telling the truth or not. Maybe he was. Or maybe Mistress Krystal had cracked him one a little harder than usual. "I ran into Finlay Johnstone at the club tonight," Clem continued. "He's one cracked nut."

If he was telling the truth about seeing Finlay then maybe Clem had gone to the gym to work out after all, Tara surmised. She knew Finlay and had always liked him. Or maybe Finlay was merely an unwitting alibi. Tara stuffed her mouth with a forkful of lettuce. She felt a coldness towards Clem she'd never felt before. Consciously or unconsciously she was detaching herself from him emotionally.

"He hasn't got two cents to rub together yet he's as happy as a damn clam. Doing another triathlon. The guy doesn't seem to have a care in the world."

Tara was more interested in eating than talking. For some odd reason Clem was Mr. Communicator on the one day that she didn't really feel like saying anything to anyone. "Guess if you have nothing, you have nothing to lose," Clem continued.

"I'm gonna pour myself a glass of wine, take a bath, then go to bed," Tara announced as she walked back into the kitchen in search of a wine glass. Tara slept soundly that night.

# CHAPTER 11

Lorraine's early morning yoga class at Bodyworks Fitness had just finished and the class unwinding. Tara felt invigorated. She walked over to Lorraine who was unplugging her iPod from the sound system.

"Hi, girl." Lorraine was pleased to see that Tara had made an appearance. "Glad you made it to class. Where have you been?"

"Nowhere," Tara lied.

"Look, if you need it, and I know it's none of my business, but I've got the name of a highly recommended marriage counselor."

"Thanks but I'm dealing with it. Great class. What was that last song called?" Tara asked, deliberately changing the subject. She didn't need any advice now that she had chosen her own plan of attack. Lorraine took the hint.

"Okay -- I'll mind my own Goddamn business."

"How's your new man?"

"Curtis?"

"Yeah."

"Useless motherfucker. You know what that jerk did? Let's grab a protein shake. I'll tell you what he did…" Lorraine was about to begin a rant but Tara didn't have time for that right now. She tossed her towel over her shoulder as she headed out of the yoga room.

"Next time. Sorry. Gotta run."

Lorraine pulled a face as she watched Tara hurry away. She was more than a little suspicious that all was not what it seemed in her friend's world.

Tara made a bee line to the women's locker room.

"Tara!" a male voice shouted. She turned around to see a black-eyed Finlay Johnstone walking towards her.

"Hi, Finlay," Tara smiled.

"Hey, babe. Haven't seen you in a while. Did Clem tell you I ran into him last night?" Finlay beamed like an enthusiastic college kid.

"Yes, he did actually."

"Think he fucked his rotator cuff," Finlay laughed as if that was a good thing.

"Yeah, he was icing it last night." Tara was intrigued. Clem's story seemed watertight though she couldn't help but stare at Finlay's shiner. "What happened to your eye?"

"Awww, I was playing squash with this crazy guy last night and he dinged me good," Finlay grinned, as if wearing a badge of honor.

"Jack Perkins?"

"Yeah, Jack! You know him? Man, that dude's dangerous!" It was almost as if Clem had primed Finlay on what to say if he ever ran into his wife.

"Seems like it. Look, I gotta run but good seeing you, Fin."

"Later gator!"

As Finlay headed out to the pool, Tara dashed into the locker room to get showered and changed.

Tara drove down Valley View Road to Trader Joe's. So, Clem had been telling the truth after all, she thought. Unless Finlay Johnstone was in on it, too. *No, that was ridiculous.* She was becoming paranoid. Lorraine's words were coming back to haunt her. Tara was starting to become very resentful of Clem. The trust was gone. She *had* to learn the truth and she knew she was on the right track.

Aside from her feelings towards her husband, Tara felt

yesterday's session with Mistress Krystal had given her a glimpse of a secret world. It had opened her eyes to a Pandora's box of perversion she knew existed but had never seen so up close and personal before. She was starting to understand why a woman would get some sort of sordid egotistical pleasure by being so in control. To be able to make a circuit court judge get down on his hands and knees, and then thank you for slapping, kicking and belting him must be incredibly empowering. Mistress Krystal was certainly a fascinating woman with one foot in the real world and the other on the dark side. She was everything Tara wasn't -- tough, street smart and oozing with sex appeal. This was a woman you were not going to mess with because she knew how to look after herself. There was no reason for Tara to like this woman but now she was starting to envy her.

Tara's plan was now underway and she had to follow it through to the letter. She'd driven by an adult store a few times that sold sex toys and fetish clothing on her occasional trips out of suburbia and now that was precisely where she needed to go. As much as she didn't want to admit it, the thought of dressing up in all that tight leather excited Tara. She remembered how hot Michelle Pfeiffer and Halle Berry had both looked all dressed up as Catwoman in those movies a few years back. If Clem was going to show up at Mistress Krystal's apartment, she needed some sort of disguise so he wouldn't realize it was his own wife flogging him. Yes, if she was going to do this, there was no doing it by halves. She was going to have to go the whole hog.

*Madame X* on Lyndale Avenue had an impressive selection of leather and latex wear. Everything from masquerade masks and bodices to thigh high boots and full body cat suits. Hanging from the ceiling was a steel cage. In the middle of the store was a large wooden spinning wheel with clamps for wrists and ankles. Over in a corner were several strange contraptions made of metal that Tara could only imagine were more torturous devices. It seemed as if half the stuff on display had come out of the Middle Ages in Europe.

Tara flicked through the clothing racks and checked the prices.

This stuff wasn't cheap but it all looked like it was very well made. A heavily tattooed and overly pierced sales assistant with her head half shaved approached.

"We custom design all our latex and leatherwear in our studio upstairs," the surprisingly sweetly spoken young woman told Tara.

"Oh, I'm just looking, thanks," Tara lied.

"That's why you won't find anything in our store with 'Made in China' on the label like in some other fetish stores I could name."

"Oh, really? That's good to know," Tara smiled, casually flicking through the corsets on a rack but now with a greater appreciation of the workmanship.

"The calf leather we import directly from Italy and the corsets and bodices are hand sewn in-house by our designers. Everything is handcrafted. We get online orders from all over the world." It was very apparent that this was a serious business.

"Very impressive," Tara nodded, hoping the punky sales girl would leave her alone though one particular black leather bodice caught her eye.

"Try it on," the sales girl suggested. Tara held the bodice up to her lean torso and stared at her reflection in the full-length mirror. The sales girl pointed to the changing rooms.

"No, really. I'm just looking," Tara insisted.

"Y'know, if you're just looking for a fancy dress costume there's one of those party stores over at Ridgedale Mall."

"No, I'm in the right place, thanks." Tara gave her a flat smile, hoping she'd leave her alone. The girl took the hint. As Tara looked around at the enormous variety of fetish items on sale, she realized this was more than just kinky behavior for strange people. This was a lifestyle choice that involved serious financial investment.

Tara must have spent an hour inside *Madame X*, trying on various leather and latex garments and flicking through the pages of various books on the subject of female domination. It was the vast array of shiny black shoes and boots that most piqued her interest and by the time Tara left the store over an hour later, she was several boxes heavier and more than a few hundred dollars lighter. A black-lipped checkout girl had neatly wrapped and packed Tara's purchases into two large carrier bags each with a large purple Madame X logo. This was clothing that Tara knew would never be hanging in her closet and those shopping bags would have to be shredded.

Back home, Tara spent the rest of the afternoon reading *The Art Of Domination*. She plowed through through the pages like an A grade student cramming for exams. She read up on all aspects of the subject and studied the historical imagery - from its Samurai origins of rope-tying to bondage trends in modern mainstream fashion. There were exquisite Victorian drawings of scantily clad women spanking naked men to articles on the psychological aspects of fetish behavior. It was incredulous to Tara that this sort of freakiness had been going on for so many years and in so many cultures.

The more she read more on the subject of female domination and why men felt the need to go to a dominatrix, the more she thought about how it all related to Clem. Had he *always* been like this? If so, how come she didn't know about it? Was she that blind? Did he marry her because she had a dominating personality? *Surely not.*

All these thoughts flashed through her head though she really couldn't come up with any definite answers. But Clem did fit the profile of someone who might crave an urge like this. He had been under so much pressure in his work environment and he was a man who had considerable power. By all accounts, he was the poster boy for BDSM.

Her female intuition was telling her that this was the only route she could pursue to understand her husband's secret life and to keep her marriage intact. Mistress Krystal would teach her everything she needed to know so that she could satisfy Clem's secret desires, then he would have no need to pay some strange woman to do all these nasty, painful things to him. And God knows how much money he'd spent for these kinds of services throughout their marriage.

Sure, she was still mad as Hell that he was deceiving her but was he having actual sexual intercourse with her or not? That was the big question. It would change everything if they were fucking. If he wasn't, and she had to know for certain, Tara felt she could save her marriage. If he was, then that was it. Done. Over. And that made her very sad. But until she could prove it either way, Clem had a stay of execution. Tara voraciously absorbed the information. She read and read and read....

*Dominatrix, Mistress, Maitresse, Fem Dom: female controller of men or women. They are to be obeyed. If instructions are not followed as strictly ordered, the submissive kneeling before her accepts full responsibility for the punishment they will endure for their disrespect and disobedience.*

*The male species is brought into this world by the strength of a woman then raised in the protective custody of a mother. And into adulthood, he will seek the comfort of a female. Through all these passages in life he will become enslaved emotionally by the power of a woman. He now kneels before the Fem Dom, eagerly awaiting and anticipating his fate.*

*These males remember all too clearly how they were spanked, slapped, scolded and punished for errant behavior at the hands of their larger, stronger female governess, mother or teacher when they were much younger. Some learnt that they enjoyed the harsh treatment they received when they were bad. They would deliberately misbehave and act out to be severely physically reprimanded. To be punished only excited them as it does today. It gave them a pleasure they could not quite fathom or understand at that tender age. And perhaps they still don't fully understand why this excites them so. But this is what they crave. This is what they need - like an addiction to a drug they cannot and will not try to kick.*

*The Fem Dom is that Governess, that teacher, that strict mother who can take them back to a time when children did as they were told or faced the consequences. She will take them on a psychological mind trip back to when they were powerless children with no responsibilities, no worries and no concerns. These men are submissives in her presence. They are weak and obedient. They kneel, crawl, and grovel to her. They worship her. They adore her. But away from her control, they can be very different beasts. These very same men often hold power in society — politicians, CEOs, lawyers, doctors, bankers - men who spend their days, weeks, months even years, controlling others. Their jobs and their decisions make or break the lives of others. But the constant need for them to appear strong and wise takes its toll. They can never appear weak or indecisive in their public life. They need an outlet to release the pressure they are constantly under. It is these men that seek out the services of a professional Dominatrix. They need to reverse their roles and become the servant. They need to be able to emotionally let loose - to wince, whimper and cry — but away from the eyes of those who would judge them and topple them. They need the privacy and sanctity of a discreet individual who understands them and protects them.*

*A Dominatrix: a Fem Dom, is the answer for these men of power. She is their outlet, their only opportunity to feel 'normal' again far away from their role-playing in real life. Being with their Fem Dom is more real than their 'reality.' This is where they can feel whole again. Only she understands them, only she knows their needs and won't judge them. She is their therapist.*

*They may leave battered and bruised physically but mentally they are invigorated. Their strength is renewed to be more powerful again tomorrow.*

Tara stopped reading and took a breath. *Wow, these were men with deep psychological problems. Could Clem really have all these issues?* This was stuff she knew could never be discussed with some by-the-book marriage counselor. In any case, why would Clem open up in therapy if he couldn't be honest with her? Tara wondered. Maybe it all started with the relationship Clem had with his mother or father when he was a child. *Did either of them ever spank him? Was he bullied at school?*

Tara felt a void of knowledge about the man she'd known all these years. Or thought she knew. As she turned to another page of the book, she heard the garage door open. *Surely, that couldn't be Clem?* It was way too early for him to be home. She quickly slammed the cover shut and looked for a place to hide it. She stuffed it in her underwear drawer and arranged her panties and thongs to conceal it. It seemed as good a place as any considering the state of their sex life.

Tara skipped down the stairs and wandered in to the kitchen, feeling like she'd been busted. It flustered her. Clem tossed his jacket on the island counter.

"You're home early. Everything okay?"

"No, I wasn't fired," Clem reassured her.

"Well, I hope not," Tara breathed a sigh of relief. Clem seemed in an unusually good mood for once.

"It's beautiful outside. Let's go for a bike ride." Clem kicked off his shoes and started to unbutton his shirt as he headed upstairs to change. This was taking Tara totally by surprise. She smiled nervously and eyed him suspiciously.

"Have you been drinking?" Tara called up to their bedroom as Clem put on a t-shirt and shorts.

"No! Not at all!" Clem yelled back down. Tara looked outside. It certainly was a truly glorious afternoon and with Minnesota's cruelly short summers you enjoyed while you got it.

"Do we still have bikes?" Tara shouted, genuinely not sure as it had been so long since they had cycled anywhere.

"Probably need some air in the tires," Clem yelled back, already running down the stairs.

"Okay, I guess I'll put some shorts on too then," said Tara, not quite sure what had gotten into her husband.

By the time she had changed into more appropriate biking attire, Clem had pumped up the tires and wiped the accumulation of dirt and dust off their two mountain bikes. Out on the driveway, Clem was saddled up and ready to go.

"Let's hit that trail down by the lake."

They both cycled off down the driveway onto the sidewalk of Dunkirk Crescent. Within a few minutes, Clem and Tara were peddling along the trail to Caribou Lake. The tree-lined bike path was dappled in golden beams of sunlight bursting through the branches and myriad shades of green. Several small deck boats and runabouts were speeding over the water, pulling skiers and tubers. Squeals of delight echoed as moms and their young kids played on the small man-made beach near the ice-cream cart. The scene looked like a photo shoot out of a 1950s edition of *Time-Life magazine.*

As they cycled the picturesque vistas along the north side of the water, Clem started to pedal slower. Tara knew something was up.

This just wasn't normal behavior for Clem — sure, it used to be back in their California days when they cycled the beachfront boardwalk — but not in recent memory. In fact, judging from his cranky moods over the previous few months, this was totally out of character. But *this* was the Clem she missed. This was the guy she wanted back but something wasn't right about all this.

Clem cycled up to a ridge that overlooked much of Eden Prairie. It was hot now and Tara was struggling to keep up with him. He got off his bike and stared out at the view. Tara pushed her bike up the remaining few yards to join him.

"Wow," said Tara as she looked out down at the thousands of homes and the large shopping mall that now occupied what was once open prairie just fifty years ago. The lake sparkled in the sunlight as ripples of waves gently lapped up to the sandy shoreline.

"Imagine how great it looked before we built all *that* crap," Clem said ruefully, pointing at the transmission towers that blighted their view. They stood silently for a moment.

"That's progress for you," Tara said, wistfully.

"We need to talk."

Tara's heart sunk. Whatever was eating at Clem was about to be divulged.

"About what?" Tara asked innocuously, not wanting their brief moment to be ruined by what she knew was coming next -- the confession she'd been waiting for. Or would this be merely a version of the truth? She held her breath in anticipation.

"If I lose my job, we don't have a lot of options," Clem sighed.

*Huh?* This wasn't the conversation she was expecting. Maybe this was Clem's way of working his way around to the real subject he wanted to talk about.

"What are you talking about? You're gonna make CEO."

"Maybe, maybe not."

"Look, if you lose your job we leave Minnesota and move back to California. What's so complicated about that?" Tara prompted, feeding Clem's train of thought and actually rather liking the idea.

"We can't afford to go back."

"We've got money, Clem. We're not broke."

Clem didn't respond. He stared out at a small deck boat leaving a trail of white water in its trail as it sped across the sparkling lake.

"My point is, the ad biz is in real bad shape. Everyone I know in New York, Chicago and L.A. is getting laid off. These are guys who could've hired me a few years ago but they're gone now. This fucking economy is brutal. Retail is getting its ass kicked and now everyone's cutting back."

Tara had not heard Clem speak negatively like this before. He'd always been the eternal optimist, even when he'd come home tired and grumpy, he'd always figured it was for the greater good in the long run. This wasn't the conversation she wanted to have with her husband but rather than wait for any kind of personal confession, Tara pressed him for more insight into his work situation. What did Clem know that he wasn't letting on? She thought.

"So you're obviously thinking Fitz will make CEO, is that it?"

"Shit, I don't know anymore. Rebakor is now going with some campaign Fitz presented behind my back. The old man must be in on this." Clem wasn't a quitter but he was sounding like a beaten man, figuratively and literally. "I need a knockout punch to win this now because it seems I'm way down on points."

Tara had never met Kurt Fitzgerald. All she knew about him was what she'd heard over the years from Clem and some of the other employees at Bergenson & Adler when she'd gone to the occasional company event: he was a womanizer and ethically corrupt.

"I don't think I'd like him if I met him," said Tara as she watched two quacking ducks fly out of the reeds below. Clem didn't say anything. "So, anything else you want to tell me?" asked Tara, hoping Clem's introspective mood might turn the conversation to the topic of her husband's sexual exploits.

Clem looked at her with a quizzical expression.

"Like what?" he asked. Tara shrugged.

"I don't know. What else is on your mind?"

"Oh yeah," Clem answered quickly, snapping out of his mood, "I have a six o'clock meeting in town with Daniel Ellerby on Friday that'll keep me tied up for a while."

*Tied up?* Tara wasn't sure if that was a Freudian slip on Clem's part but that was the day she would be visiting Mistress Krystal's apartment again. *Shit!* This could be the day of reckoning. Everything was coming to a head.

"And you'll be tied up for how long?" Tara asked, desperately hoping to sound nonchalant but really pushing for more details.

"Who knows?" Clem looked back out at the view. That irritated Tara. Clem was being vague and she didn't like it.

"So who's this 'Daniel Ellerby' character?"

"He's flying in from L.A. Said he wanted to meet me. Very last minute."

"I've never heard you mention *that* name before," Tara pressed. Clem turned to look at his wife, sensing her unblinking stare.

"He's a headhunter." Clem frowned at the apparent grilling Tara was now giving him. And she wasn't finished.

"Okay, so you're meeting someone called Daniel Ellerby on Friday night at six. Anything else you want to tell me?" Clem really didn't appreciate Tara's tone. He'd wanted a peaceful bike ride on this fine afternoon, not an argument. Clem jabbed back.

"No, Tara. There's nothing else I want to tell you. Jesus. What's gotten into you?"

"Y'know what, Clem? You don't have a monopoly on being pissed off. Other people can be moody, too."

And with that, Tara put a foot on a pedal and pushed off. Clem stood on the ridge and watched Tara cycle away with no clue what could possibly have set her off like that. As Tara cycled back through the park any empathy for Clem she might have felt at the start of their ride had now evaporated and the anger had returned. *Why was she bothering to save this marriage?* Now he was concocting more stories to cover for his perverse sexual addiction.

Maybe there *was* someone called Daniel Ellerby but that's not who he was going to meet this Friday. Why would she want to stay married to a man who would go to such lengths to be so deceitful towards her? Tara imagined the scenario playing out in her head of confronting Clem with his sexual indiscretions. He'd either explode or lie. Clem wouldn't break down and confess, she knew that for sure. Some men, maybe. But no, not mister-manly-man, Clem Drew – professional bullshitter.

Tara pedaled harder and harder. What she did know for sure was that when Clem finally did show up for his next appointment with Mistress Krystal, she'd take over proceedings and give him a beating he'd never forget. That'd teach him a lesson never to lie and cheat on her again. Best of all, Clem would never guess in a million years that it was her all dressed up all vixen-like behind her Catwoman mask. He'd have no idea he'd just paid to have his own wife slap him around. That would be sweet revenge for Tara. Yes, Tara would be in control then. Complete and *utter control*. And whether they stayed married or got divorced would be *her* decision.

That night Tara and Clem didn't talk. Tara slept in the guest bedroom. Their perfect bike ride had turned sour and left a nasty taste in both their mouths. Dealing with Tara's increasing moodiness was not Clem's priority right now. He had to stay focused on work. He knew the reality of him ever finding a job that came anywhere near matching his current salary at Bergensons was extremely remote, even if he left the state and relocated. He was seriously concerned about the future while it seemed to him that Tara's only worry was what time he would be home on any given night. Through his eyes, she just didn't seem to fully grasp the seriousness of their situation. He was frustrated at work and just as much so at home.

Next morning, after Clem had left for work, Tara left for the gym. With all the money she'd spent at Madame X, she wanted to look as fit and fabulous as she could. That meant being as lean and toned as possible, even if she would only be dressing up for perverts. It served her own ego to look her best.

After her yoga class, Tara was completely shot. She laid on her mat like a wet noodle. Lorraine walked over to her and smiled.

"How's life treating you, girl?" Tara looked up. "You were good today."

"I just needed a little motivation." Tara propped herself up on an elbow and sipped her bottled water.

"Wanna grab a protein shake? I really need to tell you the latest episode with Curtis."

Tara stood up and wiped the back of her neck with her towel. She didn't want to get embroiled in another long lunch listening to the various ways Lorraine was going to murder Curtis and dump his lifeless body. And neither did she want or need to hear Lorraine's warped psychoanalysis of her marriage to Clem. What's more, Tara knew Lorraine would think she was totally off her rocker if she told her she was learning to become a dominatrix and being taught by the very same woman her husband was secretly seeing. Lorraine simply wouldn't understand any of it. Anyway, she liked this new feeling of empowerment she was experiencing. She couldn't wait to get home and play dress up.

As she walked towards her SUV, Lorraine came running after her. "Hey, girl!"

Tara really didn't want to talk. She got in the driver's seat and slammed the door shut. Lorraine tapped on the window. Tara slid it half open.

"Sorry Lorraine. I've got to get going."

"I just want to apologize -- I get so caught up in *me* sometimes. How're you and Clem doing? I forgot to ask you."

"It's all good now," Tara lied with a weak smile.

"But that freaky card?" Lorraine frowned.

"Totally bogus. Okay. Gotta go. See you at the next class, okay?" Tara reversed out of her parking space and drove away. Lorraine watched her friend leave, not sure if she'd just be blown off.

Opening the boxes from Madame X, Tara started trying on her new outfit. First, the black lace panties and then the black silk stockings. One benefit of not having any children to breast-feed meant Tara's size 34c boobs still looked as perky and firm as when she was a twenty-one year old. She clipped the black stockings to her garter belt. Opening another box, Tara took out the black leather bodice that tied at the front. She pulled hard on the lacing, squeezing her breasts together, upwards and out. They bulged over the top of her corset like two perfect orbs trying to escape. But her favorite item was still boxed. She flipped open the lid and inside were the two longest, shiniest black latex boots she'd ever seen in any fashion magazine. She'd had no choice but to buy them. Tara pulled them up over her stockings and just above her knees. They were so tight and so unbelievably shiny that it made her laugh — they looked like insanely kinky pirate boots.

As she posed in front of her bedroom mirror, Tara saw herself metamorphosing but she wasn't finished yet. Next, came the black latex gloves all the way up to her elbows and finally, a Catwoman mask which covered her eyes and the top of her head with two little pointy ears. Damn! She looked hot and decidedly dangerous.

Transformation complete, Tara postured and posed. She loved how she looked. She felt powerful. She practiced a few kickboxing moves as if fighting off a Ninja attack. *What man could resist her?* Would Clem even recognize her if he walked in on her right now? Not in a million years. *God, what if he did walk in?* How would she explain that? It would be a complete giveaway and Clem would know she was on to him. Fearing that ugly scenario, she quickly peeled herself out of her latex and leather and hid the boxes back under the bed.

At Bodyworks Fitness, Tara signed up for the evening cardio-boxing classes and assumed Clem wouldn't miss her. So what if he did? She wasn't concerned about it. Tara was acting like a fighter in training prepping for a title fight. She was more interested in her next lesson with Mistress Krystal that coming Friday than to worry about Clem's feelings. Maybe it was time he started worrying about *her* for once, she thought. Anyway, she was still punishing him for not being honest with her the day before.

Tara beat the crap out of the heavy punching bag that night. She didn't know a left hook from an uppercut but that didn't matter.

*Baaam! Baaam! Baaam!*

Sweat streamed down her reddened face. Ringlets of her hair stuck to her forehead as she vented all the bottled up rage inside her. Push-ups, sit-ups and jumping jacks for the next hour left her in a hot, sweaty, sticky mess. She felt tired but she felt strong.

By the time Tara finally got home, it was a familiar scene. Clem had fallen asleep in front of the TV, an empty bottle of wine beside him. Perfect. She could sneak up to bed without having to talk to him.

# CHAPTER 12

It was Friday. This was to be the day of reckoning. Tara knew how to find her way to the back entrance of Mistress Krystal's apartment from Starbucks but chose to park a lot closer this time; on a quiet side street where she wouldn't be towed. Clem might recognize her black Lexus SUV if she was too close to the apartment building so she gave herself a short walk. Tara wanted to be incognito walking up the iron stairwell to Mistress Krystal's back door. Though wearing dark glasses with her jacket collar pulled up hiding much of her face probably made her look far more conspicuous than inconspicuous.

Tara rang the doorbell and was buzzed in to Mistress Krystal's apartment, her nerves began to jangle. She couldn't tell if it was fear or excitement. It was early afternoon but at six o'clock, Clem would be showing up for his appointment and that was freaking her out.

As Tara entered, she could see her tutor prepping the playroom. She was laying down plastic sheeting over much of the floor. Tara stood and watched curiously. Mistress Krystal glanced up at her.

"Three hundred cash."

Tara waved a wad of twenty-dollar bills. Mistress Krystal smiled.

"I went shopping." Tara held up the large duffle bag she'd brought with her.

"Guess you must be serious then. Get changed. Today's lesson begins in fifteen minutes. This one's very punctual."

"So soon?" Tara said, walking into the kitchen and immediately feeling anxious. Mistress Krystal followed.

"You can get dressed in the bathroom back there."

While Tara got changed, Mistress Krystal grabbed a cookie from a jar and downed it in one bite. She glanced up at the clock as she paced the kitchen floor. Everything was set for her first client of the day. She could hear Tara banging around in the bathroom.

"Need a hand?" she asked through the door.

"No, I'm good. Won't be long."

Mistress Krystal checked her own appearance in a mirror then grabbed another cookie while she waited for her newbie student to reappear. The bathroom door suddenly swung open and Tara finally emerged dressed for *sexcess*. She posed for Mistress Krystal, knowing how fabulous she looked.

"Well? What d'ya reckon?" Tara beamed, looking for approval. She felt a surge of adrenalin.

"Hmmmm....you spent some dough."

"Not too shabby for a housewife from suburbia, huh?" Tara said, feeling both excited and rather proud of her own commitment to her master plan. Mistress Krystal looked her up and down with an approving glance.

"Five minutes. Ready?"

Suddenly Tara didn't feel particularly at ease. She felt conflicted: empowered by her own striking Amazonian appearance but feeling somewhat idiotic at the same time. *What the fuck was she doing seeking approval from this woman?* The two of them looked completely out of place in the shabby apartment.

"I feel kinda silly. Like I'm some sort of extra in a Batman movie or something," Tara confessed.

"Embrace it. Get into the part. You're role-playing and you're not an extra -- you're playing the lead."

Tara's stiletto heeled, thigh-high latex boots stepped noisily into the playroom and stage where she would be performing if asked.

"Why the plastic sheet?" Tara asked with some trepidation.

"This one's a pisser," Mistress Krystal replied matter-of factly.

"Ugh! That's...."

"Disgusting?" Mistress Krystal finished Tara's sentence.

"I didn't say that."

"No, but you thought it and I hear your thoughts, remember?" Mistress Krystal taped down the last edge of the plastic sheeting.

"I was going to say *messy*," Tara lied again.

"I call this one *Mr. Winkle*," Mistress Krystal continued without smiling, as she straightened her stocking tops. "Now all you need is some weaponry and a little creative thinking," she quipped. Tara had never thought of this being creative but then this *was* like acting out a scene from a movie. Except there were no cameras filming.

*Bzzzzzzz!*

Mr. Winkle had arrived right on time. The two women waited in the kitchen for him to enter.

A large, tough looking guy who looked to be fifty-something entered wearing jeans and a leather bomber jacket. He walked silently down the hallway and stopped at a side table. He pulled out a fat roll of dollar bills and counted them into a neat pile. For what he wanted, the fee was more. His large fingers placed the notes with an unlikely deftness on top of each other. What Mr. Winkle did for a living was anyone's guess. Though if Mistress Krystal had vetted him then he was kosher.

"I thought all your clients were high end," Tara whispered to her teacher.

"Don't judge a book by its cover, Angelina."

The two women watched him through the cracked open kitchen door. Mr. Winkle entered the dimly lit playroom.

"Get undressed! And get on your knees! Wait right there until I'm ready for you!" ordered Mistress Krystal to her bulky male client. She motioned to Tara to stay in the kitchen as she lit a cigarette and took a long drag. She puffed out the smoke with a little cough.

"God I hate these things."

"Then quit," Tara whispered.

"I never started. It's in our script."

Mistress Krystal took another drag and examined the burning tip. Blowing off the ash, she walked back into the playroom where Mr. Winkle was now kneeling naked in the middle of the room. She took a blindfold off a wall hook and put it over Mr. Winkle's eyes. He bowed his head as Mistress K took another long drag of the cigarette causing the tip to glow red hot. She stood close then blew the smoke into his face. He inhaled deeply.

"Have you missed me?" she asked without any warmth in her tone.

"Yes, Mistress." His voice was strong and deep.

"I'm glad to hear it."

She dragged on the cigarette again and blew more smoke in his face. Again, he tried to capture all the smoke into his lungs.

"Thank you, Mistress."

"I've got a present for you."

"Thank you, Mistress."

"Do you know what it is?"

"Yes, Mistress."

"Of course, you do."

"Thank you, Mistress."

Tara watched from the kitchen as Mistress Krystal sucked in another deep breath of smoke. The tip of the cigarette glowed red hot. She blew away some of the burning ash to make it glow even hotter - then she stubbed it into Mr. Winkle's hairy chest.

A black circle of ash burned into his flesh causing it to smoke. Mr. Winkle took a deep breath but uttered no sound of pain. The soft sigh he made seemed to indicate he felt a deep-rooted pleasure. Tara pulled an expression of pain on his behalf though Mr. Winkle had no clue he had a secret audience of one watching this strange ritual.

"Thank you, Mistress," said Mr. Winkle. "Again, Mistress."

His Mistress obliged and fulfilled his request nine more times, leaving Mr. Winkle a singed, scorched mess of burnt chest hair and skin. The smell of his fleshy burns made Tara feel sick. But things were just warming up.

Mistress Krystal removed Mr. Winkle's blindfold and replaced it with a multi-strapped and zippered black leather gimp hood. She pulled it over his head and face. Then she buckled the buckles and zipped up the zippers leaving Mr. Winkle unable to see or hear and barely even able to breathe. He was now in a state of almost total sensory deprivation. And that's how she left him.

Tara wondered what was going to happen next to the hapless man kneeling in the other room. Mistress Krystal walked back into the kitchen and closed the door behind her.

"I'll let him enjoy that for a while."

"Can he breathe in that thing?" Tara worried.

"Barely. I need a cookie."

"What are you going to do with that?"

"Eat it. This is hungry work. I need something to take the taste of that nicotine out of my mouth." Mistress Krystal took a bite and looked at Tara.

"Ready?"

"For what?" Tara asked. She had no idea what that meant but it was too late to ask as Mistress Krystal returned to her client in the playroom. Tara gulped as her tutor motioned for her to join them. She quickly checked her appearance in the mirror like someone about to go for a job interview, then duly obeyed.

Her stiletto heels banged slowly across the wooden floorboards like two small hammers. Feeling horribly nervous, she approached the unseeing, unknowing, unsuspecting Mr. Winkle. Mistress Krystal handed her a wooden paddle.

"Here. Take this."

Tara gripped the handle tightly. She had never had any desire to play Ping-Pong let alone smack anyone with a wooden bat but that was a bit late now.

"Hit him!" ordered Mistress Krystal, sounding like a cruel Nazi commandant giving an order. Tara looked at the hooded Mr. Winkle kneeling naked before her. She could smell his burnt flesh.

"Where?" Tara mouthed silently while holding the paddle in the air.

"He can't hear you. He's in his own world now. Just hit him anywhere. This is what he pays me for."

Tara swung the paddle and hit Mr. Winkle's shoulder.

*Smaaackkk!*

It was a fair whack but not sufficient to make him budge or utter a sound. Mistress Krystal was unimpressed.

"I said hit him, not tap him. He won't get anything out of that. Do it again. Harder this time," she demanded of Tara.

Pulling her arm back further, Tara swung the paddle down on Mr. Winkle's fleshy thigh, making a loud slapping sound.

*Thwaaackk!*

Again, no reaction from Winkle.

"Harder!" yelled Mistress Krystal. Tara took a wild swing and crashed the wooden paddle down hard.

*Whaaammm!*

Mr. Winkle moaned softly.

"That's better. You're getting the hang of it."

Tara felt bad about the whack but also somewhat pleased that her teacher and Mr. Winkle seemed to approve. Mistress Krystal paced slowly around her client. *Was this what Clem liked?* Tara's mind raced as her thoughts abruptly jumped to her husband's impending arrival at six o'clock. *What were his requests when he came here?*

Her hand stopped swinging the paddle but Mistress Krystal was quick to reprimand her.

"Don't stop! Another six strokes should warm him up," she snapped, as she turned away to study her collection of whips and floggers on the rack behind them. "Go at it, Angelina."

It seemed both Tara and Mr. Winkle were under the control of Mistress Krystal as they were now doing whatever she demanded of them. Tara did as she was instructed with each stroke of the paddle coming down harder and harder. Mr. Winkle's thighs and back were turning redder and redder with each strike but he seemed a very willing subject. Mistress Krystal took the paddle from Tara and handed her a small whip.

"Here. It's all in the wrist."

Mistress Krystal demonstrated how to twirl the leather flogger. Tara seemed to handle it like a pro, flicking the knotted tips back and forth against Mr. Winkle's wide and visibly sore back. Grabbing her client by his hood straps, Mistress Krystal pulled him up to a standing position. Mr. Winkle's large frame stood willingly in the middle of the floor, naked except for the tightly bound gimp hood that prevented him seeing, speaking or hearing. Every breath sounded like a gasp reminiscent of Darth Vader. But this wasn't science fiction – it was as real as it gets and it was obvious that Mr. Winkle was struggling for air.

"Flog his chest," Mistress Krystal ordered. Tara duly obliged, spinning the flogger rapidly. As the tassels whipped his flesh, Mistress Krystal abruptly kicked Mr. Winkle hard between his powerful thighs, slamming him in the crotch. He let out a muffled yell.

*"Ooophhh!"*

His knees buckled. Tara stepped back immediately worried that Mr. Winkle might be seriously hurt. He composed himself and stood upright again, still moaning in obvious pain. Mistress Krystal kicked him hard in his nutsack again.

*Thhwaackkk!*

Mr. Winkle doubled over, reeling in pain once more. Tara stared nervously at the two of them, not sure how this was all meant to play out. "Okay, stand back. Here it comes," warned Mistress Krystal.

"What?" Tara's eyes widened as Mistress Krystal swung back her stiletto and let fly.

*Baaaaaam!*

The third kick opened the floodgates and Mr. Winkle's winkle sprayed the room with a spout of urine. Mistress Krystal stepped out of the way of the stream while Tara ducked for cover.

"Jesus Christ!"

Whether Mister Winkle had orgasmed or not was a matter of conjecture. Though that was the last thing Tara cared about. She was far more concerned that her expensive hand-stitched leather bodice hadn't been pissed on than giving any regard to Mr. Winkle's level of sexual satisfaction. Mistress Krystal pushed her client's head down, forcing him to sit in his own excreted body fluid. She unbuckled the straps that covered his ears.

"You're a dirty boy!" Mistress Krystal scolded. "A dirty, dirty boy! Lick it up! Lick it all up!"

Tara had seen enough. She walked out of the playroom and back into the sanctuary of the kitchen. She pulled off her Catwoman mask and paced the room. Mistress Krystal followed a few moments later.

"Did you have to make him do that?" Tara asked her teacher, repulsed by what she'd just been part of.

"It's in the script," Mistress Krystal said, wearily. "That's why he comes here. It's the same every time -- cigarette, wood paddle, golden shower. I need a towel." She opened a cupboard door and grabbed several towels and rags from a stockpile. She dried herself off as Tara peered back into the playroom to see Mr. Winkle still down on his knees slurping up his own piss. Mistress Krystal tossed the damp towels into the playroom and closed the kitchen door.

"Now what?" Tara asked.

"Nothing. Show's over. Tea?"

"Er…yeah, I guess."

Mistress Krystal filled her teakettle with water and turned up a burner on the electric stove. Tara sat at the kitchen table and shook out her hair.

"Personally, I don't like the golden shower stuff but I sure prefer it to scat. I draw the line at that kinda crap, pardon the pun."

"Huh?" Tara responded innocently.

"Pissing is called 'golden showers'. 'Scat' is when they shit. Had a client once who wanted me to take a dump on him. Another liked to smear his own poop all over himself. I've got my limits."

"Why do they want to do it in the first place?" Tara sneered in utter repulsion. "That's not sexy!"

"It's not always about sex, hun. A thousand bucks for an hour's work? It's good money for some. This is a business, remember?"

Back in the den of iniquity, Mr. Winkle toweled himself off, got dressed and departed, no doubt still smelling of his own urine.

Tara was still trying to process everything. "How did you ever get into this line of work? I mean, it's crazy."

Mistress Krystal handed Tara her tea and raided the cookie jar again. "Long story short -- I was going to be a nurse. Maybe fifteen, sixteen years ago. Dropped out of college in my final year to run off to Florida with a guy I thought I was in love with."

"Were you?"

"I dunno. Anyway, that was a dumb move. He was a dreamer -- code for loser. We had great sex and nothing else and that don't pay the rent plus Tampa's a miserable fucking place. How anyone lives in that heat and humidity down there is beyond me."

"So how did you end up so far north?"

"Coldest place I could find after that scorching heat. Figured I'd go back to nursing. That never happened. Anyway, now I have my own patients in a different kinda way."

It was the first time Tara had seen Mistress Krystal lighten up and relax like this. She was starting to see Mistress Krystal a little differently. The human side of this hard-nosed dominatrix was starting to emerge -- the real woman behind the tough persona. But there was no getting past the fact that she was a professional Fem Dom with little or no affection for her clients. She simply dished out pain for cash. She didn't even know the real names of these strangers. Sure, she knew the odd tidbit about them but from her point of view, the less she knew the better. It seemed her only concern was not being caught by the authorities. This woman wasn't right in the head and this was as far from nursing as you could get.

"Why didn't you just get yourself a regular job?" Tara asked. "Something more normal."

"Normal? What's 'normal' to you?" Mistress Krystal chuckled. "Sitting in an office behind a desk half your fucking life? Is that what you call *normal?*"

"You know what I mean."

"All this might not seem normal to you but it's *my* normal. Is fucking in the missionary position normal?"

"I've never thought about it before. No sex at all has been my 'normal' these past few months," Tara mused.

"Us humans used to do it doggie style -- for thousands of years. Then the church comes along and says it wasn't *normal* for us to fuck like animals. Face to face was the only way we should be having sex, they said. Missionary position. So religious nutjobs decided how we should fuck! If it ain't missionary position it ain't 'normal.' Gimme a break."

Tara really wasn't in the mood for a lecture on the history of religion, how humans hump and who should be in charge of defining what 'normal' is? Tara sipped on her tea.

"So, how'd it feel in there?" Mistress K. asked, standing up and putting her empty mug in the sink. Tara frowned.

"Empowering. But -- I mean, it's all pretend, isn't it?"

"Is it? Did you pretend to whack Mr. Winkle with that paddle? Did I pretend to stub out a cigarette in his hairy chest ten times?"

"No but...."

"Exactly."

Tara could feel the nape of her neck break out in a cold sweat. Her mind came back to Clem again. She was starting to feel anxious. Maybe she should leave before six and then avoid any confrontation with her husband. What if Clem and Mistress Krystal had sex? Tara couldn't just stand there and watch. She'd freak out.

Mistress Krystal poured more boiling water into the teapot.

"Another cup?"

"No thanks," Tara answered.

"There are some Doms who really get off doing this. They have a sadistic nature in their DNA. It isn't acting to them."

"Are you acting in there?" Tara asked, tentatively.

"Sometimes I am. Sometimes I'm not."

Tara didn't like that reply. "Really? I thought there was a pre-determined script you worked to?"

"Sure, but a little improv doesn't hurt every now and then. Livens things up!" Mistress Krystal smirked. "You wait till the next one comes in. He's something else."

# CHAPTER 13

Clem took the call he'd been waiting for. It was James Molinaire.

"Hello, Clem. Returning your call."

"James! Hi there. Thanks for getting back to me…"

"How's your golf game?"

"My golf game?" Clem was caught off-guard. He knew he was out golfing when Fitz was meeting with Rebakor in Louisville but how did James Molinaire know that? That asshole Fitz must've told him which meant Fitz must've known where Clem was. He gave a quick pat answer. "Average at best. Why d'you ask?"

"Pity you were too busy to present your agency's new campaign recommendations for Rebakor."

"That's why I called," Clem quickly gathered himself. "I wanted to follow up and see how the meeting went." He was on sticky ground. He had no idea what campaign had been shown to Molinaire and the Rebakor marketing department. Naturally, if he'd known about any meeting taking place he certainly would've been there.

"I heard that the meeting went well," Clem lied, truly hoping the meeting had been something of a train wreck.

"Mr. Fitzgerald presented a fine campaign. Impressed all of us here."

Clem wasn't sure how much Molinaire knew of his involvement, or lack of it, in the creative work that had been presented. He felt very uneasy. He was between a rock and a hard place. Either way, he could come out of this conversation looking a helluva lot dumber than before it started. If he let on to Molinaire that he hadn't seen the creative work he'd look asleep at the wheel. If Clem said he liked it, he could be endorsing the biggest piece of garbage to ever leave the agency. He hedged his bets and went for the bluff.

"Great. Glad to hear it. Let's see what the focus groups think." There was an awkward silence.

"Apparently the response of the focus groups was extremely positive. Why more testing?" Clem knew for an absolute damn fact that there was no way Fitz could've had any time to organize focus groups.

"For more accurate results," Clem double bluffed.

"More accurate? You've seen the metrics, I assume."

Clem was feeling distinctly uncomfortable with where this conversation was going. No, of course, he hadn't seen the metrics. *There were no fucking metrics other than the bullshit numbers Fitz had pulled out of his asshole.* Clem realized he had absolutely no fucking idea what was going on with the account he was supposed to be running.

"I gave Fitz power of attorney on the focus groups, James. He organized them and takes full responsibility for the results. He's more of a number cruncher guy."

"I see."

"I apologize for not making it to Louisville but Kurt Fitzgerald's my right hand man now and he's one smart cookie, trust me." Clem couldn't believe he was saying the words that were coming out of his mouth but he could spread the bullshit as well as any ad man. It was the only tact he could take now.

"Yes, he is," Molinaire replied flatly.

That was the last thing Clem wanted to hear. What kind of voodoo had Fitz put Molinaire under? He wondered.

"Well, delighted you and Fitz got to meet. I'll start looking at director's reels and start getting bids from production companies. I'll get Justine and your assistant to look at our calendars."

"Fitz has already set that up." Clem gritted his teeth.

"Okay, great," Clem lied. "Lets all move forward together now. I think this first campaign will be a doozy." Clem blurted, inwardly praying to the heavens that the work Fitz had presented to Molinaire was something the agency could be proud of.

"Just one question, Clem."

"Shoot."

"Tell me, who exactly is running my account at Bergenson & Adler when you're off playing hooky?"

*Click.*

The line went dead. Molinaire had hung up on him. He hadn't bought into Clem's bluffery. And he was obviously pissed. Clem was left feeling like a cuckolded husband. Fitz had succeeded in severing the ties that binded Clem and Molinaire. It was obvious now that Fitz and the old man were working together as a team. He had to see that campaign right now and assemble all the parties involved. The shit was about to hit the fan.

Frank Bergenson sat at the head of the large maple conference table. Clem sat at the opposite end while Chuck Svensen and his team of pissed off copywriters and art directors faced Kurt Fitzgerald, Charlie Knutson and Patrick and Gerard, the creative team responsible for the ad campaign Molinaire had seen and approved.

In the middle of the table was the 'God Speed' campaign; several large print ads mocked up on white boards. The mood was somber as everyone waited for Frank Bergenson to say something. All eyes were on the aging CEO. The silence in the room was palpable and you could cut the tension in the room with a blunt plastic knife.

Clem wanted the guilty to explain their behavior to the witnesses in the room who might not be so aware of the politics behind these shenanigans. Clem wanted to show Chuck Svensen and his creative teams that he was not the man responsible for this almighty cluster fuck that the account, and the agency, was now in. The trial began.

"Now, let me understand this correctly, Kurt. You presented this campaign to James Molinaire at Rebakor and he liked everything he saw," said Frank Bergenson.

"Lock, stock and two smokin' hot barrels," smiled Fitz with an expression of smugness Clem found nauseating. Frank Bergenson didn't seem too amused either.

"This campaign was not approved internally!" Chuck Svensen shouted, looking directly at Fitz.

"So what? Client's happy. Let's move on," Fitz grinned.

"That's not your call, Fitz," barked Frank Bergenson. Fitz was unfazed. He looked at Chuck and his three pissed creative teams sitting across the table glaring at him.

"Sorry guys but we kicked your ass on this one," Patrick grinned as he and Gerard hi-fived each other. No one else in the room was amused, particularly not Chuck Svensen.

"All creative work has to be approved internally by me. I'm the Creative Director, in case any of you forgot. Fitz, you broke agency protocol going behind my back."

Everyone was well aware of that.

"Well, Chuck, these guys came up with something great over the weekend and I made an executive decision to present it while Clem was playing golf," Fitz said smugly.

"How did you know I was playing golf, Fitz?"

"A little birdie told me," Fitz jabbed.

"You're not running the show here, jerk," Clem hit back.

"I run the show here," Frank reminded them all.

"I went by my gut and my gut was right," Fitz said flatly.

"The same gut that did those imaginary focus groups? You told Molinaire a bunch a bull about focus groups that never happened, you lying sonofabitch! You're gonna have to dig yourself outta that hole yourself."

Frank Bergenson was not amused by Clem's accusation. "Is that true, Fitz?" Fitz leaned back in his seat.

"Yes, I did. I anticipated how the focus groups would play out and now that they're underway it seems I was right on the money."

The collection of creatives groaned. Whether Fitz was lying or telling the truth was irrelevant to them. Positive focus groups meant anything they'd created wouldn't be getting any further up the approval ladder. But Clem had to save face in front of Chuck and the creative teams or it would be very hard to get them to do anything in future. His credibility was on the line at the agency.

"Frank, you gotta reel this guy in. He's a liability everyone who works here," Clem looked at Frank as if no one else was in the room.

"These ads suck," one of the writers chimed in before Frank could respond.

"Fuck you, Adrian," yelled Gerard, defending his work.

"I would never have approved that dumb line," seethed Chuck Svensen. "God Speed? That doesn't mean anything."

Fitz sat back in his chair and smiled at everyone at the table.

"Wow, you guys have some serious ego issues here. Sorry, I presented a campaign that the client loved. Maybe it proved you guys aren't as essential to the creative process as you all think you are."

That hit a nerve with everyone in the room.

*"That's not the point!"*

*"You have no respect for what we do!"*

*"How the shit....?"*

Frank Bergenson watched Fitz handle the barbs that were flying in from all around the room with a cocky easiness, as if they were tossing paper planes at a man wearing a Kevlar suit. Clem was fuming that Fitz had made him look totally out of the loop in the client's eyes. It was a deliberate attempt to undermine Clem and everyone at the table knew it. Tempers were frayed as a shouting match ensued.

"Shut up all of you! This isn't a fucking zoo!" Frank boomed. The room went quiet as all eyes turned towards the old man. "What's done is done. And we're not going to try to undo it," he announced sagely.

Everyone other than Charlie, Gerard and Patrick was waiting

and wanting Frank Bergenson to tear Kurt Fitzgerald a new asshole but it wasn't happening. And no one expected what came next out of Frank's mouth.

"This campaign nails it. It's got legs - it can run in all media. It's simple, it's smart and I love it."

The deflated expression on the faces of Clem, Chuck and the three creative teams said it all. And it was only emphasized by the glint in Fitz's eyes. Clem was livid but felt powerless. He had one last shot at trying to get a fair shake for his creative guys and get himself back in the game.

"The least we should do now is present the campaigns Chuck's teams have concepted and let Molinaire decide," Clem suggested calmly.

"Oh, Clem, put your fucking ego to one side." Frank glared across the table at Clem as if he was the cause of all of this. "We've hit a home run right off the bat. Molinaire's happy. That makes me happy. And if I'm happy, you all better be fucking happy, too."

The old man rose to his feet. Clem pounded the table with his clenched fist. Everyone jumped. "This is bullshit, Frank and you know it!" he shouted.

Fitz's grin broke into a smile. "Temper, temper."

"Fuck you!" Clem blasted, glaring back at Fitz. Everyone was angry now but Fitz just rocked back in his chair, feeling victorious.

"No, I think this is more of a fuck *you*, Clement," beamed Fitz.

Frank headed for the door. "Meeting over. Fitz, I want to see you in my office. Now!"

The old man walked out of the conference room. Clem wanted to beat the living crap out of Fitz but his nemesis exited after his boss before Clem could get around the table to throttle him. Fitz glanced back at Clem and winked.

As everyone shuffled out of the conference room with several despondent rumblings, a bewildered Chuck Svensen approached a very unhappy Clem.

"What the fuck's going on here, Clem?"

"No idea. I just know that the old man is so fucking past his sell-by date."

"He shouldn't be backing Fitz on something this big. This sets a really bad vibe down in the creative department."

"Not just your department, Chuck."

Inside Mistress Krystal's apartment, Tara looked up at the clock. It was close to five thirty and it gave her palpitations. Six o'clock was when Clem had his so-called dinner appointment with the mysterious Daniel Ellerby. A weird tingle shot down Tara's spine. She jumped off her bar stool and started to pace the kitchen floor.

Mistress Krystal decided it was time to break out the good stuff in the tea department.

"Royal Doulton makes the finest bone china. Earl Grey tastes so much better in these cups," she said, taking two rose-patterned china cups with matching saucers out of the cupboard.

"I've had enough tea, thanks."

"If you're hungry I've got more cookies in the cupboard."

"I'm good."

Mistress K went off to check her eye make-up in the bathroom mirror but Tara was still ruminating on her previous quip about going off script. "What sort of improv?" Tara called out, not sure she really wanted to hear the answer.

"Whatever takes my imagination at the time," replied Mistress Krystal, walking back into the kitchen.

That was another cryptic answer that did nothing to reassure Tara. Mistress Krystal walked off into the playroom and began to roll up the plastic sheeting. Tara followed her. "Who's your six o'clock client?" Tara asked bluntly, not expecting a name.

"Just another guy who needs to get his rocks off. This one wears me out." Mistress Krystal huffed as she got down on the floor and carefully started rolling the sheet.

"So…..do you ever have sex with any of your clients?"

"Depends."

Tara was getting frustrated not getting any straight answers out of her teacher. She wanted to know what she should expect at six o'clock. After all, *this was why she was here.* This was the culmination of her master plan. It was making her antsy and now she was getting snappy.

"What does that mean? It's a simple enough question. Yes or no?"

Now it was Mistress Krystal who was down on her knees as she rolled up the wet plastic sheeting. Tara stood over her. *So who was in control now?* Mistress Krystal looked up at Tara.

"Occasionally."

"So you *have* had sex with them then. Why?"

"Because I wanted to, not because they asked for it. It's about control, remember?" She stood up. They were now at eye level again. "These guys give that control over to me when they come into my domain."

Mistress Krystal dumped the soiled plastic in a big black trash bag. "They come here willingly. They wanna be told what to do. They want me to control everything. That's what gets them off. I'll take what I want out of it."

"Like…..what?"

"Sometimes I might let them suck a nipple or lick my pussy. Depends on my mood. There's one guy I like to blow every now and again 'cos he's kinda cute. He's got a great body and a really nice cock."

Tara didn't want to hear that, especially as Clem perfectly fit the description. These weren't the answers she was hoping to hear.

"I know you enjoyed that last session. I could see it in your eyes when you gave him those last few whacks," Mistress Krystal smiled. "Maybe one more session after this and you'll be ready." Tara raised an eyebrow.

"Ready for what?"

"Look Angelina, I'm not an idiot. You wanna go into business working as a pro dom. I'm not that dumb. The money's good and I don't blame you."

"But that's not true!" Tara protested.

Mistress Krystal laughed. "Hun, I don't give a shit. I've got my clients and you'll soon find there are a boatload more out there."

"No, that's not what I want," Tara insisted. Mistress Krystal waved a dismissive hand.

"You could use this place, too. We can work out a deal, split the rent."

"No, no, no, that hadn't crossed my mind at all. You've got the wrong end of the stick. I just want to...."

"Spice it up in the bedroom with your husband? Hun, you don't need to pay me three hundred big ones cash to learn how to do that. Anyway, think it over. It's a good offer."

Tara was blindsided by the suggestion. It had never entered her mind. She had absolutely no intention of becoming a professional dominatrix though she felt strangely flattered that Mistress K thought that she could hack it if she wanted to. Tara simply wasn't made of the same mental toughness that her tutor possessed. Inflicting pain on strangers, day in, day out was not her bag.

She was growing impatient and now her adrenalin levels were starting to soar as the clock ticked closer to six.


Back in Frank Bergenson's office, the mood was very different. Fitz was all smiles as he sat in the serenity of Frank's corner office. Frank walked over to his drinks cabinet and poured himself a large dram of Glendronach but didn't offer any to Kurt Fitzgerald.

Fitz's phone rang. Molinaire's name came up on the caller ID.

"Hang on, Frank. I'd better take this."

"Go ahead."

He picked up the call. "James, what can I do for you, sir?" Fitz sounded like a willing servant eager to please his master. He listened to his instructions. "Absolutely. I'll Fed Ex those out to you today."

Frank Bergenson reclined silently in his plush leather chair, drink in hand, while Fitz continued his call. "No problem. Anytime." Fitz hung up and smiled at Frank. "He's happy."

"Good," said Frank Bergenson as he sipped the amber nectar in his whisky glass. "Seems you and our favorite client have hit things off rather nicely."

"Clem just can't admit that anyone else can do anything better than him. He'd never have approved a campaign he wasn't involved in," said Fitz, feeling victorious.

"Trouble is, Kurt, you two assholes are going to kill each other if I don't resolve this thing soon and announce my successor," Frank frowned. "I thought Clem was the man to fill my shoes but if he'd stolen that account to start his own agency we'd be in huge financial trouble and we'd be stuck with you in control of this place."

Fitz's comfort level suddenly went down a notch.

"Stuck?"

"You know what I mean, Fitz. I'm sure Chuck Svensen would feel that way."

"He'll get over it."

"We both know Rebakor is a trigger-happy client who's fired every agency they've ever had. They're big bullies who are used to getting their own way. Why should they treat us any differently?"

Where was this soliloquy leading? Fitz wondered.

Frank continued. "Now, I don't know whether you're a better man than Clem Drew for the job but I've averted a potential crisis and created a situation."

"Situation? Stuck? What are these words you're using, Frank?" Fitz was puzzled. He didn't like being slighted like this.

"I don't know precisely what went down in Louisville between you and Molinaire but I'm getting the distinct impression you threw Clem under the bus."

"It was all *your* idea, Frank!" Fitz raised his voice in disbelief.

"I wanted you to get tighter with the client so he would get used to working with you and not just Clem. And you went and told him Clem was out playing golf?"

Now Fitz was on the defense. "So what? Molinaire loved the

campaign!"

"I can't believe you said that."

"I didn't. Charlie blurted it out."

"Well, you need to go and fire Charlie Knutson!" Frank shouted. Fitz took a deep breath. He sat quietly for a moment thinking hard.

"Can't we just reassign him?" Fitz suggested. His unauthorized attempted coup de gras at Rebakor was now coming back to bite him in the butt.

"Sure, we can reassign him -- to another ad agency, preferably in another town." Frank finished his drink. He banged his empty glass down on his desk and appeared frustrated with the situation that he'd created. He'd wanted Fitz to create a wedge between Molinaire and Clem, not a canyon. But he was running out of time now. He stood up and wandered over to the window view. As he stared out at the downtown skyline, Fitz's eyes followed him across the room.

"Do you know Mike Beresford over at Fallon?" Frank asked, as he watched a passenger jet fly off into the distance.

"Yeah. Creative Director over there, isn't he?"

"What do you know about him?"

"Smart guy. Won a ton of awards." Fitz had no idea where this conversation was going.

"Is he happy over there?"

"Damned if I know. He's a creative man. Those guys are never happy. Look at Svensen. You gonna bring Beresford over here?"

"No. Chuck's a good CD for us."

"Why d'you ask then?"

"Beresford's been getting tight with Clem. He called Clem out the blue the other day. Wants a meeting with him."

Fitz raised an eyebrow. "Yeah? How'd you know that?"

Frank turned around and walked back to his desk. "Because I know everything, Fitz. Even before it's happened."

"I need to get that package out to Molinaire." Fitz stood up to leave but Frank wasn't finished with him yet.

"That's why I know you're an arrogant asshole, Fitz. That's also why I hired you."

"Geez, am I meant to take that as a compliment?"

"Yes. Because *I'm* an arrogant asshole. That's how I got to be where I am today. This business has no room for nice guys."

"What are you getting at?" Fitz looked puzzled by his boss's statement. "Jesus, is this trash Fitz day?"

"On the contrary, I want you to come to our board meeting next week. I want the directors to meet their new CEO."

"Seriously?"

Frank was handing him the job of CEO on a plate right there and then. If there had been any doubt in Frank's mind it had now, suddenly, been resolved. The simple fact was that Rebakor was the cash cow and Molinaire seemed to like the scheming Fitz. To Frank, it was a no-brainer. To Fitz, it was everything he thought he'd lost and the nail in Clem's coffin.

"Fantastic. I'd love to." Kurt Fitzgerald felt a powerful surge of fabulousness spread throughout his entire body that made him want to punch his fists in the air and scream from the top of the Kemp building. He'd done the impossible. He'd trumped Golden Balls. The old man had finally laid his cards on the table and they had come up trumps for Kurt Fitzgerald.

"Not a word, hear me," Bergenson warned him, knowing how Fitz must be feeling. "Keep this under wraps."

"Absolutely, Frank. You can trust me on that."

Bergenson leaned across and shook Fitz's hand. The deal was as good as done.

# CHAPTER 14

It was close to showtime. Tara sat back on the barstool and pulled her latex boots high up her thighs. She'd drank enough tea to last her a lifetime. Now she was ready for something decidedly stronger.

"This next one's an interesting character," announced Mistress Krystal. Tara's eyes widened.

"In what way?"

"He's some big shot in advertising. He's a licker."

Tara leapt to her feet as a bolt of adrenalin shot through her like a gallon of Red Bull suddenly hitting her central nervous system. This was it, the moment she'd planned for but it was now the moment she was dreading. *Clem was a licker? Please Lord, no.*

"What's his name?" Tara asked fearfully.

"Sissy Boy."

"Sissy Boy?" Tara's heart was beating way too fast and with a name like that it didn't bode well.

"What's his real name?"

"Hell if I know."

"And what does Sissy Boy like to lick?" Tara asked, really not sure she wanted to hear the answer. Mistress Krystal's expression changed to a devilish smile.

"You'll find out soon enough, Mistress Angelina."

All Tara cared about at that moment was whether Clem would recognize her. She'd deliberately purchased an outfit that hid her identity. Her Catwoman hood and mask concealed her eyes and most of her nose. The dim lighting would help too but her voice would be a dead giveaway. She would have to disguise it as much as possible or maybe she wouldn't say anything.

"Well, it's gone six. He's late."

"He'll be here."

Tara paced anxiously. "Okay, so what's the script for this guy? I need to know ahead of time before you bring me in on some more weird stuff."

Mistress Krystal smiled. "Relax. Don't worry, it'll be weird."

"Exactly! That's why I'm getting nervous. I don't want to screw it up."

"Screw what up? Look, hun. You don't even know this person."

*Bzzzzzz!*

Sissy Boy had arrived. Mistress Krystal took up her position in the playroom standing with legs astride waiting for him to enter.

"Stay in the kitchen," she ordered Tara. "I'll tell him you'll be running today's session."

"What?"

"Relax and enjoy it," Mistress Krystal smiled, oblivious to the internal meltdown Tara was now experiencing.

"But what do I do?" asked Tara, in a panicked whisper. "What's the script?"

"It's loose."

"Loose? What does that mean?"

"Stay cool, hun. Whatever you want. He wants to be told what to do and he'll take any punishment you want to give him. He really just wants to lick."

That did nothing to reassure her as she paced even faster back and forth in the small kitchen and realizing for the first time just how much tight latex and leather made you sweat.

*Bzzzzzz!*

Mistress Krystal buzzed him in. Sissy Boy walked down the hallway and placed a bunch of money on the side table. He was smartly dressed in a well-fitted suit. Mistress K had a direct line of view into the hallway from her playroom and mentally counted the bills with him, not that anyone had ever chiseled her before. After all, if they did, it would be their last appointment.

"Good afternoon, Sissy Boy," Mistress Krystal uttered in her usual patronizing tone. Sissy Boy said nothing. "You may enter the playroom. Take off that very nice suit and hang it up over there. I want you naked. Do it."

She stood and watched Sissy Boy strip off. Tara could only hear from the secluded kitchen, she couldn't see what was happening and was too freaked out to look. She hadn't heard Clem's voice respond yet and now she was about to be introduced to her naked husband. This was not going as she'd imagined. She didn't think she'd feel this way but it was too late to back out now. He was sure to recognize her the minute she stepped into that room and he would simply die of embarrassment. So would she, dressed up in this ridiculous costume. *What was she thinking?*

"Today, we're going to be doing things a little differently," Tara heard Mistress Krystal say. Still Sissy Boy remained silent. "You're going to meet a new mistress. Her name is Mistress Angel." Mistress Krystal glanced over towards the kitchen and extended a beckoning arm. "Enter, Mistress Angel and meet Sissy Boy."

Tara was frozen to the spot. *She couldn't do it. No, she wouldn't obey her demand.*

Mistress Krystal repeated her order, louder this time. "I said *enter*, Mistress Angel and meet Sissy Boy!"

It was useless to think of changing her plan now. Tara had no way to escape now. She took a very deep breath, pushed open the kitchen door and slowly walked into the playroom, her eyes downcast in the dim light.

Sissy Boy turned to see who would be taking over the session. His eyes widened when he saw the black leather and latex clad vision of sexuality walk across the floor towards him. Tara looked up slowly and to her utter astonishment she saw a naked man she'd never seen before.

Clem sat in his car and banged his head against the headrest. He clenched his jaw tight. *Where had it all gone so wrong?* Fitz had stitched him up good and proper and not only had he gotten away with it, he also had the boss's blessing. What Clem couldn't fathom was whether Frank Bergenson had turned on him or had Fitz finessed the old man so sweetly that he was letting Frank do his bidding?

Clem wondered how events could play out if he took the best of Chuck Svensen's campaigns to Louisville and used it to try and un-sell the campaign Fitz had pitched. But it was double jeopardy. If Clem pitched to Rebakor and Molinaire didn't buy it, then that'd weaken Clem even further. If Molinaire liked it, he would be the hero and it would oust Fitz. But this would have to be a strictly clandestine operation. No one should know he was going. Not even the creatives who'd worked on it. If Fitz could pull off that stunt then he certainly could too. There was still time. It was Friday and the meeting with Rebakor and Molinaire was still scheduled for Tuesday of next week. Clem did a U-turn and headed back towards downtown. He needed to get those campaigns Chuck Svensen's guys had concepted before they got trashed.

Hurrying out of the elevator and back towards his office, Justine was still finishing up for the day. Clem went straight into his office.

"I need those layouts."

"What layouts?" Justine followed him.

"The ones Chuck brought to the meeting two hours ago. I'm gonna fly down to Louisville and sell them to Molinaire. You can't mention this to anyone, understand?"

"Clem. Can I have quick word?"

"Now where the fuck are they?" Clem rummaged through a pile of old layouts on his desk. Justine closed the door behind her.

"You can't go to Louisville."

"Oh, really? Just watch me. I've gotta find those damn ads."

"Clem. You're wasting your time."

"What are you talking about?" Clem looked up.

"Rosanne told me Mr. Bergenson invited Fitz to meet the board next week. He's got the job, Clem."

It was like the blood had suddenly drained out of Clem's face as he turned a whiter shade of pale. Justine certainly hadn't planned on being the bearer of bad news especially as she cared so much about her boss but she had to stop him from making a fool of himself. Like Clem, she also knew the consequences of Fitz getting into power at the agency. There would be a cull and she would be the second casualty for sure after Clem when the axe fell.

Clem sat down and slumped forward holding his head in his hands. Justine's eyes started to well up. She knew how conscientious he was and how hard he'd worked every day since she'd been his personal assistant.

"Sorry you had to hear it from me, Clem. Please don't shoot the messenger," Justine pleaded. He looked up at her with the expression of a beaten man.

"Thanks for telling me, Justine. Go home. Enjoy the weekend. It's going to be pretty out." Clem gave her a gentle hug. "And cancel my trip to Louisville next Tuesday. Waste of fucking time that'd be."


Sissy Boy stared salaciously at Tara's thigh high shiny black boots. Mistress Krystal slapped his face, not hard, but with enough force to get his attention. Tara said nothing; still surprised and very relieved that she wasn't standing face to face with her husband.

Mistress Krystal winked at Tara.

"Sissy Boy will do whatever you tell him to do, won't you Sissy Boy?" Mistress Krystal glared daggers at the naked man who finally broke his silence.

"Yes, Mistress. I will do whatever Mistress Angel desires."

"Yes, you will."

"Mistress Angel is very beautiful, Mistress."

"Yes, she is. And she will be obeyed. Understand?"

"Yes, Mistress."

"Mistress Angel, he's all yours. Do with him what you will."

Tara nodded as Mistress K gave Tara a reassuring glance then left her alone in the playroom with Sissy Boy. "I will be watching everything," she told them both.

Sissy Boy and Tara stared at each other for a few seconds but it seemed like an eternity. This man wasn't like the others. He didn't act submissive. Tara was terrified of this unknown naked male standing before her waiting to be told what to do. She hoped her hooded mask disguised any look of fear on her face.

"You're very beautiful, Mistress Angel," Sissy Boy said quietly.

"Don't say a word," Tara ordered. He was much younger than the judge and in far better shape than Mr. Winkle. He was handsome too, and he was talking out of turn. Tara didn't like being spoken to. It was making her very uneasy. This Sissy Boy character had an air of mischief about him.

"Can I lick you, Mistress Angel? Can I? Please?"

"Shut up," said Tara, more firmly this time.

"I want to lick you," Sissy Boy insisted, giving her a smile which creeped her out. "Let me lick you, please."

"And I told you to zip it, Sissy Boy." Tara knew that if she so even glanced to wherever Mistress Krystal had gone, she would lose any control she might have in the room. "Shut up means shut up. Unless I ask you a question. Got it?"

"Yes, Mistress Angel."

Tara didn't have the first clue how she was going to start the session. She looked at the rack of equipment hanging on the wall but that only confused her more. She needed guidance but it was too late to ask teacher now. To looked back at her naked subject.

"What would you like me to do today, Sissy Boy?"

"Anything you want to, Mistress," Sissy Boy replied quietly, not helping any. She took hold of a small flogger and turned and stood behind the naked man. She was surprised to see his back was heavily tattooed. It looked like demonic depiction of Hades with skulls and flames and naked torsos.

"What the.....? Stop!"

Sissy Boy grabbed her left ankle and frantically began licking her boots. She jumped backwards and out of his grasp then swung back her right leg and kicked Sissy Boy hard in the back, instinctively trying to protect her expensive footwear.

*Whaaam!*

"Oooooofff!"

He fell forwards and lay sprawled on the hardwood floor. Tara immediately felt compelled to help him up but stopped herself as she saw Sissy Boy begin to crawl back to her footwear and resume his compulsion to smear her boots in his saliva.

*He wasn't in pain, he was in Heaven.*

Tara swung back her leg and slammed a Beckhamesque right-footed kick, this time straight into Sissy Boy's mouth.

*Craack!*

Sissy Boy fell backwards holding his jaw, a trickle of blood ran down on to his chin. Tara had caused him some real pain now but was annoyed and scared with her client's manic behavior, though she daren't show any fear. She had to maintain *control.*

"Have you any idea how much these boots cost? Damn you!" Sissy Boy bowed his head in shame as he lay face down at her feet.

"Sorry, sorry, Mistress Angel. I deserve to be punished, Mistress. Please punish me," he begged.

As Tara looked down at the pathetic, bleeding Sissy Boy, his long tongue began to dart in and out between his bloody lips, like a salivating lizard.

"No, you don't!" Tara had had enough of this crap. She didn't want his spit on her boots let alone blood. She wasn't putting up with this shit anymore. "Stand up!"

Sissy Boy stood obediently. Tara took the small flogger back to the rack and put it back in its place. *This guy needed to be taught a lesson.*

She grabbed the biggest whip on the rack and cracked it. Sissy Boy looked around at her.

"Don't look at me. Look straight ahead."

"Yes, Mistress."

"And shut up. On your knees. Lean forward."

Sissy Boy crouched down, exposing his tattooed back. Tara stood several feet away and took a practice swing. Then she flashed the bullwhip down hard across his back.

*Craaaack!*

He stayed motionless, not uttering a sound. Whether she'd left a mark was hard to tell with so much ink on his back. She brought the lash down on him a second time.

*Craaaack!*

Again, no reaction. Tara wondered if her whippery was not really up to snuff or if her client had no working nerve endings. She walked over to her prostrate victim and dug her stiletto into his side. He groaned. She could see the flesh on his back welting up. She'd made her mark all right but it seemed he wanted more. As she pondered her next move, Sissy Boy leapt across the floor onto her latex boots once again flashing his tongue out like a Komodo dragon.

He wrapped his arms around both her feet and frantically started licking her footwear again. But now his penis was fully erect. Tara struggled to keep her balance. She cracked the butt end of the whip down hard on the back of Sissy Boy's head but he had her firmly in his grasp. She fell backwards landing with a thump on her rear end. She kicked herself free and quickly got back up on her feet again.

"Crap!"

*Whaaam!*

Tara booted Sissy Boy hard in the side of his neck with a kick of such viciousness, he fell backwards.

"Take that, you sick fuck!" Tara screamed.

*"Whaaaaamm!*

She swung her leg back again and smashed him in the mouth this time, at which point Mistress Krystal decided it might be a good idea to take over proceedings. She motioned for Tara to leave the playroom.

Blood was now pouring from Sissy Boy's mouth. His lip was badly swollen and it seemed he'd lost a tooth but if he was in pain he wasn't making much fuss about it. He smiled and wiped away the blood as Tara slammed the kitchen door behind her.

"You've annoyed Mistress Angel, Sissy Boy," Mistress Krystal said sternly.

"I apologize, Mistress. Sorry, Mistress Angel," he mumbled through his swollen, bloody lips as he crawled on all fours towards Mistress Krystal's black stilettos and began gently licking them like a kitten lapping a saucer of milk.

Behind the closed kitchen door, Tara was shaken up. She wiped the saliva and blood off her beautiful heeled boots with a paper towel. She felt her first one-on-one session had probably gone as badly as it could have. But that was a creepy guy and she really didn't have any regrets about kicking the living daylights out of him. What really irked her was that the pervert had enjoyed it. *And where the fuck was Clem?*

Back in the playroom, Sissy Boy was now licking his way up to the top of Mistress Krystal's stockinged leg while stroking his stiff penis.

"If you promise to behave, Mistress Angel will come back out here and join us. Won't you Mistress Angel?" Mistress Krystal yelled out loud enough for Tara to hear. That was the last thing she wanted to do.

Tara took a deep breath and obeyed her teacher's instruction. She pushed open the kitchen door and walked slowly back in to the playroom. Sissy Boy looked up to see her approach him but this time she kept her distance.

"Stand right there, Mistress Angel. That's right. Sissy Boy wants to look at you while he has his fun."

Tara stood a good ten feet from the now squatting, masturbating man. As he jerked himself harder, his groaning got louder with each messy lick of the top of Mistress Krystal's stockings but all the while his unblinking eyes gazed fixedly on Tara. Mistress Krystal just stood there letting him do his nasty thing while Tara's expression of utter disgust seemed only to turn him on even more. She looked away not wanting to watch what she knew was coming.

After a few minutes of groans culminating in a series of pig-like grunts, Sissy Boy climaxed ejaculating sticky dollops of white semen over his mistress's black stilettos.

"Ahhhhhhhh….ahhhhhhhhhhh…." he groaned ecstatically. The two women stood silently by as Sissy Boy convulsed and jerked in an orgasmic spasm that Tara found totally repugnant.

"Clean it up!" Mistress Krystal ordered.

A far more docile Sissy Boy obeyed, licking up his own semen from her soiled footwear but still his eyes watched Tara stomp back towards the kitchen. Tara paced up and down, still high on adrenalin. Moments later, Mistress Krystal joined her.

"That was, without question, the freakiest most fucked up thing I've ever had the misfortune to be part of. What a creep!" Tara yelled, angry that Mistress Krystal had dropped her in the deep end with the depraved Sissy Boy.

"You'll get over it."

"Creepy, creepy! Crap! I can't believe I just saw that." Tara kept pacing but Mistress Krystal seemed unfazed. "Why'd you pick him to be my first solo client?"

"You did great, hun," Mistress Krystal grinned, giving Tara a compliment she wasn't expecting and didn't appreciate.

"All that blood! Ugh! I think I kicked out one of his damn teeth! Disgusting."

"You sure did," Mistress Krystal said, handing her Sissy Boy's missing molar.

"I don't want it!" Tara squealed, pulling a sour face.

Mistress Krystal opened the fridge and took out a bottle of Moet & Chandon.

"Look in that cupboard. There's a couple of Champagne flutes in there."

Tara breathed a huge sigh and took out two elegant slim glasses as Mistress Krystal popped the cork off the bottle of bubbly.

"We should celebrate your first solo performance! What an outstanding debut! You were terrific. That was some hot foreplay in there."

"Foreplay?" Tara was bemused. "I kicked the sick fuck's tooth out."

"Ha! He's got plenty of teeth. He won't miss one. That's the quickest I've ever got him finished. Wanna grab some dinner?"

"Sissy Boy is still in the playroom," Tara reminded her.

"Pah, he'll be gone in a few. There's a cool Sushi place up on Grandview."

Mistress Krystal raised her glass and took a sip of her chilled Champagne. Tara downed her glass in one gulp. She couldn't think of any reason why she shouldn't accept the offer to go out and eat.

"Sure, why not?"

Sushi Tango was slammed with diners but both Mistresses Krystal and Angel were well anchored at the sushi bar and back in their regular attire. The failure of Clem to appear at six o'clock was a huge weight off her shoulders but she was still reeling from the experience with Sissy Boy. Tara chased down her glass of Moet with a cup of warm sake.

"So how can you ever be sure one of your clients isn't a raving nut job with a criminal record or something?" Tara asked, as she dipped her yellowtail nigiri into a small bowl of soy sauce.

"You learn pretty quick how to spot the wackos," Mistress Krystal said, looking more like a normal human being without all her dramatic make-up and wild hairstyle. "And I video every session in case I need police evidence," she added.

"Seriously?"

"I've got two little cameras way up high in the corner. Plus, my heaviest weaponry is close at hand and it's got live ammo in it."

"Everything is recorded on video?"

"Insurance."

"And you got a loaded gun?"

"Magnum. Same as Dirty Harry."

"Wow. I didn't realize you were so buttoned up in the security department!"

Tara was impressed and intrigued. That meant that there would be video evidence that Clem was one of her clients. Mistress Krystal looked around for a sake server as she gulped down her third cup. The more she drank, the looser Mistress Krystal's behavior became. Tara saw this as her opportunity to glean more information about this woman and some of her other clients though the combination of Champagne and sake wasn't sitting too well with Tara.

"So what's your real name?" Tara asked.

"What's yours?" Mistress Krystal shot back. Tara didn't like that reply so she changed the subject.

"You must have a lot of videos then?"

"Tell me about it."

"Y'know, you could record directly onto your computer, or get an external hard drive," Tara suggested.

"Nah, I'm old school," replied Mistress Krystal, who still hadn't touched her food.

"So Sissy Boy's in the ad biz, huh?" Tara asked nonchalantly, probing for more information.

"Yep. I need another drink. Where's our waitress?"

"Any other advertising executives on your roster of illustrious clients?" Tara asked pointedly.

"Not that I know of. I've got eleven regulars -- a judge, an ad guy – that's Sissy Boy -- doctor, a lawyer, some CEO, and the others I have no clue what they do nor do I care."

"Don't forget Mr. Winkle."

"Oh yeah, and Winkle."

"So you must have some type of normal conversation with these characters sometimes."

"Sometimes."

"But you honestly don't know any of their real names?" Tara pressed, still wanting to know for sure if Clem was on her roster. Mistress Krystal looked Tara in the eye.

"Look, hun. I told you. I don't need to know their real names. And I don't particularly care to. Less I know the better. I suppose all this will be in the book you're writing, huh?"

"What book?"

"Or article, or thesis, or report," Mistress Krystal jabbed.

"No. I'm no writer," Tara laughed.

Mistress Krystal scanned the restaurant. "These damn waitresses are serving everyone in here except us. Hey! Can we get another round of sakes over here?"

One of the pretty young Oriental girls finally appeared with a fresh warm pot. Tara realized that Mistress Krystal wasn't going to reveal any details about any of her clients however much booze she knocked back. She probably knew all the real names of all of them but there was no way she was going to spill the beans. Tara was dealing with one shrewd cookie muncher even though she was now fairly inebriated. Maybe Clem was this woman's best client and she'd twigged that he was married to Tara. After all, she couldn't have been the first suspicious or jealous wife she'd had to deal with. Tara was being out-maneuvered with sublime brilliance by a mistress who was a master -- of the human psyche. This would be a battle of wits she couldn't win.

*But what if she could get to see those videotapes?*

"I need a vacation," Mistress Krystal announced with a hint of a slur. "Been waaaay too long."

"You're your own boss. I'm sure your clients could survive a week or two without you."

"No, I'm talking about a real vacation. Like three months on a beach somewhere."

Tara dabbed her yellowtail nigiri in the green wasabi and put the whole piece in her mouth. "Mmmmm...yeah, I see your point," she mumbled as she looked hungrily at the ten pieces of nigiri tuna still on Mistress Krystal's plate.

"You could do this job," Mistress Krystal slurred.

"No, I couldn't." Tara's focus was still on the uneaten raw slices of fish.

"Why don't you run the show while I take a break?" Mistress Krystal smiled.

"I hope you're not being serious."

"Three months. The time will fly, believe me."

"No way. I don't want Sissy Boy jerking off on me and Mr. Winkle urinating all over the place and God knows what your other clients get off doing."

"Look, Angelina. You're younger than me, prettier than me and in better shape than me. I'm forty-nine years old and I need a damn vacation."

"You said you were forty-seven," Tara reminded her.

"Forty-seven, fifty-two, ninety-one, who cares? Close enough. Look, Sissy Boy nearly creamed his pants the second he saw you. All my clients will just fawn all over you."

"That's what I'm afraid of," Tara added.

"Then why the did you go and buy all the gear? That was a wad of cash, hun. I know you're getting off on this shit."

"I don't have the stomach for it. But I'll admit it's interesting, in a very creepy, depraved way."

"Interesting? Interesting? That has to be the understatement of the century. Working in a laboratory is *interesting*."

"I meant learning how the mind of the male species works. That's a real education."

"They're wired totally differently to us, that's for sure. It's all visual to them. You know, hun, there are plenty of women out there in this line of work. And once you get a few regulars, you want to keep them."

Mistress Krystal wasn't giving up. She seemed determined to throw Tara in the deep end even though she could still barely swim.

No, this was not why Tara was doing this but she couldn't tell Mistress Krystal the truth. Not at this late stage in the game.

"It's sure as shit more interesting than what you're doing right now," Mistress Krystal muttered as she finally started to tuck into her food. She was right about that, too.

"Don't you ever worry about running into one of your clients?" Tara asked, wanting to change tact.

"No. Why should I? They're a lot more worried about running into me."

"So you don't date and you're not married?" Tara was prying now.

"I never said that," Mistress Krystal shot back.

"I just assumed -- I mean your apartment on Calloway is quite small to work and live"

Mistress Krystal gave Tara a quizzical look. "What apartment on Calloway?"

Tara laughed. "The one we were just at!"

Mistress Krystal laughed out loud. "Hun, what are you smoking? My place is on Robertson."

Now Tara was the one with the confused expression. She then realized she'd only ever entered the apartment from the rear of the building.

"Robertson?"

"Maybe you're just a ditz."

Mistress Krystal leaned over to bite into another piece of sushi while Tara paused and thought hard. She'd never actually seen what the front of the apartment building looked like. In fact, Tara had never even been on that street as she'd always entered via the back way under the iron stairwell. She'd simply assumed that it was 1611 Callaway, as Jack Kelsey had told her when he showed his videotape of Clem arriving and leaving. Now she was really confused about everything. If Mistress Krystal didn't live at 1611 Callaway, who did?

"How long have you lived there on Robertson Street then?" Tara asked.

"I've never lived there, I just work there," Mistress Krystal replied, shoving in another mouthful of tuna and washing it down with more sake. "I don't want anyone knowing where I live."

Now Tara's mind was racing. If Mistress Krystal worked on Robertson Street, who in the world was Clem secretly visiting on Callaway? Maybe it was Justine after all. Or maybe it was some other mystery woman. Her ingenious plan to trap her husband in the act was an abject failure. She'd gotten it all wrong. She'd been at the wrong location all along. Now she would have to re-think everything.

"I think we're done," Tara announced emphatically. Mistress Krystal still had three succulent pieces of sushi on her wooden tray waiting to be devoured and wasn't ready to leave.

"I'm not done, Angelina. I also want another drink," Mistress Krystal slurred. Tara counted out forty dollars and slapped it down on the sushi bar.

"I gotta go." Tara stood up, threw down her napkin and made her way through the crowded sushi bar towards the exit. Mistress Krystal shrugged and carried on eating as she ignored Tara walking out. She was more interested in catching the eye of the waitress.

"Hey, another drink over here!"

As Tara drove home, she felt very conflicted. Her sessions with Mistress Krystal had made her feel good about herself in a way she had never experienced before and certainly hadn't expected. She liked the feeling of being in control. But now this was all moot. If Clem wasn't seeing Mistress Krystal there was no need for her to see her anymore. *But why was that card in his jacket?*

Maybe Mistress Krystal did live on Calloway Avenue after all and was simply lying to Tara. The only to find out who did live there was to go ring the bell at number 1611 and find out. And she might as well do it right now.

Tara took the next exit off the interstate and pulled over to the side of the road. She was still a little dizzy from all the alcohol she'd consumed but this was a sobering moment. She quickly punched the

Calloway address into her GPS and made a U-turn. It was getting late but there was still some blue in the dusky evening sky. As she headed back to south Minneapolis, Tara ran various scenarios through her head but nothing seemed to make much sense.

*Damn, it was all going pear-shaped.*

# CHAPTER 15

Ocean Breeze was an upscale restaurant in St. Paul, a ten-minute drive from downtown Minneapolis and nowhere near any ocean. Over at the bar, Clem was drinking with Daniel Ellerby, the recruiter from Los Angeles. Ellerby was a mover and a shaker with offices in Beverly Hills and on Madison Avenue and he'd placed Clem at Bergensons four years earlier. He dressed like an ad executive but had only enjoyed a brief career employed in agencies. The environment had proved too stifling for him and he was lousy at kissing up to clients. Ellerby had a classy persona but he was a wheeler-dealer better suited to operating behind the scenes. He only made money when he shuffled people around. Clem raised his Martini glass to Ellerby's.

"Bottoms up."

"Been a few years, Clem."

"Kinda surprised you called to be honest."

"Well, I couldn't get a direct flight to New York so I thought I'd stop over in Minneapolis and see how things were going. I see your name's been in all the trades recently."

That made Clem smirk.

"Yeah, well -- Guess I'm hot. Gonna try and lure me away?" Clem chuckled sardonically.

"You know, that really was a great deal I put together for you at Bergensons. These guys wanted you so bad they really would've paid anything."

"That was four years ago," Clem reminded Ellerby. "Ancient history. Different economic climate now, huh?"

"Yup. Pretty dead out there." Ellerby's words had a somber tone to them. Not what Clem wanted to hear but he'd guessed as much. If anybody knew the beat of the street it was his old headhunter.

"You're still alive and kicking though," Clem smirked.

"Living off scraps. Look, you don't need me to tell you -- retail has taken it up the ass."

Ellerby looked a class act but subtlety wasn't his strong suit. Clem was in no hurry to divulge any tales of his corporate infighting with Kurt Fitzgerald but Ellerby knew a lot of people in a lot of agencies and he could well have gotten wind of the recent monkey business at Bergenson & Adler. He'd placed account executives in the best ad shops in all the major cities over the years: Dallas, Chicago, San Francisco, Los Angeles, New York and Atlanta were his towns; his playing fields. Each of those cities had three or four big name agencies where he placed and cherry-picked the best talent. Ellerby knew the hottest gossip at every big agency in every big town whether it was true or not. That was how he made his money.

"Y'know, this could be one of those synergistic things," Clem smiled.

"Yeah? How so?"

"Well, I've been thinking. How can I top landing Rebakor? It's like I won the Superbowl for my team. I threw the winning touch down. I'm the star quarterback and I got MVP. Maybe I need a new challenge. Quit while I'm ahead."

"Are you fucking serious?" Ellerby chuckled, rather surprised. "Stay put and wait for Frank Bergenson to retire -- you're sitting on a pot of gold. Why am I even telling you this? You know that."

"No, I'm serious. And this town is so damn cold for six fucking months of the year. Tara says she's had enough of it and I can't blame her."

"You want to quit your job because you're cold?"

"It's June and there's still a huge pile of dirty snow down on Baker Road refusing to melt."

"Fuck, Clem. I told you. It's dead."

"Come on, Dan. I'm talking to the most connected man in advertising," Clem smiled. Dan's expression remained solemn. "I'm worth a fucking fortune right now and you know it. Who wouldn't want to hire me?"

"Lots of agencies *would* hire you, Clem. But they're not paying what you think. All the perks have gone. Agencies have tightened their belts big time. If you've got a job, hold on to it for grim life."

"Well, you didn't drop by just to see *me*, Dan," Clem smirked, suspicious that Ellerby was being economical with the truth. "I'm not buying your 'stop-over' line. There must be some deals going down here or you wouldn't be visiting."

"Sure, I've got some small things in the pipeline on the creative side. Nothing at your level. But if you're not happy at Bergensons, I'm advising you to suck it up and stick it out until the economy starts to make a comeback. Couple of years maybe." Ellerby looked over the menu.

"I never said I wasn't happy here," clarified Clem, and being economical with the truth himself.

"How are the crab cakes?"

"Everything tastes good here." Clem wasn't remotely interested in eating. He tossed the menu back on the white tablecloth. "I wouldn't move empty-handed. I could bring some clients with me, y'know." Ellerby held the menu up to the light.

"Why is restaurant lighting so damn trendy these days? Screw the ambience, I can't read any of these appetizers." Ellerby took out his readers and squinted more closely at the menu. He closed it shut in frustration. "Do we even have a waiter to tell us the specials?"

"Doyle Dane, J. Walter, BBDO....I'd be interested in talking to any of those shops." Clem wasn't whetting his headhunter's appetite for his business either. Ellerby looked around the quiet restaurant.

"Jesus, it's even dead in this joint. Like I said....this fucking economy….."

Clem spotted a server and beckoned him over. Ellerby took another sip of his cocktail.

"Clem, when you work day in day out at the same place, you lose touch with the outside world. Those agencies are like dinosaurs now. Big, fat corporate monsters. They know it, too. That's why every one of them is scaling back. In a few years there'll be much smaller versions of themselves and then they'll start to cannibalize each other. Pretty soon they won't exist at all – not in their present form anyway. The big old ad agency is going the same way the music industry, big box retail stores, bookstores – they're all going away. The internet is forcing businesses to rethink and reinvent themselves. It even screwed the porn industry, now how fucking funny is that?"

"Fuck Zuckerberg."

"Him, too. The web is the great destroyer because it's leveling the playing field and we can't all thrive like that. Ad agencies are next because they're too big and slow to react to market forces. If you want to leave Bergensons, start your own boutique agency with those accounts you can steal from the place on your way out."

"And spend the next three years working my balls off for peanuts?" Clem studied the olive swimming in his cocktail glass. "You've just been telling me how sucky the economy is. If those smaller accounts fail then I'm not only out of a job, I'm in serious debt with staff I've got to lay off and a lease on a building I can't afford."

Clem felt defeated and deflated. There no way that was going to happen. He probably had a month at best once Fitz was crowned king. It was always a bit of a cat and mouse game with headhunters. Daniel Ellerby must know something, or may have heard it on the grapevine, and that's why he'd contacted Clem. But the sharp shark was playing his cards close to his chest.

"So what's the word on Bergensons? What's the talk on the

street?" Clem tried to sound ambivalent.

"Everyone's jealous."

"That's it? Nothing juicier than that?" Clem sat back in his seat and took a slow sip of his cocktail.

"Nada," said Ellerby, not coughing up a single insider tidbit that might be to Clem's advantage. "But keep your eyes open because those other shops are going to try and nibble away little bits of your big fat pie so watch your back."

Clem smirked at Ellerby's choice of words. He didn't know if Ellerby was playing straight or just fishing for more information. Maybe one of Ellerby's informants had tipped him off. Good inside info could mean a little kickback for the informant and over the years Ellerby had quite an impressive little network of industrial spies. But trying to get anything out of the human trafficker was like trying to prize open an oyster with his bare hands. Of course, that didn't mean Clem wouldn't continue to try. Clem figured that Ellerby must've heard that all was not rosy up at Bergensons.

"How you getting along with Kurt Fitzgerald?" Ellerby asked casually. Now Clem's suspicions were realized.

"We get along just great," Clem smiled, lying through his teeth. "Strange question to ask," he added.

Ellerby swirled his Martini, then gulped it down, chewing on the olive. "Talented guy, even if he can be an arrogant prick sometimes."

Sometimes? Clem thought. *How about all the fucking time?*

The waiter finally made an appearance at their table. "Good evening, gentlemen."

"Get me the crab cakes to start then the Filet Mignon, medium rare, with a side of creamed spinach to follow. Another Martini too," Ellerby snapped before the waiter had a chance to tell them the specials. Clem smiled up at him sympathetically.

"Cobb salad, thanks," added Clem, more politely. He pointed to his drained cocktail glass. "I'll take another, too."

Clem wasn't going to be drawn into the subject of Mr. Kurt Fitzgerald. If Ellerby had gotten word that there was infighting in upper management at Bergensons then maybe it was Fitz who'd made the call to Ellerby. That's the kind of crap he'd pull if he felt it could further his career. Clem had always been a very ambitious man but Fitz was notorious in his striving for power. He didn't want Fitz's name to come up again. But then the penny finally dropped and Ellerby unloaded.

"Okay, I got one thing," Ellerby said. "It's not much but it's all I got and I think it's a real opportunity."

"Oh, so now the veil has dropped. Shoot."

"It's a small shop down south. You might've heard of them -- agency called Wardle & Ward in Birmingham."

"Alabama?"

"Two hours from Atlanta. Mid-sized agency, some good clients. They need someone to take the reins. Willy Wardle had a heart attack. Dropped dead on the golf course."

"Ala-fucking-bama? Are you kidding me, Dan? That'd be career suicide. You know that."

"There's a twist. Tracey-Locke in Atlanta is going to buy them out within the next six months. You walk into Tracey-Locke with all the Wardle & Ward accounts in your hip pocket and with what you can snatch here. Come on, you'll be running the whole show!"

"What's the money like?" Clem asked, more out of curiosity than real interest.

"Nowhere near what you're making now but you'd get great stock options and you'll make out like a bandit with the buyout."

"And what if the buyout doesn't happen?"

"It'll happen. The wheels are already in motion."

"But it's not a sure bet, Dan. A deal ain't a deal until the deal is done. You know that."

"Look, Clem. This is an opportunity. Birmingham's a great little town these days. It's a very progressive city. Got a totally happening arts scene." Ellerby was dangling a carrot but Clem wasn't biting.

"It's still Alabama. That's not even second division."

"It's all I've got. I know it's not at your level but they want to move quickly," Ellerby prompted. "They want the position filled in the next couple of weeks. Could start losing clients with no one steering the ship. Is it ideal? No, not for you. But it's your fastest route out of town if you're so terrified of Tara's tits freezing over."

Clem knew that moving down in the ad biz made it really hard to ever get back up on the higher tier. Birmingham, Alabama was not a serious ad town like the major cities. It was a big drop down on many levels. Clem wanted to stay in the first division. It would look obvious to the entire advertising industry that he was squeezed out at Bergensons. And he didn't think the Wardle & Ward/Tracey-Locke buyout held much mustard. That looked dubious at best.

Driving home from his dinner meeting with Daniel Ellerby, Clem was feeling more downbeat than before he'd met his old headhunter buddy. That was a reality check. In the back of his mind, Clem always thought that he and Tara could relocate to either coast and find something at one of the big shops. That was looking very unrealistic now. But what was really niggling away at Clem was that he hadn't told Tara the full extent of their dire financial situation. She had no idea that the hedge fund in which Clem had heavily invested their savings had tanked so badly. Clem was starting to think that perhaps Tara really should quit volunteering and find a job that paid her a salary.

Across town, Tara pulled up outside 1611 Calloway, parked her Lexus and got out. It was dark now and the recessed doorway was rather foreboding. This was not the most salubrious part of town by any stretch of the imagination but she was here now. She walked up to the darkened doorway. There were sixteen brass buzzers with nametags to match, some printed, some handwritten scrawls. Tara squinted, trying to read some of the names. She took out her cell phone and turned it on to shine its glow onto the nameplates. Tara scrolled down the list mumbling the names to herself. "Andresen, Lofthouse, Sungaard, Jakes…"

With no idea what Mistress Krystal's real name was this was a pointless exercise. Clem could have been going to any one of these apartments for his little trysts. A flashing blue light lit up the doorway as a police cruiser slowed down on the street. Tara put her cell phone away and walked back to her SUV. It was definitely time to go home before she either got arrested for loitering or got mugged.

By the time Clem got home, Tara was in her favorite place to go other than Caribou Lake – relaxing in the bathtub with plenty of bubbles and Nora Jones playing. Clem might be having secret trysts with someone but she'd had several sessions with naked strangers in the past week, too. The only difference being that she had been dishing out the punishment rather than taking it. Truth be told, she was being as secretive as Clem. Their marriage was one big lie; two people sharing a house and little else. Maybe Lorraine was right and counseling really was the solution after all. She would ask Lorraine to lunch on Monday after her morning yoga class. Tara had been so caught up with Mistress Krystal that she'd dropped her friend like a hot brick. Maybe it was time to let her in on what she'd been up to, though she wasn't sure whether Lorraine would laugh or chastise her. At this point she didn't care. But she needed to talk to someone she could trust.

That night, Tara slept in the guest bedroom again, still not on speaking terms with Clem. That was fine by him. He had plenty on his mind to think about without getting into a confrontation with his moody wife.

# CHAPTER 16

At breakfast next morning there was a different mood in the kitchen. Being Saturday, for Clem that meant getting up at seven and running around the lake before breakfast. Then granola, toast, orange juice and coffee with various vitamin pills before hitting the gym. It was the routine same every Saturday but not today.

By the time Tara woke up it was past eleven and her head was pounding. Sake and Champagne was proving the perfect cocktail for a stinking hangover. She pulled on some cotton sweat pants and an old t-shirt then splashed cold water on her face to try and bring herself to life. She figured Clem must be up and out somewhere as per usual as she ambled downstairs to the kitchen. She popped two Tylenol then plonked two bagel halves in the toaster.

"Hey," Clem said softly, walking up behind her and sliding his arms around her waist. He kissed the back of her neck. Tara felt her body tighten up defensively.

"What's that for?" Tara's head felt like it'd been whacked hard with a wooden mallet and was annoyed at being touched.

"That's for not paying you enough attention for too long," said Clem, showing great humility for a change. The Tylenol hadn't kicked in yet and Tara was suspicious of this sudden display of affection. This was guilt-driven. Clem looked like he'd been hit by a truck as he stood there wearing his sweat pants and old t-shirt with his usually perfect hair very disheveled.

"What's gotten into you?" Tara asked, giving him a cursory glance while holding a hand against her throbbing forehead.

"You can talk," Clem smiled as he looked at Tara, "You look like crap."

"Yeah? Well I feel like crap."

Clem opened the fridge and poured himself a glass of orange juice. Tara made herself an espresso.

"Out on the town last night?" Clem asked his grumpy wife.

"Yep. For a change."

"You never mentioned you were going out." Clem sat down at the breakfast table with his drink.

"You're right, I didn't." Tara leaned against the sink and bit into her bagel, her head still pounding.

"Where did you go?"

"To a restaurant with a friend." Tara was deliberately vague to invite more questioning from her curious husband. Then she would be ready to ask a few questions of her own.

"Have fun?"

"Yes."

Clem drank the rest of his orange juice and stretched. It seemed that was the end of Clem's interest in Tara's social adventure.

"Don't you want to know who I was dining with?" Tara asked.

"Sure, if you want to tell me. You're not exactly gushing with the details so far."

"Do you even care?" Tara snapped.

"You're my wife. Of course I care," Clem frowned. Tara sipped her espresso.

"Went to a place called Sushi Tango with some hot guy I met at the club."

Clem smirked. He could see through Tara easily. His wife was a lousy liar but he decided to play along.

"Hope he paid for dinner."

"Damn right, he did."

"What's his name?"

"His name?"

"Yeah, what's his name?" Clem smirked. Tara stalled.

"Jimmy."

"Jimmy?" Clem did his best to not laugh. Tara switched gears seeing as Clem didn't appear remotely jealous or even bothered.

"Yeah, Jimmy. Cute guy. So how was your night? Weren't you meeting your old headhunter?"

"Yeah, Dan Ellerby."

"Daniel Ellerby," Tara repeated, as she turned her attention to the espresso machine for a second caffeine blast.

"He's the headhunter who found me the job at Bergensons, remember?"

"So where did you two lovebirds go?"

"Ocean Breeze. It's a nice restaurant."

"I wouldn't know. You've never taken me there." Tara was in a combative mood and Clem knew she was spoiling for a fight. "And why were you meeting him?"

Tara folded her arms and leaned back against the counter as she watched Clem swallow a handful of vitamin pills.

"Because it looks like I'll be needing him," Clem said flatly. Tara bit into her bagel. If this was Clem trying to play the sympathy card she going to react the way she figured he expected her to.

Tara snapped. She threw her half-eaten bagel into the sink.

"Are you having an affair, Clem? Tell me the truth!" Her eyes drilled into Clem's. He stared back at Tara in disbelief.

"What are you talking about?" He looked stunned.

Tara walked over to where he was sitting and stood over him with her hands on her hips. She repeated the question with precisely the same tone. "Are you having an affair? Simple question. Yes or no?" She was as furious as Clem had ever seen her.

"No, I am not having an affair. What is wrong with you?" Clem said firmly, completely dumbfounded by the allegation.

"You're lying to me, Clem. I know you're lying."

"Where the fuck is this coming from, Tara? Is that why you've been acting so weird? This is why you haven't been sleeping in our bed?"

Tara's unblinking eyes stayed on him like a tracer bullet locked onto its target. Clem stood up and glared back at her. "You're being ridiculous, Tara, I don't have time to have an affair even if I wanted to."

"What's more I know who she is," snapped Tara.

"Then please tell me because I've got no damn idea what or who you're talking about."

Tara walked up to Clem, got right in his face and said it.

"Mistress Krystal."

"Who?" Clem looked completely dumbfounded. Tara pulled the business card from the pocket of her sweat pants and held it up in front of his eyes. He studied it closely then read it aloud.

"Mistress Krystal. *Professional services?* Who in God's name is that?" He shrugged.

"You tell me."

"How should I know?"

"It was in your jacket pocket."

"*My* jacket pocket? That's insane."

"Is it? You're telling me you don't know how it got there?"

"Nope. No clue."

"What do you think this card is?" Tara asked, already knowing the answer more than she'd ever admit.

"Could be a fucking magic act for all I know or care. Jesus!" Clem shook his head seriously wondering about his wife's mental state. He snatched the card out of Tara's hand and studied it more closely. He flipped it over and read the scrawled writing on the back.

"Tuesday – 5 o'clock."

"Recognize the handwriting? Huh?"

"Not mine. Looks like mine," Clem admitted. "But it isn't." Tara waited for a better answer but it wasn't forthcoming.

"Well, naturally you're going to deny it."

"Tara. Calm down. I honestly have no idea who in God's name this Mistress Krystal person is."

"Who's your friend on Calloway Avenue then?"

"My friend? Have you been following me?"

"I'm not a complete idiot, Clem."

"You *have* been following me, haven't you? What's wrong with you?"

"I hired a private investigator."

"What?!"

"I've got videotape of you at 1611 Calloway Avenue so there's no point in you denying it!" Tara clenched her fingers as her whole body tensed up. Clem was guilty and there was no way out now.

He looked at Tara and smiled. He ran his hands through his already messy hair, as Tara stood like a black widow spider ready to devour a fly stuck in her web. She was red with rage. But now Clem looked at Tara with a quiet calmness that annoyed the crap out of her even more. He had no intention of trying to calm her down. In fact, he decided to fan the flame that was burning inside her and get some payback.

"Yes, I pay a woman for her services and yes, I've seen her a few times. So what?"

"You fucking bastard! You're unbelievable! How long has this been going on? Tell me! How long?" Tara demanded.

"Oh – long enough." Clem sat back down.

Tara wanted to beat the living crap out of him. Why didn't *she* have a rack full of implements she could tear him up with? She paced the kitchen in a fury, tears welling up in her eyes. How could Clem be so blunt about it? He didn't even seem to give a shit.

"In fact, I'm going to see her this afternoon. Why don't you come along, too? I'd like you to meet her," Clem said, coldly.

"How fucking dare you!"

*Smaaack!*

Tara slapped his face hard. It hurt but Clem kept his cool.

"Two o'clock. Come with me," Clem suggested, deciding it was his turn to eat breakfast. Tara couldn't believe what she was hearing.

"Don't be such an asshole, Clem!" Tara wasn't sure whether he was being serious or sarcastic.

"I'm serious, Tara. You need to meet her. It's only right we clear the air with this." Clem walked over to the toaster and dropped in two slices of wholegrain bread. Tara was lost for words. She paced the kitchen some more, thinking of what response to give Clem. Her future flashed in front of her; separation, divorce, selling the house, leaving Minnesota…

"Okay! Two o'clock. You fucking asshole!" shouted Tara as she stomped back upstairs.

While Clem finished his breakfast, Tara was so uptight from their conversation that she had to let off steam somehow. She took off to the gym and spent the next hour punching the heavy bag alone in the cardio-boxing studio.

*Baaam! Baaam! Baaam!*

As she wailed away, so many thoughts were running through her mind. Every time she imagined Clem with Mistress Krystal, or whoever this mystery woman might be, she pummeled the bag with harder and harder right crosses and left hooks and uppercuts and haymakers…

*Baaam! Baaam! Baaam!*

She felt like beating both of them to a bloody pulp and breaking their bones. Maybe that's exactly what she would do. After all, she'd learnt how to throw a punch and what better way to show how you really feel?

*Baaaaam!*

Tara slumped down to the ground exhausted. Where had her *control* gone? She was now totally devoid of all control. She didn't have Clem where she wanted him at all. Quite the reverse, in fact. Caught on tape and guilty as sin, yet he was still the one controlling their situation. *But why was he being so fucking blasé and unemotional about it, like it was no big deal? Did he have no remorse whatsoever? No feelings for Tara in the slightest?*

It was just past noon when Tara emerged a sweaty mess from Bodyworks Fitness. There was no way she could go to Calloway Avenue looking like that.

Back at Dunkirk Crescent, she showered and got dressed. She rehearsed what she was going to say to Mistress Krystal or whoever the fuck this whore might be. First of all, she'd tell her the truth and that she wasn't Angelina. After that, she had no idea what she would say. *Fuck, this was it!* Maybe Clem would prefer to be with this person rather than be married to her. That's why he was acting like he didn't give a shit about their marriage. *Boy, this could be a brutal meeting between the three of them.* Her attempt to shame and embarrass Clem and his bitch could backfire and she could end up looking stupid. This had all the hallmarks of being totally disastrous.

Tara put the finishing touches to her make-up and went downstairs. It was one thirty and Clem was waiting, dressed very casually in the same sweat pants and tee shirt he'd been wearing all morning. At least he'd run a brush through his hair.

"Ready?" Tara sneered as she walked past him towards the door to the garage. Clem followed silently. "I'll drive," she said.

Neither of them spoke on the way to Calloway Avenue but Tara was getting increasingly anxious the closer they traveled towards their destination. Clem looked out the window like a kid going on a day trip. His ambivalence was infuriating Tara but she bit her tongue, too wrapped up in her own emotions to engage. This was about to be a pivotal moment in their marriage and Tara's life. Her stomach was in knots and Clem's attitude was confusing her. She wanted to scream and to cry at the same time but she had to keep it together. Her mind was racing a million miles an hour. *How could he be so callous? Didn't their marriage mean anything to him? Had he ever truly loved her?* Her heart pounded as they drove in stone silence to their destination and to Tara's destiny.

Within what seemed like minutes, Tara was turning onto Calloway Avenue and driving slowly down the street with its mix of retail and residential structures. Daylight made the apartment building more easily recognizable than the night before. She pulled over and stopped her SUV outside the front entrance of number 116.

"We're here," said Tara, stating the obvious.

"Thanks. See you in an hour or so," Clem said, getting out.

"Wait! You're not going in there alone," Tara scowled as she got out and hurried around the vehicle to join Clem on the sidewalk. They walked together towards the front entrance.

"I guess you can watch," said Clem quietly.

"You are such an asshole."

Clem opened the door to the building and they both walked into a small lobby full of apartment mailboxes and nameplates. The place was shabby with a very low rent look and smell about it. He pointed to one nameplate and read it aloud.

"Lundquist."

"That's her?"

"Yes. That's her."

Tara stared hard at the nametag. That was a typically Minnesotan name. Mistress Krystal was from Chicago. That couldn't be her real name. So if this Lundquist person wasn't Mistress Krystal, who in the hell was she?

Clem rang the rusting brass button and the door buzzed open. Clem led Tara up two murky flights of stairs and into a long, dimly lit hallway. The interior had an ominous, spooky feel about it but Tara was beyond caring about the décor of the seedy place. She followed Clem towards one of the faded white doors. He stopped at number 304 and rang the bell.

As they both waited silently for the door to open, Clem shot a slick grin at his jealous wife.

"I hate you," Tara said venomously. Her heartbeat was now in overdrive.

The door slowly opened and standing before them was a young

woman with dark brown hair and a warm smile.

"Hello, Clem."

"Hi, Christine. My wife gave me a ride here," Clem turned to his seething wife and introduced her. "Honey, this is Dr. Lundquist, my wonderful chiropractor."

Tara was dumbstruck. Dr. Lundquist held out her hand to shake Tara's.

"Nice to meet you Mrs. Drew," the chiropractor smiled warmly. "Please come in."

Tara felt dumber than a box of rocks.

"No, no. That's okay. I'll just do a little shopping and pick you up in...?"

"Oh...an hour should have me cracked and realigned, I reckon. Right doc?" Clem smiled.

"Absolutely," Dr. Lundquist confirmed.

Tara gave her husband the best fake smile she could muster. Clem puckered his lips to give her a goodbye kiss. Tara reluctantly offered him her cheek and he pecked it.

"What a cute couple you two are," Dr. Lundquist smiled. "Now. Let's get to work on that stubborn back of yours."

"Bye honey. Don't be late now." Clem gave Tara a little wave before going inside.

*Clunk!*

The door closed shut.

*Chiropractor? Chiropractor?*

The word screamed out inside her head as she walked back down the stairs to the street. No wonder Clem was so relaxed. He obviously wanted to teach her a lesson. It was payback time for Tara and her ridiculous accusations against him. She was relieved but emotionally spent. Tara stood outside and took a breath of fresh air. She stood for a while in shock and then burst into tears. This was all so ridiculous. *What was happening to her?*

As she walked back to her SUV, feeling completely drained, she felt a huge sense of relief that she'd got it all so terribly wrong.

She didn't care about being in control anymore. All she wanted to do right there and then was let out an ear-shattering scream. But she didn't.

Tara didn't drive anywhere for the next hour. She just sat in her vehicle on Calloway and stared out the window. She'd put two and two together and got five. But none of this explained Mistress Krystal's business card in Clem's jacket pocket. Someone must have planted the card in Clem's jacket. It was probably that asshole Kurt Fitzgerald. Had her visits to Mistress Krystal been a complete waste of time and money? The money she'd spent on Jack Kelsey was a big, fat waste for sure. But she also felt a huge weight had been lifted off her heart. Clem wasn't cheating on her or lying to her. She had been wrong and was very happy about it. But now what?

Tara was so wrapped up with her thoughts that when Clem finally appeared out of the brownstone and opened the passenger door, it felt like only a few minutes had passed. He smiled at Tara.

"I'm sorry I had to do it like that. You okay now?" Tara flung her arms around Clem and hugged him tight.

"I'm sorry, too," Tara said, burying her head in his chest, too embarrassed to look into her husband's eyes.

"I didn't want to put you through that little charade but I figured it was the only way I'd be able to convince you I was telling the truth. You were ready to kill me back at the house. You were so furious, you weren't go to believe anything I told you."

"I know, I know. I was so mad at you." Tara opened her purse and tore up Mistress Krystal's business card.

"I agree that does look like my handwriting. But it's totally bogus. I've honestly never seen that card before – ever. I swear to you. I have no idea how it got into my pocket but it's obviously a fake card."

Tara knew there was *nothing* fake about that card. For the first time in a long while, she believed him. Tara pushed the start button of her Lexus and they headed for home.

"Why didn't you tell me you were seeing a chiropractor?" Tara asked, as she turned onto the interstate.

"I've only just started seeing her. I go to see a chiropractor once – just once – and you hire a P.I. because you think I'm having an affair?"

"That was the first time you'd seen her?"

"Yes!"

"Oh, boy. I'm sorry. I don't know what I was thinking. You've been gone so much that when I found that card I just.... oh, I don't know. I guess I was just getting lonely and missed you. That's what women do. We overthink stuff. I'm truly sorry." Tara couldn't help but smile at her foolish assumptions. "I've been such an idiot."

"And I've been a prick getting so crazy with work. I apologize for being so fucking wrapped up in my world and not including you."

"As long as you still love me," Tara smiled, teary eyed.

"Of course I do, you nitwit."

"And you don't love anybody else?"

"Well, I kinda fancy Jessica Beal and that Sofia Vergara chick," Clem smiled.

"That's okay. I'll let you have those two." Tara laughed as they set off for home. Nothing that Clem said now could have such a devastating effect on their life. All was good. Then Clem broke the real news.

"But we do have a problem, Tara. A real problem."

"Don't mess around, Clem." Tara looked at Clem and she knew by his serious expression that he wasn't messing around. "Oh, shit. What now? Don't do this to me."

"Fitz made CEO. I'm done." Clem sounded almost apologetic for failing to win the prize he'd so coveted for so long.

"Don't be ridiculous!"

"I'm serious."

"You know that for sure?" Tara knew the consequences of Fitz getting the nod over Clem. Their life would be changing dramatically.

"I've been well and truly stitched up. Fitz out-maneuvered me. My days at Bergensons are numbered."

Tara let the news sink in as she kept her eyes on the road and her hands on the wheel.

"Well, we're just gonna have to sell up and downsize. At least we've got our savings."

"That's the problem," Clem started.

"What?" Tara glanced over at him. "You invested it all right?"

"It's all gone. Poof!" Clem waved his hands like an old school magician making a bunny rabbit disappear into thin air.

"Clem!"

"That hedge fund went belly up. We lost everything."

"Holy shit!" Tara swerved over to the curb and slammed on the brakes. "You mean we really do have *nothing?* Why didn't you tell me this?" Tara was incredulous.

"I didn't want to worry you. I couldn't change it. I figured I'd make CEO and get a big salary bump with bonuses and stock options and we'd recover our losses."

Clem looked as downcast as Tara had ever seen him. What an emotional roller coaster this drive was turning out to be.

"I don't know what to say. All our money's gone?" Tara stared at her deflated husband.

"Ever been to Birmingham, Alabama?"

During the remainder of their journey home to Dunkirk Crescent, Clem told Tara about what Justine had heard from Rose and that Frank and Fitz had been conspiring together to undermine him. He told her how his meeting with Hank Britney had proved fruitless after all, after which Daniel Ellerby had painted a pretty grim picture of his prospects for landing any job anywhere even close to his level. And even living dangerously on the squash courts with Jack Perkins hadn't left any impression with the board: only several on Clem.

They talked about the logistics of relocating to Birmingham and how much money they'd lose on the sale of their Eden Prairie house. Their future looked financially bleak and uncertain. Suddenly, the freezing Minnesota winters didn't seem quite so bad after all.

Tara listened as Clem finally opened up about everything that had been going on at work and it became very obvious to her why he'd been so detached. She felt useless. Her fate was tied to his. Tara's allegations regarding Clem's faithfulness seemed trivial by comparison. While her fears had all been imaginary, his fears were now very real.

That night, Tara Drew felt an intimate closeness to her husband that she hadn't experienced for a very long time. Ironically, it seemed their adversity had brought them closer together, both emotionally and physically, than they had been for a very long time. Tara made a Greek salad for dinner and they sat out on their deck with some Chianti and warm bread. It was a calm and peaceful summer's evening and the perfect way to chill out at the end of what had been the strangest of days in their long relationship. It'd been both an antagonistic and reconciliatory day. Clem was now in a philosophical mood. Opening up about everything had made both of them feel so much lighter inside, even if the news was not all good.

"What are we bitching about? We've been living in this big house and living the life many people still dream of enjoying. And let's be honest, we've been no happier here than when we were both broke living in that crummy apartment in North Hollywood all those years back."

Tara frowned. "True. So just how much money did we lose in that hedge fund?"

"Hell, it's only money!"

"Jesus, Clem. That was over two hundred thousand dollars – just gone?"

"I know, I know. No use crying over spilt milk."

"That's a few drops more than spilt milk! That's the whole dairy and the cows."

It was a beautiful evening and the sun glowed orange as it sunk below the tree line. Clem put his feet up on a small ottoman.

"So we can wait and see what fate has in store for us or we can dictate our own destiny."

"What do you mean by that?"

"Well, rather than just wait around and let outside forces impact our future, we can decide for ourselves where we go and what we do next."

"And what do we do next?"

"Damned if I know."

The two them stared out at the sunset. When it came to having control, neither of them seemed to have much of it now. As evening turned to night, they stayed out on the deck in the warm air and reminisced about the past and how they'd always seemed to get by. When they'd met, neither of them had much money and now here they were worrying about losing a lifestyle they never dreamed they'd ever have anyway. They both saw the irony in that and couldn't help but chuckle about it.

That night, Tara and Clem had sex for the first time in months - gentle, passionate, loving sex. It was something they were both in dire need of. Tara couldn't remember the last time she'd had an orgasm that wasn't a solo effort. The events of the day had changed both of them and for the better it seemed, so maybe it wasn't all so bad after all.

The two of them slept in the same bed that night and so soundly that it was almost Sunday afternoon before they started to stir. Both of them were nursing wicked hangovers when they finally awoke. It was Tara's second thumping headache in two days.

"Holy moly. How much did I drink last night?"

Clem felt his pounding forehead as Tara rolled over towards him and hugged his warm naked body.

"I don't remember…. but let's do it again tonight."

Over a very late breakfast, they both seemed like different people compared to the crazed versions of themselves they had been just yesterday morning and over the previous weeks. Clem's usual get-up-and-go appeared to have finally got-up-and-gone while Tara was relieved that her marriage was not the train wreck she thought it was.

That was more important to her than the money.

Clem gulped down two pills with his OJ and stared out of the kitchen window at some neighbor's kids cycling down the sidewalk towards Caribou Lake. Tara chewed on a bagel as she walked over to be beside him.

"That's Brian and Heidi's kids, isn't it?" Clem asked his sleepy wife. "Heck, they've grown up fast. Haven't seen those two in a long while."

"They're always playing outside. Even in winter."

"Where does the time go?" Clem sighed. Tara wrapped her arms around him.

"Y'know, I still can't figure how that woman's card got into your jacket pocket," Tara mumbled. Clem turned away from the window and grabbed his half-finished juice.

"Yeah, that's a mystery." Tara looked at Clem for any sign that he could be lying to her. "I'm going to talk to Justine about it," Clem continued.

"Why Justine?" Tara frowned.

"Because I always put my jacket on the back of my chair when I get to work. Who else goes in my office all the time?"

"Justine wouldn't do something like that. Why would she? If it was meant to be a gag it really wasn't funny. Especially not with your handwriting."

"That wasn't my handwriting," Clem insisted.

"Why copy it then?" Tara asked, suddenly wondering if Clem knew more than he was letting on. But what Tara did know, was that she'd tried to catch her husband in a lie on more than one occasion and had failed with flying colors. Her female intuition appeared to be malfunctioning, so going on her gut instincts was a definite no-no.

"Amazing how destructive something like that can be."

"Who would do something that could create such havoc in a marriage? I mean, that's just plain vindictive."

"That's the kind of crap Fitz would pull but he'd need to be alone in my office with my jacket to do it. I'll talk to Justine about it when I get to work on Monday." Clem smiled and kissed Tara's head.

They spent the rest of their lazy Sunday afternoon sitting around reading the newspaper and talking about what the future might hold if and when Clem parted ways with the agency. Tara read through the jobs in the business section. It just felt so good to have the old Clem back.

Late afternoon their hangovers had subsided. Tara was starting to feel human again.

"Come on! Let's get out of here and get some fresh air."

Moments later they were strolling through the park towards the lake. Tara reminded Clem that it was his birthday on Monday and that they should go out and celebrate in some manner though the thought of more alcohol really didn't appeal to either of them.

"Why don't you come up to Bergensons? We can go out for dinner afterwards."

"Okay, sounds good." Tara smiled, looking forward to actually going on a date again with her husband.

# CHAPTER 17

Heading to the office along Interstate 62 on Monday morning felt strange for Clem. It was his birthday but he felt ten years older than his forty-four years. His usual motivation to bust a gut to get into the agency was no longer in him but he still had a job and a paycheck. At the end of the day he was still a professional who took pride in his work but he really wasn't in the mood for all the bright pink and yellow balloons waiting for him when he arrived.

"Happy birthday, boss!" Justine squealed as she greeted him with his usual morning cappuccino but today he got a slice of banana and walnut cake with a blue sparkler stuck in it. It made Clem smile at least. "Remember, you have an internal photo shoot at one o'clock for the big Rebakor press release we're doing," Justine reminded him.

"Is Molinaire coming in?" Clem sipped his caffeinated brew.

"Apparently," said Justine, pecking her boss on the cheek with a birthday kiss.

Clem spent the morning calling old connections on both coasts. He needed an exit strategy and knew he couldn't depend on Daniel Ellerby to find him anything other than the dubious Alabama gig at Wardle & Ward. Seemed Ellerby wasn't kidding about the state of affairs in recruitment. Everyone was more concerned about hanging on to the jobs they had. No one was about to help Golden Balls take another step up the ladder that they were barely clinging to. But then that was the ad biz; a dog eat dog world.

As desperate times call for desperate measures, so Clem started surfing the web. After exhausting Linkedin for any leads, he turned to the murky postings on Craigslist. Sure, there were hundreds of ads for 'marketing positions' but they were barely more than internships.

Clem's calendar was looking auspiciously empty for July and August with only a few internal meetings on his schedule. He'd delegated the handling of his other accounts to fellow account execs as clients were all cutting their budgets so there was no need for him to get back involved. Those accounts were ticking over just fine without him. But it seemed word had got out that Clem Drew was not going to be the chosen one as everyone had been expected. His rivalry with Fitz was common knowledge and everyone was very aware that whoever became the new broom would sweep the agency clean. Word had gotten out about the Rebakor debacle and it'd shot around the agency gossip grapevine very swiftly. Frank Bergenson's imminent retirement was becoming something of a lightning rod. Employees had to make sure they didn't get on the wrong side of the next king. There was no doubt that Clem was far more popular than Fitz within the agency rank and file but as Clem knew only too well, people jump ship when it starts sinking.

One o'clock came around quickly. Clem skipped lunch and headed down to the photography studio on the forty-second floor. All the main players were in attendance -- Frank Bergenson, Earl Chambliss, James Molinaire, Kurt Fitzgerald and Fitz's creative guys, Gerard and Patrick.

Chuck Svensen was a notable senior management absentee and understandably so, considering that no one gave a flying fuck about consulting him to approve the campaign they were all gushing about. At least he could piss off Frank by being a no-show.

Molinaire and Fitz were chatting away like bosom buddies. Clem ignored the agency staffers and made a beeline for the two of them.

"Hello, James." Clem smiled warmly, though not attempting to shake anyone's hand.

"Hi, Clem."

Molinaire's response was cordial but somewhat aloof. The last time the two had spoken was when he'd chastised Clem over the phone. Fitz stood his ground next to Molinaire saying nothing. He seemed more laid back than usual, probably comfortable in the knowledge that his future was now looking distinctly rosy. Clem knew Molinaire probably felt *dissed* so he knew he had to handle him carefully. After all, Clem was still very much a loyal agency man.

"So you made it to the shoot, Clem. Congratulations."

Molinaire's sarcasm was duly noted and ignored by Clem though Fitz had a smile sneak across his face. Clem wanted to tell Molinaire to stop acting like the pious prat he was but thought better of it. He'd missed one meeting and canceled a second with Rebakor and so now Molinaire was acting like a dumped girlfriend, such was the ego of the man.

Clem acted as if all was fine and dandy and left Fitz to kiss up to his new buddy. He did the customary glad-handing with the rest of the Rebakor marketing executives in the studio but to him, Fitz was now invisible. As for Frank his feelings of betrayal towards him were immense.

The agency photographer arranged the assembled executives around a giant Rebakor logo.

"I need Mr. Molinaire in the center with Mr. Bergenson on one side and Mr. Fitzgerald on the other."

If Clem needed another clue that Fitz was being lined up for the CEO gig that was it. The three men duly obliged the photographer and smiled weakly for the camera.

*Click.*

"One more, please."

*Click.*

"Okay, now I need the rest of you to take positions either side of them. Try to balance each end."

Clem felt miffed being stuck on the end of the group.

*Click. Click. Click.*

"Thanks. That's a wrap," said the photographer and walked off to load the images into his computer. The group relaxed and started chatting amongst themselves again.

"Clem," called out Frank Bergenson, walking over wearing a smile that defied its insincerity. "Hope you and Tara will be coming to my retirement party this week."

"You can count on me," Clem smirked, aware of the irony.

"Sorry I can't make your birthday party this afternoon though." Frank smiled that famous fake smile again.

"What birthday party?"

"Apparently it's your birthday today."

"Yes, I'm aware of that. I didn't know there was going to be a party to celebrate it."

"Maybe it was meant to be a surprise."

"Well, I don't like surprises."

"Life's full of them, my friend. Meet me in my office in ten minutes." Frank walked back over to the Rebakor clan.

Maybe the Rebakor guys didn't know the political landscape at Bergensons. Maybe they did. It really didn't matter; the dye had been cast. Fitz continued his chumminess with James Molinaire, hogging the man so Clem couldn't get in on their conversation even if he'd wanted to. Not that Molinaire seemed too interested in conversing with him, so Clem headed for the exit.

He knew damn well what Frank wanted to see him about. He was going to give some bullshit speech about why he appointing Fitz CEO and not him. Maybe he'd get some answers though and some rational *Frank Bergenson* reasons why he was doing this.

"No calls till we're done, Rosanne," said Frank Bergenson as he led Clem into his office and closed the door behind them.

"Sit down, Clem."

Clem sat on the white mohair sofa. Frank sat on the end of his desk. Clem knew what was coming and he was ready for it.

"Molinaire loves the new campaign," Frank said, making a point that really didn't need to be made.

"Yeah, I know Frank. Thanks for rubbing it in. I guess it appeals to his God-fearing sensibilities." Clem rolled his eyes.

"Look, Clem. I know you're still pissed about the way this whole thing with the presentation went down."

"You think? You mean the creative strategy that my team spent four months developing, which everybody approved internally, then got mysteriously ignored when it came to executing? That campaign, Frank?"

"Here's the deal, Clem -- without the Rebakor account, this agency would be in some serious trouble financially. Our other accounts are tightening their budgets and they've all cut back on their media spend for the foreseeable future. It's the same across the nation and I know you know that."

"Then why are you telling me what I already know?"

"Because...."

"Frank, please spare me the lecture on the world recession. I'm not an idiot, I know what's going on."

"Let me finish, Clem."

"Fine. Knock yourself out."

"I'm appointing Kurt Fitzgerald CEO and I'll announce it at my retirement party next week."

Clem stared back at Frank and let his words hang in the air. Hearing it straight from the horse's mouth meant for sure that he was officially the big loser in all this. But now it was Clem's turn.

"Why, Frank? What fucked up thinking brought you to chose Fitz and not me?" Clem shot back. "Just give me one reason why you think that's a smart move for this agency?"

"It's business, Clem. Just business," Frank answered without a hint of emotion.

"Well, it's bad fucking business. He has totally schmoozed you,

Frank. Good and proper. He's successfully bullshitted the bullshitter. I don't know what kinda crap he had on you but it's fucked up your thinking." Clem was incensed.

"Here's why, Clem. Kurt Fitzgerald pretty much ran this agency for the four months you were embroiled in the Rebakor pitch."

"It ran itself, Frank. No one was spending any ad dollars," Clem pointed out.

"You wanna spend the next five years kissing Molinaire's butt cheeks?"

"If it's for the good of the agency, Hell yeah."

"You're better than that, Clem. Let Fitz run Rebakor and you can run everything else."

"What are you smoking, Frank? The second you appoint Fitz CEO, he'll fire my sorry ass."

"No he won't. I won't let him," Frank scowled.

Clem stood up angrily. "How, Frank? How you gonna stop him? You won't be here. You're retiring, remember? And no one's gonna give a damn about you or what you want anymore. The second you vacate this office, you're ancient history!"

Frank looked at Clem as if his protégé had just stabbed him in the gut and not the other way around. But Clem wasn't finished.

"You should've retired years ago."

"Then you'll be pleased to know I'll be gone next week."

"And not a moment too soon as far as I'm concerned you egotistical, manipulative old fuck!"

Clem stormed out, smashing the door behind him. He thought about turning back around and kicking it down and giving Frank Bergenson a real piece of his mind. But what he really wanted to do was punch Fitz all the way back to New York City.

"Happy birthday, handsome!" said Rosanne as Clem walked past her desk but he was too angry to hear her. As he walked down the corridor towards the elevators, the agency photographer passed him carrying photographs from the Rebakor PR shoot.

"Here ya go, Clem."

The photographer handed him an 8" x 10" of one of the newly printed pictures. Clem took it and ripped it up without even glancing at it.

Justine had decorated Clem's office with more colorful balloons and a good gathering of Clem's favorite employees were waiting with party poppers and Champagne on ice to greet him. Tara arrived early much to Justine's delight.

"So glad you're here, Tara! I haven't seen you in ages."

"I know. You've probably seen more of Clem than I have these past months."

"So you know about everything?" Justine winced.

"Yup. Clem told me. Unbelievable."

"Oh – don't get me started. Clem has done so much for this company. It makes me so mad, I can't tell you."

"You're preaching to the converted, Justine. Our marriage has been a distant second."

Justine felt bad for Clem but hadn't realized how much it had affected Tara. "He needs this little party to lift his spirits. Thanks for doing this for him, Justine."

Clem walked into his office to much applause as the room broke into a rendition of Happy Birthday. Timing-wise it couldn't have been worse but he had to put on a brave face. He took a big breath, huffed it out and managed to force a weak smile as he looked at all the happy faces singing to him. Justine popped a bottle of Moet.

"Speech!" a voice from the back of the room shouted. Everyone applauded. Clem sucked it up and took another breath.

"Hey, guys. Thanks for coming to my 90th birthday."

"I thought you were only eighty-nine," someone quipped.

"Very funny. Thanks for coming, guys."

"Here's to our next CEO!" a young, un-informed trainee from the media department shouted. He was obviously out of the loop. Everyone clapped their hands supportively though more out of respect to Clem knowing the toast was redundant. Tara walked over and hugged her husband.

"Yes, here's to our next CEO," Clem muttered into Tara's ear as they embraced. "Shame he couldn't be here," said Clem sarcastically. "Guess he's busy upstairs blowing the old man."

As the gathering broke into smaller groups, Clem wandered over to his desk. Tara approached him with a sympathetic smile.

"So *this* is where you spend all those long hours," she said, clinking her Champagne glass with his. He noticed another copy of the same Rebakor PR photograph he'd torn up earlier with Fitz's dumb grin looking at him alongside Molinaire and Frank Bergenson. Clem was in the shot but way off to the side.

"Jesus," Clem huffed. "How many times do I have to rip up that damn photo?"

Tara picked up the glossy picture. "Not a great shot of you, honey." Tara took a closer look. "Holy shit!" she blurted out.

"Come on, it's not that bad. I just didn't feel like smiling." Tara stared intensely, engrossed in the photograph.

"Who's that?" Tara asked, pointing to the grinning Fitz.

"Who d'you think?" Clem sneered. "That's the company asshole -- Kurt Fitzgerald."

"That's Fitz?"

"Yeah, ugly bastard, isn't he?" Justine added, looking over Tara's shoulder at the picture. Tara stared hard again at the photo and put it back down on Clem's desk.

"More Champagne anyone?" asked Justine, topping up Clem and Tara's glasses. "So great you could come today, Tara. I know we talk on the phone every now and then but you need to come up here more often!" Justine gushed, though all three knew that the likelihood of that ever happening was now highly unlikely.

As Tara and Clem spent the next hour socializing, Tara had a moment of clarity. The tables had now turned. Clem didn't have any secrets that he was hiding from her. She was the one with the secret and maybe she should level with him.

That night, Clem and Tara dined downtown at Manny's Grill

just up the street from the Kemp building. It was an old company hang out for Clem as he'd had many a business lunch and dinner there, so they'd snagged a quiet booth away from the throng of noisy diners.

Clem told Tara about the awkwardness of the photo shoot and the flat reception he'd gotten from Molinaire. He also told her about his come-to-Jesus conversation with the old man and that the out-of-the-blue phone call from Daniel Ellerby probably hadn't been quite so random after all. Clem was reflective and subdued.

"Anyway, Bergenson is going to make the big announcement at his retirement party."

"Can I go?" Tara asked. Clem was surprised.

"Why would you want to? I don't want to go myself but I made a promise I would to my team. Don't know why you'd want to suffer through wearing some stupid costume."

"Costume?" Tara frowned.

"Well, just to show what a wonderfully, fabulously creative guy he's been all his professional life, the crazy old bastard wants to make it a costume party. Jesus."

A wry smile crossed Tara's face. "How fun! A costume party! Well, that's perfect."

Clem shot Tara a look. "No. It's not fun. It's not fun at all, Tara. I hate dressing up. Now I'm going to look an even bigger loser when Fitz gets the nod over me in front of everyone and I'm standing there dressed up like some friggin' pirate or someone equally ridiculous."

Clem couldn't understand why Tara seemed so enthused by the thought of wearing fancy dress.

"Clem, it's perfect. Everyone will be in disguise. No one will know who's who."

"Big deal."

"It's a license to behave badly. Yes, you can be a pirate and I'll be....oh, I don't know. I'll think of something."

Next day, after Clem had left for work, Tara had unfinished business with Mistress Krystal. She called her on the phone and got her voicemail. She started to leave a message.

"Hi, it's Angelina. I want to apologize for running off the other night..." Tara was in mid-sentence when Mistress Krystal picked up the call.

"Apologize for what?"

If Mistress Krystal wasn't offended there wasn't much point in apologizing.

"Can I come over? I think I left something at your place," Tara asked.

Mistress Krystal was cleaning up after a session when Tara arrived at her apartment.

"Mr. Winkle, I presume?" Tara said, knowingly.

"I should charge him extra for all the cleaning costs," Mistress Krystal complained. "What did you forget?"

"Sissy Boy's tooth. I decided I want to have it as a memento," Tara smiled. Mistress Krystal pointed over towards the kitchen.

"Second draw on the right. I always keep any body parts that fall off or fall out just in case the original owners want them back," Mistress Krystal chuckled. "Sissy Boy has been asking about you. Wants to know when his next session with 'Mistress Angel' is going to be."

Tara found the shiny white molar wrapped in tissue paper. She pulled a face, and then tucked the tooth away in her purse.

"Why? Does he want me to knock out more of his teeth?" Tara snarked. Anyway, thanks."

"That it? That's all you came over here for?" Mistress Krystal asked, walking into the kitchen.

"Uh huh," Tara replied.

"Now, hang on, hun. You kinda stomped off the other night," Mistress Krystal reminded her. "And you gave me some little speech about being done with class. I don't know if that was the booze talking or not because, I gotta be honest, I wasn't really listening."

"Oh, yeah. I think we're done. Classes are finished for me. You were a great teacher, so thanks. I learnt what I needed to know."

Tara knew this would be the last time she'd ever see Mistress Krystal and felt, strangely, a little sad now knowing that she never was the monster her mind had tricked her into believing.

"I've been thinking…" Mistress Krystal started. "…about just quitting and moving out west."

"What about your regulars? They'll be lost without you."

"Tea?" Mistress K smiled.

"Oh, sure, why not? I'm in no rush." Tara sat down as Mistress Krystal put the kettle on the stovetop and got out the Royal Doulton.

"They'll all want to find other mistresses, for sure. Unless…" Mistress Krystal hesitated.

"No. Don't bring that up again. I'm not interested. I told you that," Tara reminded her.

"Why not? You could so easily take over this gig."

"Oh, no, no, no. That's never gonna happen!" Tara laughed at the thought.

"Several of my clients know who you are now and they love you. Especially Sissy Boy."

"Nuh-uh. That's not love."

"And I'd be handing you a great source of income on a plate."

Nothing could have been further from Tara's mind. Mistress Krystal searched the kitchen cupboards for a black bin liner.

"I've had three lessons with you. I'm just not into this stuff."

"You think I get off doing this shit, day in, day out? It's a job. I think you could be terrific as long as you stay on script. And you know what? Even a lousy mistress is better than no mistress."

"Well, that's not exactly a ringing endorsement," Tara laughed. "Was I a lousy mistress?"

"Well, I've never had a student before. You were the one and only, so that makes you the best student I ever taught."

As they two them laughed, Tara couldn't even contemplate working as a professional dominatrix. How could she ever tell Clem?

He'd suggested she might want to quit her volunteering to get a job that paid but this could never have been what he had in mind.

"Think it over, hun. Anyway, there's a client I see once every blue moon. I call him Coco because likes to dress up like a clown, the crazy bastard - makes animals out of balloons, too."

"That sounds rather fun. Why does he need to do that with you?"

"Well -- while he's making his little balloon animals, he likes me to stick a baseball bat up his ass." Tara looked at Mistress Krystal.

"No. Forget it. It's over. I'm totally done with all this. It…it just wasn't what I thought it was going to be," Tara said bluntly. "It's not sexy."

"It is to Coco," said Mistress Krystal in all seriousness.

"No." Tara stood up. "I definitely won't be needing any more classes but I wanted to come over here and thank you in person for opening my eyes to a brave, new, scary world."

Mistress Krystal was visibly disappointed. "Okay, hun. Well, I enjoyed showing you the ropes." She tapped out a cigarette and lit it, then spluttered a cough.

"The judge is back so soon?"

"Yep. They kinda think of you as an old friend after a while," Mistress Krystal smirked, still trying to twist Tara's arm.

"By the way, my real name is not Angelina – it's Tara."

"Yeah, I know," Mistress Krystal took another drag to keep the cigarette tip burning. Any guilt Tara had for being deceitful was immediately replaced by surprise.

"You know? *When* did you know?"

"The day you first called my number. You can find out anything on the internet these days." Mistress Krystal gave her a wry smile. Tara felt silly now.

"I thought you were old school and not into technology."

"Don't believe everything people tell you, hun. I guess when you realized your husband wasn't one of my clients you figured it was time to quit." Tara was gobsmacked.

"What? How the --?"

"You're a pretty easy read, Tara."

"Am I? Really? Well, then you deserve an even bigger thank you for taking on someone you knew was being so economical with the truth." Tara was amazed she'd been so easily rumbled.

"It's all business," said Mistress Krystal. "It was easy money." She handed Tara a cup of tea. "So how *did* you find my card?"

"It was in my husband's suit jacket."

"Yeah? How'd *he* get it?"

"I'm still working on that one."

"And he's not one of my clients?"

"Unless he looks like this guy." Tara took a small picture of her and Clem out of her bag and showed it to Mistress Krystal.

"Nah. He's not my type."

"Good to know!" Tara smiled.

"Well, I'm leaving town in a month. If you change your mind, you'll make quite a few needy men very happy. Especially Sissy Boy."

"Well, then. Maybe I'll think about it."

"You should. Seriously."

"Do you really think I could hack it doing this?"

"I know you could. I'll give you a couple of free lessons to get you a little more up to speed on a few things."

"Y'know, I'd really like to see myself in action. You said you video everything, right?"

"Yep."

"Can I get a copy of me and Sissy Boy?" Tara smiled coyly.

Mistress Krystal frowned. "No way. I never let anyone see those tapes. They're confidential."

"But if you want me to take over the show, I need to study my technique. I gotta learn to keep the customer satisfied, right?" said Tara, doing her best to look sincere. Mistress Krystal sipped her tea. "When would you need me to start?" Tara winked.

## CHAPTER 18

"Did you ever figure out all that bull crap with the dominatrix chick? 'Mistress Kickass' or whatever she was called?" asked Lorraine, as she and Tara sunbathed on loungers by the club pool.

Tara smiled to herself. The sun felt good on her face. "Oh, that was all a misunderstanding," Tara replied casually but Lorraine wasn't buying it.

"No, no, no, no, no, Tara Drew. Don't blow me off with that answer. I recall how upset you were. And now it's no big deal? Do I look that naive? Come on!"

A young blonde Bodyworks server appeared with a drinks menu.

"Hi, ladies! Can I get you two something to drink?" Lorraine shooed her away as she waited for Tara to spill the beans.

"Clem was never seeing that Mistress Krystal woman after all," Tara shrugged.

"Really? So, let me get this straight: He wasn't seeing her even though he just so happened to be carrying around her business card in his pocket with *Tuesday at five o'clock*, written on the back of the card in his *own handwriting?*" Lorraine rolled her eyes. "Puh-leeze!"

"Clem swore he had no idea how that card got into his pocket. And it wasn't his handwriting on the card either."

Lorraine was incredulous. "Good grief woman! You must be the most gullible wife on the planet. What else was he going to say? Guy rule number one is 'deny everything, admit nothing' for Chrissakes. You should know that at your age. Oh, I'm so mad I wanna jump in that water right now!" Lorraine boomed.

Tara smiled knowingly. "Go ahead, jump. I believe him. Call it my woman's intuition -- I know he wasn't lying."

"I would've hired a private investigator to follow his sorry ass around town till I got slam dunk evidence." Lorraine bitched.

"Don't be ridiculous, Lorraine. I would never do something like that!" It seemed Tara's ability to lie had be honed in recent weeks.

"Well, I sure would have. All men are pigs. So you know for *sure* he wasn't seeing this Mistress Krystal?" Lorraine was still appalled at Tara's naiveté.

Tara answered quietly. "Yup."

"How?"

"Because *I* was seeing her."

"Huh?"

"I was seeing Mistress Krystal."

"You went to see her? You? As in you, Tara Drew?"

"Several times."

"I don't believe you."

"Yup."

"What? Why?"

"I wanted her to teach me how to do what she does."

"Oh, no you didn't!" Lorraine squealed.

"Oh, yes I diddy," Tara mocked back with a twinkle in her eyes. Lorraine was now confused, bemused and totally intrigued. She leaned over in her lounger to get closer.

"Are you shitting me, Tara Drew?"

"Nope. I called her up and asked her to give me lessons," Tara admitted. "She said it would cost me three hundred bucks a pop so she became my teacher."

"Holy crap! I cannot believe you really did that. You did that? Why?" Lorraine was both horrified and impressed at the same time.

"I needed a job," Tara lied again.

"As a dominatrix? Are you kinky crazy? If you want a job take mine! My damn back's killing me doing this yoga shit every day. Get back to your story."

"That's why I know for sure Clem *wasn't* one of her clients."

"So did you get to whack some of these perverts?" Lorraine was stunned that *Little Miss Goody Two Shoes* wasn't quite as goody-goody as she'd always assumed.

"I did meet some interesting characters that's for sure."

"And you got to whip them?" Lorraine's eyes widened.

"Few times." Tara confessed.

"Tell me more about this woman," Lorraine pressed, wanting to know all the juicy, gory details.

"Actually, I liked her. Nice woman." Tara said, admitting for the first time to herself that Mistress Krystal was actually pretty cool.

"Nice woman? Give me a fucking break. Guys don't pay her to be nice to them."

Frank Bergenson's chauffeur-driven black Lincoln Town car sped through downtown Minneapolis. Sitting in the back seat were Frank and Kurt Fitzgerald.

"Did you break the news to Clem yet?" Fitz asked.

"He knows," Frank replied in his gravely voice.

"Good," Fitz grinned.

Frank stared out the window at a large retail store that had gone out of business. "I don't for a New York minute think that you're a religious man, Fitz."

Fitz chuckled. "Maybe not but if Molinaire asks, I was in the choir at Saint Patrick's Catholic Church."

"That 'God Speed' tagline is dumb. You know that."

Fitz seemed unfazed. "Client is always right. Even when they're wrong."

"It's not going to put my name on any awards," Frank said, pointedly. "We'll take the money this year. But next year you'll need to bring home a Clio or two."

"Don't worry about next year, Frank. You'll be basking on your yacht in the south of France by then, sailing into Monte Carlo."

The black Lincoln turned onto Hennepin Avenue and stopped at a red light. Fitz was getting twitchy with excitement but Frank was feeling reflective.

"Yeah, I'm going to miss the place. I've been in this business for sixty one years."

"Jesus. How old are you?"

"Seventy four. Started when I was thirteen in the mailroom at Ogilvy & Mather. Seems like just a few years ago." Fitz gave Frank an admiring glance.

"Helluva run, Frank. Damn -- to survive that long in this cut throat business – that's legend."

"That's because I was the guy cutting the throats," Frank said without missing a beat. The light turned green and their car pulled away slowly along Washington Avenue.

"I'm making the announcement tomorrow night at the party. I hope I've made the right decision picking you as my successor."

Fitz smiled. "You've molded me into your own image, Frank. How can you possibly be wrong?"

The Lincoln pulled up outside the television studios of WKBO, the local ABC affiliate, where Frank was being interviewed for the six o'clock news segment. The Minneapolis-St. Paul business community had voted Frank Bergenson *Business Leader Of The Year*. The award was more out of respect for the fact that Bergenson & Adler had become a Minneapolis institution. It seemed a fitting gesture as the old man stepped down and into retirement.

"Whatever happened to your old agency partner Lewis Adler?" Fitz asked Frank as they walked towards the building. "He vanished without a trace."

"I caught him fucking my wife," Frank said bluntly. "So I fucked his career and married his secretary."

"Outstanding!"

Fitz had learnt more about the man he was replacing in one short car ride than in his two years at the agency. It was really only now that Fitz fully appreciated that he was stepping into the shoes of one bull-headed, hard-ass survivor, and he had every intention of carrying on where Frank Bergenson was leaving off.

"Where do you want us?" Fitz asked the floor director as he and Frank walked into the television studio.

"We only need Mr. Bergenson."

"This is about me, not you, Fitz. Sit down and shut up," Frank teased. "I still run the show till tomorrow, remember?"

"Then why'd you ask me along?" Fitz asked, a little miffed he wasn't going to get his on-screen moment.

"Over here, Mr. Bergenson." The floor director beckoned and pointed to an armchair beside a fake fireplace. Frank wandered over with a glance back at Fitz.

"I just wanted make sure I was handing over the keys of the house to the right guy, that's all. By the way, what are your plans for Clem?"

"Clem who?" Fitz snarked back, still irked.

"Yeah, I thought so," said Frank, as he took his seat in front of the cameras.

A make-up girl dabbed a little powder on Frank's face as the crew took their places. Lucy Gerhardt, the attractive and leggy local news anchor at the network walked onto the set. Dressed sharply in a navy blue dress suit, she brushed passed Fitz who was standing in the wings. He winked at her and got a flash of a fake news anchor smile in return.

"Hi. I'm Kurt Fitzgerald." Fitz gave her a wiggly-fingered wave. "I'm from the agency, too. I handle the Rebakor business."

"Oh, am I interviewing you as well?" she asked, seemingly rather intrigued by the slick ad man.

"No. You're interviewing my grandpa over there by the fire," Fitz joked.

"I heard that Fitz, you sonofabitch!" Frank shouted from the studio where he was still getting powdered. Lucy Gerhardt laughed.

"You must be Frank Bergenson, the legend!" she called out as she headed over to the fireplace. She glanced over at Fitz who was grinning back at her like the Cheshire cat. The news anchor shook Frank's hand.

"Be nice to the pretty lady, Frank!" Fitz called over to them.

"That's the jackass who'll be taking over my agency when I retire next week," Frank said loudly as he shooed away the make-up girl.

"And if that isn't a ringing endorsement, I don't know what is," Fitz said to the floor director who could care less.

"Going live in forty-five seconds!"

"Excuse me for a moment, Mr. Bergenson." Lucy Gerhardt walked over to the floor director and whispered something in his ear then headed over to Fitz. The floor director turned to his crew.

"Hey, we need another chair. Lucy wants to interview these two together. Make it snappy!"

"I think you should be in this interview, too," said Lucy to Fitz. "Let's get you a dab of powder."

Fitz walked on the set and sat down next to Frank as the make-up girl reappeared to dab his forehead. Lucy took a seat next to the two agency men.

"What's he doing here?" Frank looked seriously irritated.

"Okay guys, I want to have you, Mr. Fitzgerald sitting here next to Mr. Bergenson because then we'll have the old guard next to the new guard," Lucy beamed, pleased with her own idea. Frank wasn't happy about the new arrangement.

"Don't hijack my interview. Who's retiring? Me! Who's Man of the fucking Year? Me!" Frank grouched.

"Going live in fifteen!"

Frank's ego was feeling more than a little bent out of shape. He didn't want anyone stealing his moment in the spotlight and he was getting even more pissed now that Fitz was blatantly flirting with Ms. Gerhardt. Frank leaned forward in his armchair towards the attractive news anchor.

"Listen, hot pants. It's not public knowledge who my successor will be so I'd appreciate it if you didn't mention it, okay?"

"Absolutely. Don't worry, Mr. Bergenson," Lucy reassured her agitated guest. The intro music to the news program began to play in the studio and everyone on set got very quiet.

"Going live…..standby….and three…two….."

The red 'live' light came on. Lucy Gerhardt looked directly into the camera. "Welcome to Twin Cities Primetime Live. I'm your host Lucy Gerhardt and tonight I'm talking to advertising legend, Mr. Frank Bergenson, who is this year's recipient of the prestigious Twin Cities' Business Leader of the Year Award, which is given by the Minnesota Chamber of Commerce. Now, Frank. You will be retiring next week after sixty years in the business…"

"Sixty one," Frank corrected her.

"Sorry, sixty one years. And most of that time at the helm of the Bergenson & Adler advertising agency. Frank is Chairman and CEO and, as you've probably read in the news, his agency has recently landed the $200 million Rebakor account, thanks mainly to the man sitting next to him, Mr. Kurt Fitzgerald."

Back in the Kemp building in his office on the forty-third floor, Clem sat with Justine watching Frank's interview on WKBO.

"Jesus Christ, I wanna puke."

Clem got up off the sofa and walked back over to his desk to busy himself with some paper shuffling to avoid watching the TV. Justine watched in stunned bewilderment as Fitz basked in all the glory of the agency's Rebakor win.

"Why is that asshole even there? This is meant to be about Mr. Bergenson's retirement."

The camera cut to a tight shot of Lucy Gerhardt.

*"What are your best memories of working in the advertising business all these years, Frank?"*

The camera cut to Frank sitting in his cozy armchair beside the fake fireplace, now with fake flames flickering.

*"Creating jobs for thousands of people over the years and bringing in some of the finest advertising talent from all over the country to come and work for me and make my agency extremely successful and me a lot of money."*

"At least he's being honest," Clem said, still refusing to watch but listening to every word. The camera cut to a close-up of Fitz looking even more cocky than his usual self.

"Ugh." Now Justine stood up in anger. "I should've reported him when I had the chance."

"Reported him?" Clem said, turning his attention to Justine.

"Oh, he's always all over me whenever he sees me around the agency. He gives me the creeps."

"You can't report him for giving you the creeps, Justine."

"Why not? Listen to him kissing up to Frank."

Clem and Justine turned their attention back to the television where Fitz was now on eulogizing Frank.

*"….and I just want to say that working with Frank Bergenson has been such a great honor. Personally, I'd love him to stick around for a few more years. We could all learn a lot from him."*

Fitz's insincerity sounded totally believable. The camera cut to Frank cracking a smile then cut back to Lucy Gerhardt.

*"Tune in tomorrow night and we'll have a Primetime Live camera crew live at Frank Bergenson's retirement party which seems is going to be quite the grand occasion from what I hear. Thanks, guys."*

"And out. Break to commercial," yelled the WKBO floor director as he waved an all-clear sign and wrapped Twin Cities Primetime Live. Frank Bergenson and Kurt Fitzgerald stood up and unclipped their lapel mics.

"Thanks guys, nice piece," said Lucy Gerhardt, shaking hands with the two of them

"I need to take a piss," Frank mumbled, looking around for a restroom sign.

"Through that door." Lucy pointed the way though Frank was

already headed off in the opposite direction. She turned to Fitz who seemed enamored by the TV anchor.

"Pretty impressive, Mr. Fitzgerald."

"Thanks for getting me the face time."

"I meant landing the Rebakor business. That's huge."

"Awwww….I can't take all the credit."

"Hey, why be modest about it? Good for you. And good for the Twin Cities, too. I'm sure we'll be hearing a lot about you now that you're going to be the big cheese over at Bergensons."

"Why don't we grab lunch sometime? Maybe I'll let you in on the secrets of my success. And call me Fitz. Everyone does."

"Okay, Fitz. Maybe I'll take you up on that," Lucy said with a mischievous grin. "And I'll be at the big event at the Pavilion, too."

"That'll be very cool. It's a costume party so look out for the king being crowned king." Fitz snarled his upper lip Elvis-style then slid his business card in the lapel pocket of her jacket.

# CHAPTER 19

It was the night of Frank's retirement party. Clem adjusted his eye patch in the bathroom mirror. The bandana around his head and large ornate belt buckle made him a pretty passable pirate, albeit a rather squeaky clean one.

"Well, it's not Johnny Depp but it'll do," he said, checking his appearance. "I think we should get there late and leave early, so take your time getting ready."

"Oh, I'm ready," said Tara, calling from the bedroom.

"So what costume are you wearing tonight? You never told me," Clem called back.

"Ready to find out?" Tara shouted as Clem made more minor adjustments to his own costume.

"I guess so. I just hope you're not a pirate too because I've got this nailed down."

"Okay, I'm coming out!" Tara announced. Clem ignored her as he fiddled with his irritating eye patch. The bedroom door swung open and Tara took a step forward into the bathroom. She stood directly under one of the recessed spotlights in the ceiling.

"So, what do you think, Cap'n Jack?" Tara smiled, presenting herself.

"Whoa...! Fuck!" Clem did a double take as he caught her

reflection in the mirror. He spun around and lifted the patch off his covered eye. "Who the heck are you meant to be?"

Tara looked like sex on legs and just about the most stunning vision of eroticism Clem had ever set eyes on. Tara knew how hot she looked as she struck a pose for Clem's benefit.

"You like?"

"Like? Yeah, me likey, all right. But seriously, Tara you can't go out in public dressed like that."

"Oh, no? Just watch me."

"Where did you get that outfit? What's with the whip?" Clem ran his eyes over her body from head to foot, from corset to boots to her Catwoman mask to the latex gloves up to her elbow.

"Well, it sure wasn't from the same place I found your pirate costume," she smiled. Clem had never seen his wife looking that hot before and he loved every kinky inch of her.

"Let's stay in tonight and fool around. I mean, seriously, you cannot go out dressed like that. You'll get arrested."

"We're going out and we're gonna have some fun for once. Heck, we'll never be seeing any of these people again once you get fired, assuming that's what's going to happen to you."

"Damn! I'm a pretty boring pirate next to you. Who are you meant to be anyway?" Clem asked, still admiring his sexed up wife.

"I'm a Fem Dom," Tara said smugly.

"Fem Dom? What's that?" Clem followed Tara downstairs and out towards their garage.

"You must be a newbie," Tara teased.

"A newbie at what?"

"Female domination. Think of me as a kind of Catwoman with a twist."

"Hmmmm….Very twisted."

The novelty of a costume party certainly added to the spectacle as hundreds of colorfully attired guests showed up at the stylish Depot Pavilion in the heart of downtown Minneapolis. A large flock of black stretch limos were lined up unloading their fancy dressed invitees. Over the years, Frank Bergenson might have made a lot of enemies but judging by the turn out he had plenty of friends, too. Many of the old money local socialites were showing up along with noted lawyers, academics, pro-athletes and politicians amongst the growing throng. Cameras flashed and locals videotaped.

By the time Clem and Tara arrived at the venue, the party was in full swing. The valet guys were as busy as all get out but still found a second to smile approvingly as Tara stepped out of the silver Mercedes with her pirate chaperone.

Inside, a Beatles tribute band were on stage looking every bit like John, Paul, George and Ringo in their collarless suits and mop top haircuts.

"This is pretty wild," Clem shouted over the strains of *Back In The U.S.S.R.* and seeing if he could recognize anyone with his one seeing eye. There were cowboys, witches, ballerinas, several Indiana Jones's, more pirates and various incarnations of Star Trek and Star Wars characters. Clem counted at least three Harry Potters, two Barack Obamas, eight clowns and someone dressed as Ron Burgundy from *Anchorman* doing a pretty decent impersonation.

"Looks like a Hollywood back lot!" Tara yelled, making her way through the throng.

"Where's the bar? I need a stiff one!" Clem shouted, still trying to be heard.

"Hey, if we get split up, just look out for my little pointy ears!" Tara yelled back at Clem, just as the errant arm of a flapper girl pulled him onto the dance floor. Clem grabbed onto Tara, dragging her with him just as the song ended much to the flapper's disappointment.

"Who's she?" Tara asked with a teasing expression.

"No idea. Now where's the bar?" Clem looked around sounding somewhat desperate.

As George Harrison changed a broken string on his sunburst Rickenbacker, the decibels dropped to a more tolerable level for a few minutes.

"Hi, guys!" Justine squealed at Cap'n Jack and Mistress Angel. "Glad I found you two in this madness! Wow, Tara! You look amazing. That is seriously sexxxxxxxy!"

"Well, y'know," Tara feigned bashfulness. "And look at you in that adorable….fairy dress?"

"I'm Glinda!" Justine posed, waving a fairy wand.

"Who?" Clem asked.

"Clem, you look ridiculous," Justine smirked.

Clem smiled sarcastically. "Gee, thanks. And for the record, I also *feel* ridiculous standing next to this kinky woman."

The bogus Ringo up on stage cracked his snare drum to kick off *She Loves You*, so Justine led Clem and Tara towards the VIP lounge before all their eardrums took a hit again.

The volume was much more conducive to conversation in the roped off lounge with its plush red leather sofas and cocktail bar. Several overly large TV screens were looping the Bergenson & Adler showreel playing every commercial the agency had ever produced. Several people were smiling while watching some of the older spots from the late seventies with their dated production values and cheesy acting.

"I'll take a Fuzzy Cosmo," Tara told Clem.

"Is that a real drink?" Clem frowned.

"I think that's more like two drinks," Justine giggled. "I'll take one as well then."

Justine was fully in the party spirit as she started grooving to the music. Glinda and Mistress Angel sang along to the chorus bleeding in from the ballroom. *"Yeah, yeah, yeah, yeaaaaah!"*

Tara looked around at all the gussied up partygoers. She didn't really know any of the faces to match to the names that Clem always talked about. Even Justine was having trouble figuring who was who under all the weird, wild and wonderful outfits.

"Any sign of this Fitzgerald character?" Tara asked, as the two scanned the room waiting for Clem to return with their drinks.

"I heard he's coming as Elvis," Justine mumbled into the side of

Tara's leather mask. "That's Frank Bergenson and his wife Lucille over there." Justine pointed to Superman with a rather old Indian squaw talking to Laurel and Hardy. Clem broke in between the girls carrying their cocktails.

"This is better," Clem said. "At least I can hear myself think."

The VIP lounge was starting to get busier by the second. At that moment a tall priest walked in with several white-gowned alter boys who were way too old to be dressed so innocently.

"Who are they?" Tara asked, trying not to laugh out loud.

"I've seen it all now. That's James Molinaire and the Rebakor marketing department," Clem observed. "I didn't know they were coming."

"Don't you want to go and talk to them?" Tara asked.

"Not really. Let them settle in and loosen up a bit first. Me too, for that matter."

Clem glanced around at the growing number of costumed guests entering the lounge as the strains of the Fab Four singing harmonies on *I Wanna Hold Your Hand* kicked up the noise level seeping in to the large room.

"Well, no one seems particularly interested in talking to the three of us," Tara remarked ruefully.

"I think you're scaring everyone off in that highly provocative leather outfit, honey," Clem joked, eyeing his hot wife up and down again. "Let's go home and....you know."

Justine looked horrified. "Awww, no! Don't go. You've only just got here. This is going to be a fun night."

"I feel stupid. Why am I at an event where I know I'm going to be publicly humiliated? And in front of the entire agency and clients."

"Our crew are all over at the bar," Justine motioned. "Chuck Svensen was looking for you earlier. Wanna go find him?"

"Yeah, I owe him a big drink."

The song ended and The Beatles started up again immediately with the opening stains of *Come Together*. Justine squealed. "I love this song! Let's go dance! Tara, can I borrow Clem?" she pleaded.

"Knock yourself out! Assuming you can get him to stop being so grumpy. I'm gonna finish my Fuzzy Cosmo then I'll join you guys later," Tara said, her eyes darting around the VIP lounge.

"Really? You sure?"

"Absolutely. You two go and do your thing."

"Okay, see you later, honey!" Clem yelled to his wife as Justine pulled him away towards the dancing throng in the main room.

On the other side of the VIP lounge, Frank 'Superman' Bergenson introduced the priestly James Molinaire to his Indian squaw wife. Tara noted the alter boys looking over and checking her out as she stood at the bar sipping her cocktail. She figured that most of the other guests in the lounge were agency clients mingling with senior Bergenson management and a smattering of wives. Some of their costuming was rather more conservative for fear of making themselves look foolish though it simply revealed who was out of their comfort zone. Tara was impressed that James Molinaire had made the effort to dress up in such a manner. But then, that was probably how he saw himself. Though following that train of thought, did Tara really see herself as a sex vixen? From her vantage point, she could see Frank and Molinaire through enough heads to still stay pretty much out of sight and that's just how she wanted it.

"See all those cameras outside?" a male voice behind her asked. Tara quickly turned around to see that one of the alter boys had broken rank and slipped over to join her at the bar. Maybe it wasn't the best place to stand after all.

"Guess the paparazzi knew I was coming," Tara purred. The alter boy leaned in closer.

"Wouldn't surprise me. You've gotta be the hottest chick in here tonight."

"Thanks," Tara said to her admirer. His youthful appearance was enhanced by his black cassock and white choir dress though he seemed to be brimming with the confidence of an ambitious middle manager without a religious bone in his body.

"Love the whip. Nice touch. Makes that dominatrix thing all the more authentic."

"Right," Tara answered flatly.

"I'm Ricky." The alter boy held out his hand to shake. Tara held onto her drink with no intention of shaking it as she looked him up and down.

"The pleasure's all yours," she quipped at the annoying pest. She already looked the part but now she was feeling ready to reveal a flash of her alter ego.

"Not that those dominatrix women look anything like as sexed up as you."

"Really?" Tara raised an eyebrow.

"No way. They're usually all fat, old sluts."

"And how would you know?"

"Ha! You're funny! Hey, do you ever do private parties….?" He grinned cheekily, oblivious to the fact that he was starting to annoy the crap out of Tara. He was ruining her modus operandi. She really didn't need this distraction and he wouldn't stop bugging her. Tara suddenly morphed into Mistress Krystal.

"Sure, I do private parties but you couldn't afford me, you little jerk." Mistress Angel spat venomously at the clueless alter boy.

"Man, that's great. You so fucking cool. Let's hit the little girl's room. I've got some blow."

"Really?"

"Damn right."

Tara grabbed the back of his hair and yanked hard, snapping his head back so he faced the ceiling.

"Owww!"

"How about I march you back over to Mr. Molinaire and tell him one of his junior executives has a serious fucking drug habit?"

"Shit. Okay, I get it. You're not interested."

She released her grip and watched him scurry back to the rest of his alter boy crew.

In the middle of the VIP lounge, Superman Frank was now

getting considerable attention as more clients and senior agency executives arrived. He was encircled by well-wishers and ass-kissers.

Tara stood alone by the bar sipping the last dribbles of her drink, shielded by an impressively costumed Hulk. She was waiting for her moment and now that Clem had been whisked away by Justine, it was just a matter of time before Kurt 'Elvis' Fitzgerald made an appearance. He was the prey she was laying in wait for and Mistress Angel didn't have long to wait.

"I'm a hunka hunka burning love!" Fitz boomed as he entered the lounge sounding and looking every bit like a bad Las Vegas Elvis impersonator wearing a white rhinestone studded suit with its collar pulled up high. He spread his arms wide to embrace his new flock of clients.

"The king is in the building!"

Tara watched Fitz high-five everyone as he sauntered over to Frank and Molinaire. All the alter boys laughed, except Ricky who was still rubbing the back of his head.

"Funny. I thought I was still the king," Frank jabbed.

Fitz looked at Frank's blue and red outfit with a giant 'S' on his chest. "Come on, Frank! Everyone knows you're Superman," he joked. "You didn't need to wear a costume for us all to know that."

More laughter. Fitz was pumped. This night was not so much about Frank retiring but more about *his* ascendency.

"Maybe Elvis will go and sing with the Beatles," suggested Earl Chambliss, dressed as a rather overweight Count Dracula.

"Later gator! Yeah, I'm all shook up to be here," Fitz drawled in a southern accent and striking a karate pose. James Molinaire patted Fitz on the back affectionately.

"Hey, you can do what you want but don't step on my Rebakor shoes," zinged Molinaire. More hilarity ensued as every one started doing bad Elvis impersonations. Tara watched from a safe distance. Everything about cocky Kurt Fitzgerald annoyed her but now it was just a matter of timing to make her move.

"Congratulations, Kurt on your impending inheritance," James

Molinaire said loudly, taking Fitz to one side.

"Thanks, James. I'm digging the priest thing you got going on there."

"Glad I didn't come dressed as the Pope as I was intending. If I'd know it was going to be so damn hot in here I would've worn something skimpier."

Frank Bergenson wandered over to join them. "Channel 5 is coming tonight, boys. They're gonna to do a live broadcast on the ten o'clock news. Probably want to get you two on camera. Hope they tape my speech because it's as funny as shit."

The VIP lounge was filling up. Frank looked around the now jam-packed room. "Jesus, who are all these people? I don't recognize anyone in these stupid fucking costumes. Whose dumb idea was it to make it fancy dress?" Frank wandered off to find his Cherokee wife. It was getting rowdier by the minute and the alter boys seemed in a rambunctious mood now. Molinaire gave them disapproving looks as any priest would as he took a swig of his club soda.

"I'm not really a party person," Molinaire announced to no one's surprise. "Alcohol turns people into morons." He looked at his own marketing guys when he said it.

"Hey! Check that out over at the bar!" one of them joked as he got a clear shot of Mistress Angel staring over at them.

"Damn," another alter boy shouted. "I'm gonna hit that."

"Good luck, buddy. You don't 'hit' on a dominatrix. She hits on you," said Ricky.

"Watch me."

"Seriously, dude. Don't do it. I think she just might be the real fucking deal."

"Bullshit. How'd she get an invite then?"

"Who gives a rat's ass? She's freaky hot."

All eyes turned to the woman in black with the whip. The wave of people who'd kept her hidden had parted like the Red Sea and now she was exposed. A gun-slinging cowboy turned to a plump Mr. Spock. "Beam me up, Spocky."

"Under the circumstances that would be illogical. You might want to stick around," Spock replied, enjoying the same view. Fitz was too engrossed in telling an Elvis joke to see what everyone else was looking at. Realizing he'd lost his audience he glanced over to see what the fuss was all about. He stopped in mid-sentence.

"Oh, fuck. No. Not here," Fitz spluttered under his breath.

"Friend of yours, Mr. Presley?" Frank asked, seeing the stunned expression on Fitz's face.

Mistress Angel looked directly at Fitz and beckoned him over with one finger.

"She wants you, Elvis!" the gunslinger laughed loudly.

Two of the alter boys nudged each other seeing that Fitz seemed at a loss what to do. His mind was racing. What *should* he do? If he didn't obey Mistress Angel's command then she might approach his entourage. This woman could seriously embarrass him in front of everybody. He was dumbstruck. His jaw fell slack as he broke into a cold sweat.

"Maybe she wants to spank us all," a voice suggested to much merriment but Fitz didn't see the joke.

James Molinaire looked even more pious than usual looking curiously at his gobsmacked ad agency point man.

"Go on, Elvis," the cowboy urged. "A little less conversation and a lot more action, please!"

A roar of laughter filled the lounge. This was Tara's moment. She walked slowly towards the assembled executives. Her right arm raised her leather bullwhip as the crowd stepped back.

"Shit. This is about to get really fucking interesting," said Ricky, the admonished alter boy.

An army Sargent standing close by joined in the fun. "Look out, gentlemen. Incoming! This is not a drill. Repeat. This is not a drill!"

Tara walked slowly and seductively towards the group of leering men surrounding Fitz. Her thigh-high black latex boots shimmered in with every step. Just then Frank returned with his wife and saw Fitz standing motionless more like a statue of Elvis.

"You okay, Fitz? Look like you've seen a ghost."

Tara stopped in front of the frozen Fitz.

"What the fuck's got into Fitzy?" said an axe wielding Viking. "Shame Clem isn't here to see this."

"So we meet again, Sissy Boy. Fancy seeing you here," Mistress Angel announced loudly so everyone could hear. The group roared with laughter and applause. Fitz laughed too but in nervous panic. "Remember me?"

"No, I don't," Fitz mumbled, hoping to sound convincing but looking distinctly uncomfortable. Mistress Angel smiled, drew back her whip and slapped the long leather lash into her gloved hand, close enough to Fitz to make him flinch.

A collective "Wooooooo…!" filled the room as the VIP lounge was now noticeably more crowded and less exclusive. The audience encircled Fitz and Mistress Angel. They seemed equally fascinated by this brazen display of female sexuality and Fitz's expression of abject horror. No one knew if this was some little rehearsed sideshow but whatever it was it was holding everyone's attention.

"Sure you remember, Sissy Boy! You know exactly who I am."

Frank Bergenson had seen enough. "What in the devil is this all about, Fitz? You rent this woman for some parlor act? Is this meant to be funny?"

Fitz didn't answer. The crowd was like a pack of hungry hounds as Mistress Angel circled the statuesque Fitz like a prowling cat.

"Remember my boots and how much you enjoyed licking them last Friday?" Everyone laughed, some even applauded.

"Who put you up to this?" Fitz mumbled to the circling vixen. "Clem Drew? Did *he* put you up to this?"

The gunslinger frowned. "Hey, man. What's with the Sissy Boy moniker?"

"Well, he answers to it so that tells you something," pointed out The Lone Ranger.

"Hey, Fitz. D'you actually know this hot babe? Man, you lucky bastard," a tattooed Hell's Angel shouted as Fitz's face started to turn beet red.

The crowd could sense Fitz's uneasiness and their mood was quickly changing from jocular to voyeuristic. Fitz glanced across at the disapproving expression on the face of James Molinaire and a visibly concerned Frank Bergenson.

"This woman's nuts," Fitz announced to the crowd.

"Am I?" Mistress Angel smiled.

Fitz looked for a gap in the crowd to make an exit but this was now a compelling show. He had to do something. *Anything*. He and Mistress Angel were center stage with an enthusiastic audience that wasn't going anywhere.

"Remember how we first met, Sissy Boy?" she smiled wickedly.

Kurt Fitzgerald looked scared to death and decidedly un-CEO like. Frank Bergenson's heir apparent was being made to look a complete fool in front of senior agency personnel and all their clients, most notably, the Rebakor chief. *Why was Fitz so terrified and how was this woman wielding so much power over him?*

The usually overly confident alpha male seemed to be under this woman's control. It was too late now to try and bluff his way out of it. The shock of seeing Mistress Angel had really fucked with his mojo. He tried the only option he had left in his repertoire of bullshit. He started to applaud.

"Okay. Joke over. Run along, honey. Good gag," Fitz bluffed loudly, trying to gather some sort of control of his predicament but the beads of sweat on his forehead betrayed his bogus bravado. No one was buying it.

This was Tara's moment. "Okay, Sissy Boy. Let's show everyone how we met, shall we?"

"Huh?" Fitz muttered.

Tara slid out a small remote control from inside her thigh high boot and pointed it at the large televisions. The screens all snapped to black, then footage of Sissy Boy at Mistress Krystal's apartment filled started playing. All eyes in the VIP lounge were now firmly focused on the large TVs and the raw video images of a naked, tattooed Fitz.

The crowd were silenced and captivated. They watched the footage of Mistress Angel whipping the heavily tattooed images of her prey.

Fitz could do nothing other than stand rooted to the spot and see what other horrible scenes the video would reveal.

"Oooooohhh!"

Everyone reacted as one voice as they witnessed Mistress Angel slamming her boot into Fitz's jaw and knocking out his tooth from his bloodied mouth. They were equally gobsmacked.

Fitz had seen enough. He pushed his way through the stupefied crowd only to run into a livid Frank Bergenson.

"You stupid sonofabitch."

Fitz shoved past him and disappeared deeper into the crowd.

"Turn off those damn TVs!" Frank yelled across the room. But nobody moved. It was compulsive viewing. "Jesus Christ!"

Frank pushed his way through the crowd to the DVD player and switched it off. The TV screens went black and the Bergenson & Adler showreel started playing again.

Right at that moment, the news crew from WKBO entered with video cameras and bright lights forcing a retreating Fitz back into the lounge. A smiling Lucy Gerhardt shoved a microphone in his face.

"I'm here live at the Depot Pavilion in downtown Minneapolis at Frank Bergenson's farewell party and look who's here! Elvis!"

Fitz looked like a dead man walking. Frank Bergenson shoved his way back through the mayhem to join Fitz in the spotlight. Lucy turned her attention to the old man.

"And here's Superman! Actually this is the man himself, Mr. Frank Bergenson and the man who will be replacing him as the new CEO of Bergenson & Adler, Mr. Kurt Fitzgerald…"

"I'd like to make a small presentation if I may?" Mistress Angel interrupted, deliberately stepping into frame before anyone could stop her. Frank and Fitz stood in the spotlight, terrified of what might happen next.

"Okay, sexy lady. Go ahead!" Lucy Gerhardt beamed innocently, holding the microphone in front of Mistress Angel and clueless as to what had transpired just moments ago.

"I have a special presentation for Mr. Kurt Fitzgerald."

Frank Bergenson snatched at the microphone and grappled with Lucy Gerhardt but she was too quick for him.

"Whoa, we'll get to you in a moment, Frank," the WKBO anchorwoman scolded.

With no place to hide, Fitz look terrified as the smiling Fem Dom stood in front of the news crew.

"I would like to present Sissy Boy here with this spectacular molar which I kicked out of his fat mouth at his last session with me." She held the tooth up for the camera to see.

"Wow!"

"Holy shit!"

"I told you she was for real, man," said Ricky the alter boy to his cohorts. Lucy Gerhardt looked horrified and the sound bites from the crowd didn't help.

Fitz could restrain himself no longer. He leapt towards Tara, knocking the his missing molar out of her hand hoping no one would see it. But it was too late for that. The lights and cameras filmed the scrambling Fitz down on all fours trying to retrieve it.

"Sissy Boy! This is not the time or place to start tonguing my nice latex boots now is it?" Mistress Angel scolded.

As the news crew captured the mayhem now ensuing, James Molinaire walked out in disgust followed by his alter boy gang.

Lucy Gerhardt ushered away her film crew, realizing that this was absolutely not appropriate for live television but the damage had been done.

Back in the ballroom, The Beatles broke into another classic tune as Mistress Angel disappeared out of the VIP lounge and into the dancing crowd. She had to find her husband and get the Hell out of Dodge before she got identified as Clem's wife.

Frank Bergenson looked downcast. "Jesus fucking Christ. That's a shitload of PR we didn't need. Who the fuck was that crazy bitch?"

In the packed ballroom, Tara made her way through the crowd

and found Clem sitting on the floor over in a corner with two other pirates looking pretty hammered.

"I see you found some fellow shipmates," Tara said looking at Henry and Jerry from the creative department.

"Where have you been?" Clem asked.

"Just hanging out in the lounge. Ran into some of your friends," Tara answered innocuously. Clem stood up and took Tara to one side.

"Let's get outta here. I don't fancy waiting around to see Frank make his damn announcement," Clem said, already maneuvering his way towards the exit.

"Too late," said Tara, pointing to the fake Fab Four leaving the stage. The house lights came up and the crowd turned its attention to the podium where the WKBO news crew had taken up position. A man looking remarkably like Abraham Lincoln walked to center stage to much applause.

"Ladies and gentlemen, without further ado, the man of the moment, Mr. Frank Bergenson!"

As wild applause and cheering broke out amongst the alcohol enthused gathering, Frank Bergenson walked up to the microphone, looking more like Superman's tired grandpa.

In the wings, a subdued Kurt Fitzgerald tried to pull himself together though he was still emotionally shaken up from his public humiliation. His head was a jumble of thoughts. So far, what was supposed to have been a celebratory, triumphant evening had turned into an unmitigated disaster.

*Why the fuck would Mistress Angel do that to him? His sexual fantasies were private – between him and the person he chose to dominate and humiliate him. This was nobody else's business!*

Frank began his speech.

"Hello fellow partygoers! I think you all know who I am - I'm Superman!"

The ballroom erupted into laughter and applause. Frank raised his hand to quiet them.

"Thank you all for coming tonight to celebrate my last day in the advertising business as CEO of Bergenson & Adler. I'd also like to thank The Beatles for entertaining us and blowing out my eardrums. Been quite an eventful evening that's for sure. Great to see Channel 5 are still here."

Frank looked to the wings where Lucy Gerhardt was watching. "Hey, I should send you an invoice for that free ad I just gave you." Frank waited for the laughter to subside as he switched gears to a more serious tone. "Now I'm not going to bore you to death and ruin the fun atmosphere with one those tediously dull speeches…"

"Thank God for that," mumbled Clem to Tara, watching from the rear of the ballroom. "Come on, let's go." Clem reached for Tara's gloved arm and tugged her towards a bar-stop exit door. They slowly and silently squeezed through the last layer of guests whose attention was fully focused on Frank Bergenson up on stage.

"Sixty one years in this business has taught me a lot. I've worked with some very talented people during my career, most of whom I've hired so they've got me to thank for their success." Muted laughter rippled through the crowd. "I've worked with geniuses and morons, visionaries and nitwits, so I know talent when I see it and when I don't see it. Fortunately, most of you here are people I respect though I thought I saw some jackasses earlier though that might've just been their costume."

"Fuck, it's locked," said Clem to Tara as he pushed against the exit door. They were stuck at the rear of the ballroom.

Frank paused and looked out at the two thousand or so guests that had come out to celebrate his career. "So, I know you've all been wondering who's going to be my successor and take over the reins of the most successful ad agency in the Mid-West. Well, it has to be someone special. After all, Superman is one tough act to follow. I've made my choice from the ranks within the company. This man is indeed a visionary, so I'm very pleased to announce that the next CEO of Bergenson & Adler will be none other than the very talented …..Mr. Clem Drew!"

A loud cheer went up as heads started turning around looking for Clem. In the wings, Kurt Fitzgerald stared in disbelief as if he'd misheard Frank's announcement. As wild applause filled the room, a spotlight caught Clem in its glare. Tara ducked out of the way. She'd done enough damage already.

"Speech!" someone yelled and before he knew it, Clem was being shoved towards the stage to rapturous cheering.

Lucy Gerhardt looked totally confused as she stared over at the dumbstruck Fitz who staggered past her, almost knocking her over. He pushed his way through a group of men dressed as Minnesota Vikings cheerleaders and hurriedly exited the ballroom through a side door. It slammed shut behind him.

"Elvis has left the building," said one of the news crew.

Clem made his way up on stage and walked towards the podium. Tara was so shocked and delighted that she started to tear up. The drama of the evening had finally gotten the better of her. It seemed that being in control was exhausting work, even for a real Mistress.

Clem looked across at Frank Bergenson who'd never looked happier. Standing at the podium, Clem removed his pirate eye patch and the red bandana around his head and tapped the microphone. Tara watched proudly between a cheering Marilyn Monroe and Lady Gaga.

"Thank you. Thank you, everyone." Clem's voice boomed out across the ballroom. "Thanks, Frank. Wow. Bit of a surprise." The crowd was with him. "No, really. This is a huge surprise and I'll tell you all why. A few days ago, Frank here told me he was going to announce to you all tonight that Kurt Fitzgerald was going to be our next CEO."

Frank Bergenson shrugged, trying to dilute the awkwardness of Clem's blunt honesty. A murmur went around the floor. Clem looked away from the crowd and focused his gaze on Superman.

"What happened, Frank? Fitz turn you down?" The room went dead quiet. "I learnt a lot from you over the four years I've worked here at Bergenson & Adler. You're right, this agency has some terrific people. To be CEO of this fine agency was something I'd always wanted and worked hard to get."

The reflective pirate sucked in a deep breath of air. "Like I said, I've got no idea what made you change your mind tonight but I've got an announcement to make as well. I've changed my mind, too. I don't want your lousy job!"

Clem beamed a broad smile. A roar of laughter broke out. "I'm serious. I don't fucking want it!"

Clem was still looking over at an extremely uncomfortable Frank Bergenson. The laughter subsided quickly, as if all the oxygen had just been sucked out of the place. Tara couldn't believe what she was hearing but her husband wasn't finished yet.

"And you know why, Frank?" You could hear a pin drop. "Because I'm tired of all the bullshit!"

Two very drunk Klingons at the back of the ballroom burst into applause but were instantly hushed by Captain Kirk. Frank walked over to the podium where Clem was speaking and put his hand over the microphone.

"Jesus, Clem. This is being broadcast live! Why are you doing this to me?"

Clem smiled.

"It's business, Frank. Just business."

Clem pushed Frank's hand away from the microphone and yelled out. "I quit! Thanks, guys! Been a wild ride!"

And with that, Clem walked off the stage back into the stunned audience. A few partygoers applauded but Tara's hands were over her mouth in shock at her husband's outrageous speech.

In the wings, Lucy Gerhardt turned to her news crew. "Let's go, boys. What a cluster fuck this turned out to be."

As Clem exited to some handshakes and pats on the back, various voices called after Clem wishing him luck and thanking him.

"You go, Clem!"

"Way to tell it!"

"The truth shall set you free!" bellowed a drunk preacher.

As the lights dimmed, a deejay tried to get the energy levels back on track again by playing an annoyingly loud song with a pulsating bass thump. Clem made his way through the now dancing throng towards Tara. He gave her a huge hug and kissed her on the lips with a big smack.

"Okay. *Now* can we leave?" He grabbed hold of Tara and pulled his confused Fem Dom away. Tara was still in stunned disbelief that all her hard work had been for nothing. They scurried down a hallway and out onto the sidewalk.

"What just happened, Clem? I mean…what were you thinking up there?"

Clem handed his ticket to one of the white-jacketed valet boys and stood on the pavement looking very pleased with himself. Tara wasn't quite so happy.

"Seriously. What the fuck happened back there?"

Her smiling husband appeared to have a very relaxed aura about him. "Well, I think I just retired from the ad business," he grinned.

"That was insane! That's it then?"

"That's it, I guess."

"God! One minute you're depressed you're not gonna make CEO and when they hand it to you on a plate you tell Frank to stuff it up his ass."

"Yeah. Felt good!" Clem beamed.

"Just how drunk are you?"

"Totally, unbelievably cool man!" a wasted Klingon shouted, as he stumbled out of the Pavilion's revolving door. Clem smiled and waved back at him. Tara shook her head.

"Well, at least the Klingon empire still loves you."

"I had two glasses of wine. And one moment of clarity."

Clem did a goofy little pirate jig. His mood was bordering on exuberant, a far cry from the sullen state he was in on his way to the party. For Tara, the evening had been a completely different experience. Her adrenalin rush of acting out as Mistress Angel had been seriously tempered by Clem's un-acceptance speech.

"Oh, shit." Tara shook her head as she looked at her dancing pirate. "What a crazy, crazy party this turned out to be. Sure no one slipped you a Mickey?"

Clem ended his little jig and put his hands on Tara's leather corseted hips. "Damn, you look good tonight, honey. Y'know, I've been thinking a lot over these past few days and a few light bulbs flashed on tonight."

The silver Mercedes pulled up alongside them. Clem handed a few bucks to the valet boy who held open the passenger door for Tara. Within seconds, the pirate and the Fem Dom were speeding through downtown towards Interstate 62. Tara stared over at her seemingly quite sober and lucid husband.

"So please enlighten me as to what these light bulbs were that flashed on in your head tonight. Seems they were more like exploding bombshells."

Clem seemed so relaxed and happy it was quietly freaking Tara out. "Y'know, it just really hit me tonight," Clem mused.

"No, I *don't* know. Help me out here."

"Like how much my life was making me miserable."

Tara looked at him in disbelief. "What? That's it? *That's* your light bulb moment? I could've told you that. You were making *my* life miserable, too. "

"Exactly," Clem said, keeping his eyes on the road. "I really don't know what the fuck happened in Frank's brain tonight to suddenly pull a switcheroo like that. I mean, he flat out told me that Fitz was getting the job and not me. Then he goes and pulls that dramatic stunt which frankly, I think he'd planned it all along. He did it for the cameras. Wanted drama right to the end. What a prick! The look on his face was priceless though. Fitz can have the fucking job."

Tara bit her tongue. Her show stopping performance had probably seen to it that the pitiful Sissy Boy Fitz certainly wouldn't be handed anything other than a pink slip. She had been superb as the controlling Mistress Angel, bringing her hapless victim to his knees, literally and figuratively. But it had been rendered redundant by

Clem's performance up on that stage. For a brief moment though, she finally felt in complete control of a situation and manipulated it deftly. She liked how it felt, albeit for only the few minutes it lasted. Now she was back to being plain old Tara Drew.

"Y'know, I finally realized that I didn't really want it. Maybe I *never* really wanted it. I'd turned into some workaholic asshole who ignored his wife and turned her into a jealous nut job. *That* guy wanted it. But not me. And, by the way, did I tell you how incredibly hot tonight you look tonight?

"Yes. Numerous times."

"And that I can't stop thinking about banging your brains out."

"Thanks, honey. So romantically phrased," Tara interjected, as words continue to pour out of Clem like a gushing drainpipe.

"Guys were looking at you like...well, I think they were scared and turned on at the same time!"

"Yeah, I know. It felt good," Tara admitted.

As Clem pulled into Dunkirk Crescent, it was still a warm night. The silver Mercedes turned into their driveway. It had been an evening to remember for both of them and for different reasons. Clem still seemed high on something as they got out of the car in the garage and walked into the kitchen. Tara headed straight to the wine refrigerator and grabbed an ice-cold bottle of Chardonnay while Clem continued his soul-bearing monolog.

"My point is, do you work to live or do you live to work? I lived to work. Your job shouldn't define who you are. I don't know...wait, didn't you ask me that once? Yeah, I think..."

"Shut up." Tara handed him a glass of vino to calm him down. "Don't think anymore. Cheers." Tara clinked Clem's glass. "We can figure out how we're going to live when we start the rest of our lives tomorrow."

Clem kissed Tara on the tip of her nose. "Okay."

"Of course, there's still the payment on the house which you've lectured me about more than once which we'll no longer be able to afford even though I've now got a job." Tara told him, then sipped her wine and waited for Clem's response.

"You got a job? Doing what?"

"Teaching,"

"Really? Teaching what?"

Tara smiled. "They're like one hour classes."

"Teaching *what?*"

Tara slid her arms around Clem's neck and pulled him close. "Let's talk about it tomorrow." Tara ran her hand through the back of his hair and messed it up. Clem's brain was still firing on all synapses but now he was going to focus on his sexy wife's hot body.

"House is too big for just two people anyway. I've never liked it. Wouldn't hurt to downsize."

"Damn hard work keeping this place clean all the time, too," Tara whispered.

"Have to give the car back." Clem kissed her lips.

"You don't need a car, you've got nowhere to go anymore." Tara grabbed his butt cheeks and pulled his crotch into her hips.

Clem kissed Tara again, longer this time. He pulled away and looked at her.

"Shit. Did I fuck up tonight?"

"Oh, yeah. Big time," Tara said softly. "You're definitely one of the dumbest pirates I've ever known. One of the cutest though."

"Thanks. No one's ever called me a dumb cute pirate before."

"You were a very naughty boy and I'm going to punish you," Tara teased. Clem smiled. He gently squeezed her boob and ran his finger over her nipple. Tara purred. His hand slid up to the lacing on her bodice and untied the bowed knot, releasing her constricted breasts.

"Y'know, I had no idea I'd married such a kinky woman."

"You're right, Mr. Drew. You have no idea at all," Tara smiled.

# CHAPTER 20

In the months that followed Frank Bergenson's eventful retirement shindig, events at Bergenson & Adler took a decidedly downward turn. Not surprisingly, Kurt Fitzgerald was fired and Daniel Ellerby was hired to find a CEO in place of the three missing amigos, Frank, Fitz and Clem. But the new man couldn't turn the tide of the growing recession. It was a death knell for the agency. After the live televised debacle at the Depot Pavilion, James Molinaire fired the agency and took his giant account back to the west coast and to its first ever agency, Chiat Day in Los Angeles. And as the economy slowed and retail sales slumped across the board, the ad business was hit hard everywhere. Clients weren't just trimming budgets, they were slashing them. Bergenson & Adler had to lay off nearly forty per cent of its employees. Even James Molinaire was eventually let go as Rebakor slashed its workforce after the "God Speed" ad campaign bombed.

It took quite a while for Clem and Tara to finally unload their McMansion on Dunkirk Crescent and for considerably bit less than they'd paid for it four years earlier. They had found a nice little two bedroom craftsman style bungalow to rent in the older Minneapolis suburb of Hopkins. It wasn't as upscale as toney Eden Prairie but now Clem could walk to his new job.

He stood on the sidewalk wearing tattered old blue jeans and a sweatshirt outside a small storefront. He rubbed the two-day stubble on his chin as he stared up at a fat little man on the ladder holding a paintbrush.

"Looks good!" Clem called up to him. It was a wonderfully sunny morning with not even a hint of a breeze. The chubby fellow climbed down the ladder and the two of them stared up to admire the cursive green lettering. The new sign above the store read *Bake & Brew*.

"What kinda joint is this anyway? Sounds like you can either get stoned or get hammered," the sign writer joked as he wiped his hands on a dirty cloth.

"Hmmm....never thought of that," Clem frowned. "Actually, we're a bakery and a coffeehouse."

"No beer?" The fat little man sounded disappointed. "When I see *brew* I think *beer*."

"Nope."

"Then ya shoulda called it *Bake & Beans*. That'd be a good name for this place." He collapsed his ladder and laid it flat on the ground.

"But when you say *Bake & Beans*, it sounds more like *bacon beans*," Clem argued.

"Well, gosh darn it, maybe ya need one of them marketing guys to come out here and make a few suggestions. They got all the ideas, ya know. They're smarter than guys like you and me."

"Thanks for the tip," Clem smiled, still looking up proudly at the freshly painted signage.

"Well, good luck with your new business," said the sign writer packing up his tools. "I gotta little tip for you though."

"Oh yeah? What's that?" Clem asked, as he watched him lay his ladder down on his flat bed truck.

"Advertise. That's the key to success, my friend."

Inside the store, Tara pulled a tray of banana muffins out of the oven and slid in a fresh tray of chocolate chip cookie dough. The glass-cased counter displayed a variety of baked buns, cakes, muffins and cookies. Taking pride of place on the countertop was the La Pavoni espresso machine, the only remnant from their house on Dunkirk Crescent.

"Hey! Can't a girl get some service in this place? I need a double shot cappuccino and make it a dry one!"

Clem came running in. "Double shot capp coming right up!"

At the Minneapolis-St. Paul International Airport, a Delta Airlines Boeing 757 was readying for takeoff as Mistress Krystal walked up to the baggage drop and checked in two large suitcases. The attendant printed out two labels and tagged her bags before swinging them onto the conveyer belt.

"Your bags are checked all the way through to San Diego, Ms. Gibson." The attendant looked closer at her computer monitor. "Just one way?" she asked.

"You're damned right," Mistress Krystal replied adamantly. "I never want to see snow again."

Down in Birmingham, Alabama at the Wardle & Ward Advertising Agency, the imposing figure of former football player and agency president Bucky Ward stood in front of his eighty seven employees and with a big downhome smile as he introduced his latest employee.

"Hey folks, let's show some good 'ol southern hospitality to your new chief executive, Mr. Kurt Fitzgerald, even though he's a damn Yankee!" Bucky joked, though the employees didn't seem especially amused. They gave Fitz a rather underwhelming round of applause, which didn't exactly fill Fitz with confidence. Bucky Ward leaned over and put a big strong arm around his shoulder. He whispered in Fitz's ear. "Don't worry, son. They'll loosen up over time."

On the south side of town, in Mistress Krystal's old apartment, Mr. Winkle stood naked in front of Mistress Queen Lorraine as she cracked a bullwhip across his bare flesh.

*Craaack!!!*

"Owwww!" yelled Mr. Winkle.

"What d'you say, motherfucker?" Lorraine barked at him.

"Thank you, Mistress Queen Lorraine, O beautiful African Goddess and…er…"

*Craaack!!!*

The bullwhip ripped into Mr. Winkle's flesh once more, tearing the skin on his stomach with a long slash.

"African Goddess and Bitch Babe!" Lorraine yelled.

"Please. Don't hit me quite so hard, please," Mr. Winkle asked politely.

"Shut your pie-hole, Winkle. And if you even think of pissing on my floor I'll bite your damn dick off, you hear me? You hear me?" Lorraine screamed at her terrified client.


Meanwhile, back in Hopkins, Bake & Brew was flourishing without much need for any advertising at all. Word of mouth, social media and some blogging did the trick and it didn't cost a penny. In fact, they got so busy they needed extra help, so they hired Justine, who'd recently been laid off and who was delighted to be reunited with her old boss, though it was Tara who was her new boss now.

It was suggested that the little chubby man with the paintbrush and ladder should come back out to visit them and rename their store *Kakes & Koffee* but Clem, Tara's marketing manager, insisted that would create confusion with their brand and seriously impact their demographic. As Tara liked to say to Justine – You can take the man out the ad biz but you can't take the ad biz out of the man.


Mistress Krystal never did come back from California much to the delight of Lorraine who'd finally discovered an occupation that she found immensely satisfying and fulfilled everything that was missing in her life. What's more, the tight bodice she wore did wonders for her lower back pain. And the fact that the job allowed her to exact revenge on the male species without any legal repercussions other than a wad of cash every time she vented her anger on her willing subjects was manna from Heaven.

As for Frank Bergenson, he enjoyed living in retirement on the French Riviera for two fabulously relaxing weeks before suffering a massive heart attack. He died in Saint Roch Hospital in Nice a few days later.

And in a dimly lit room somewhere in Birmingham, Alabama, a large-breasted woman who called herself Mistress Diana was entertaining a new client.

*Thhhwaaack!*

The whiplash crack of the riding crop made him flinch. But the sound of her stiletto heels on the bare floorboards seemed to excite him.

## ABOUT THE AUTHOR

As well as being an author, Tony is also an Emmy Award winning writer and filmmaker, musician and photographer. His documentary work includes *The Royal Academy* and *Mondo Bondo*. He attended Westminster City Grammar School in London and is a graduate of *Ealing College of Art & Design* in England. In 2006, Tony was the recipient of the *Individual Artist Fellowship* awarded by The Tennessee Arts Commission. He has worked professionally as a copywriter in advertising for over 20 years on both sides of the Atlantic and has lived in San Francisco, Los Angeles, Nashville and Minneapolis. Tony is married and was born in London, England.

Chardonnay Press is a Limited Liability Company